THE FURTHER I FALL

Melissa Roos

ISBN-978-1-7374960-7-6 E-book
ISBN-978-1-7374960-8-3 Paperback

Cover design by: Melissa Roos & Kristy Hoy
Printed in the United States of America

David - Ryan - Delaney
Cole & Makayla

Thank you for always encouraging me on this wonderful, crazy journey.

ONE

Tate Becker watched his best friend, Neil Sellers, push aside the word game tiles that someone had left out and laid his backpack on the long, wooden table in the high school media center. Neil pulled out his tablet and began highlighting his notes for history class.

"You and your color-coordinated notes," Tate said, shaking his head in disgust as his own notebook lay abandoned on the table, pen dangling between his lips as he chewed on the end. "You'll never catch me doing that."

"And that's exactly why you're just getting by with a C," Neil responded dryly. "You never prepare. Speaking of which, are you ready for tryouts tonight?"

Leaning back in his chair as far as he dared, Tate draped his arm over the back, completely relaxed. "What's there to be ready for? I'll either start at shortstop or I'll pitch. I'm happy either way."

"You know Eddie is vying for your spot. He wants to be the starting shortstop, always has. Thinks he's the next Cal Ripken or something. He'd like nothing more than to knock you off your pedestal."

"View's great from up here." Tate grinned around the half-chewed pen. "He can try. But don't forget, I was the one to unseat the starting senior, Dalton Turk, our freshman year. Why would this year be any different? Besides, a little competition is good. Makes all of us better in the end."

"Heard Eddie was hitting the gym all winter."

"So? I play basketball. It's not like I've been sitting around doin' nothin'," Tate said, slightly annoyed.

Holding up his hands in defense, Neil responded, "Don't shoot the messenger. I'm just saying."

"Well, don't. It'll all work itself out on the field, one way or the other."

"Look out." Neil elbowed Tate.

"What now? Can't a guy get a moment of peace around here?"

"Here comes Kimmy." Neil pointed as he spotted the petite cheerleader across the room.

"So what?" Tate asked a little too loudly.

"Mr. Becker!" The librarian spat out his name. "Please keep the noise level down. You are in a library."

"I got you, Mrs. Fritz."

In a barely audible voice, Neil asked, "Do you live under a rock? Didn't you hear that she's determined to ask you out?"

"Shit. Was that serious? I thought the guys were just razzing me."

"I think she's pretty serious. And I heard she will slash your tires if you turn her down."

"What the . . . She wouldn't. Would she?" Frustrated, Tate raked his hands through his shaggy brown hair.

"I think she would. Remember last year when she was turned down for the homecoming dance? She put sugar in that guy's gas tank."

"I just bought new tires," Tate whined as he scanned the library for somewhere to hide. "What am I going to do? I don't want to go out with Kimmy."

"I have an idea," Neil offered.

"It better be good."

"The best way to get out of it is to date someone else."

"Great idea, best friend of mine," Tate said sarcastically, thumping him on the shoulder. "But I'm currently not dating anyone."

Neil shrugged, replacing the cap on his blue highlighter. "Ask someone out."

"Yeah, like it's that easy," Tate grumbled.

"So fake date someone just until Kimmy finds someone else to try and get her meat hooks into."

"Where am I going to find a girl on short notice who's willing to play along?"

Neil snorted. "You're kidding, right? Any girl would love to pretend," Neil made air quotes with his fingers, "to be your girlfriend, even if only for five minutes."

"Whatever," Tate said, "but I don't want just any girl. I need someone who won't take the situation too seriously. I need someone I can trust."

"Therein lies the problem," Neil agreed.

"Mr. Becker." Mrs. Fritz glared at Tate over her reading glasses. "Don't make me give you detention."

"Sorry, Mrs. Fritz."

Both guys scanned the room. Neil nudged Tate. Grabbed letters from the word game and spelled out C-H-L-O-E, pointing as Chloe Harris disappeared between the rows of books with a group of students.

Tate slapped his friend on the shoulder. "Yeah, good thinking. That's believable, right?"

"Beyond. You guys are always together anyway." Neil jerked his head to the left. "But if you're going to do it, you'd better make it quick. Kimmy is on her way over here."

Tate threw his pen on the table, scooped up his notebook, and handed it to Neil. "Here. Hold this."

"Why?"

"Because I need my hands free," Tate explained.

"What for?"

"You'll see."

Questioning him again, Neil asked, "What are you going to do?"

Tate spared a glance at his friend. "Go big or go home. Keep an eye out for Kimmy." Tate hurried off after Chloe. Ducking down an aisle, he wove his way through the students she'd walked in with and found her talking to a couple of friends as they searched for books. He looked her over, and his mouth went dry.

From her sassy brown ponytail to the pale blue toenails that peeked out of navy-blue flip-flops below the edge of her frayed jeans, Chloe was truly the perfect prospect. Tate overheard part of her conversation.

"I want to write," Chloe stated.

"Write what?" Eddie asked, thumbing through a book before putting it back.

"Stories. Novels," Chloe said. "Probably mystery or romance. Maybe suspense."

Eddie took a different book off the shelf and handed it to Lucy, tapping it with his index finger. "That's the one you want."

"Thanks," Lucy said, tucking it under her arm. "You should write romantic suspense. That's a great genre."

"Or better yet, thriller," Eddie added. "You've got real talent. Makes me a little jealous."

Chloe laughed. "I don't think you have anything to be jealous of. And I'm not sure I could write a thriller. Maybe romantic suspense."

"What about you, Eddie? What do you want to study in college?" Lucy asked.

"I like editing and proofreading. I'm also interested in the publishing side of things. Not sure what the actual major would be at this point."

Tate swallowed hard when it suddenly registered that Chloe's entire Senior Composition class was in the library doing research, and half of them were in this very section. What he was about to do would be witnessed by everyone.

Taking a deep breath, Tate murmured, "Here goes nothing." He came up behind Chloe and tapped her on the shoulder. "Hey, there you are. I've been looking all over for you."

Chloe pulled a book off the shelf, turned around, and glanced at him. "You have?"

"Yep . . . yes, I have."

"Hey, we were in the middle of a very important conversation," Eddie protested.

"Sorry, man, but this is important too. Extremely."

"What's up?" Chloe asked.

Tate heard someone clear their throat loudly. Glancing over, he saw that Neil had followed him partway and was mouthing, "She's coming."

Tate looked at Chloe. "I have a favor to ask, but I don't have time to explain."

Looking back at Neil for support, he saw him motioning to hurry up. Out of the corner of his eye, Tate saw Kimmy come around the corner. He was out of time. It was now or never. "Trust me, please?" he pleaded, desperate.

Chloe barely had enough time to nod.

Without hesitating, he wrapped an arm around Chloe's waist and pulled her gently against him.

"Oh, shit!" Eddie cussed. "Here comes a PDA!"

"What are you . . ."

He didn't let Chloe finish. His mouth closed over hers and cut off the rest of the question in a soft kiss.

Eddie groaned loudly and every head turned.

"How romantic," Lucy sighed.

Chloe was stiff, so Tate drew back to judge her reaction. His free hand reached for her face and held it still. Running a thumb lightly over her lips, he asked in a voice barely audible, "Are you with me?"

Big green eyes looked up at him in wonder. He felt the heat rise in her cheek as it pressed against his palm and saw her head dip slightly in acknowledgment.

His smile was instant and genuine. "You're my hero," he whispered. Leaning in slowly, his lips testing, tempting her with his tongue. Melting into his embrace, she returned his kiss. Shifting, he guided her gently back against the bookshelves. He heard multiple gasps and whispers from the gathering crowd.

"Attaboy!"

"Since when did they become a thing?"

"OMG."

"Get a room!"

"I wish someone would kiss me like that."

"Way to go, Tate!"

Tate tried to block them out and focus solely on Chloe. Knowing that Kimmy was there, watching, he wanted to make it as believable as possible. After all, his brand-new Goodyears depended on it.

There was an audible squeak and a loud cry. "No!"

Only then did he dare crack open one eye and look at Kimmy. She stood surrounded by a flock of her peers with a huge scowl on her face, arms crossed, staring directly at them. For a split second, he thought Kimmy would come at them, but just as quickly, she turned on her heel, pushed through the crowd, and stomped away. Relief washed over him as applause erupted from the students.

Slowly, he withdrew from Chloe. A grin spread wide across his face as he examined hers.

Chloe's fingertips went to her lips. "What -- what was that for?"

The bell rang, and Neil popped through the crowd. "Come on, Tate! We're going to be late for practice!" Neil shot Chloe a cheesy grin and gave her a thumbs up.

"You were perfect!" Tate whispered into Chloe's ear. "I love you!"

"I was? You do?"

"You do?" Eddie asked, still standing a foot away.

"Eddie! Tate! Let's go!" Neil yelled over the crowd and waved for them to follow.

"Yes." He kissed her on the cheek and ran a hand down her smooth ponytail, letting the silkiness of it slip easily through his fingers. "I'll meet you after practice in the usual spot. We'll talk on the way home."

"Oh . . . okay." Chloe leaned back against the shelves as a little sigh escaped her lips.

Everyone filed quickly out of the media center, but one hand dragged across the long table, scattering the letters of Chloe's name.

❋

Hours later, Chloe leaned against the building, her back absorbing the warmth from the late afternoon sun as she buried her feet in the long grass. The wind whispered around the corner, sending voices in her direction. She was invisible from the baseball field and the parking lot was almost empty, except for a few remaining athletes' vehicles.

Chloe had too much on her mind; she needed somewhere to hide and sort out her feelings until baseball practice was over.

Which would be soon, she thought, glancing at her cell phone.

Her thoughts were jumbled and her stomach was in knots. She'd been in turmoil since Tate had kissed her.

At softball practice, she'd been off, unable to get a single pitch over the plate. Chloe couldn't help it. Every fiber of her being hummed with possibility. Was it true? Did he love her? That kiss had been the most romantic thing she had ever experienced.

She could hardly believe it. Just like that, all those years of crushing on him and thinking that he only thought of her as a friend ended in one earth-shattering kiss. Her knees were weak just thinking about the moment his lips touched hers. Chloe had waited so long for him to kiss her. The proverbial cherry on top was hearing those words from him. She'd been in love with Tate Becker forever. And now, he loved her too.

The sun was slowly sinking, bleeding toward the Pennsylvania hills, sending out a prism of colors so brilliant it almost hurt her eyes to look. Yet, she did, wondering if it seemed more beautiful this afternoon because she was in love.

As the players filtered into the parking lot after practice let out, she heard the crunch of cleats on gravel, the laughter, and the camaraderie.

Neil, Eddie, and Tate rounded the corner of the building. They couldn't have been more different: Neil with his dark auburn hair and a sprinkling of freckles and Eddie with bark-

7

brown hair sporting a mullet, glasses, and a wiry frame. Then there was Tate. He emerged like a sun-kissed god from the shadows, his favorite baseball bat slung over one shoulder, bag on the other.

Her heart fluttered.

Their words floated through the air as they peeled off toward their vehicles. Tate walked to his truck and stowed his gear in the bed before noticing her propped against the brick wall. A grin spread so wide across his chiseled features; that one dimple winked out. His light brown hair was tousled by the wind. He was covered in a thin layer of dust from the diamond, but that only made him more enticing as he walked toward her.

"How did tryouts go?" she asked, trying to sound casual.

Tate brushed an imaginary piece of dirt off his shoulder. "Had it in the bag before we even started." Grinning down at her, he reached out a hand. Without hesitating, Chloe took it, and he pulled her up onto her feet. "I've been looking all over for you. Why weren't you by the fence?"

"Well, I . . ." Chloe couldn't explain. She was having a hard time focusing on anything other than her hand in his and the intense heat that was working its way slowly up her arm.

"It doesn't matter. I couldn't wait to see you and tell you the news."

She swallowed hard. "Tell me what?" No matter how hard she tried not to, she just kept falling further for him. If that was even possible.

"It worked." He pulled her in for a quick hug and spun her around. Whispering conspiratorially, he said, "I'm in the clear."

He was so happy she couldn't help but smile as well. "You're in the clear about what?" she asked, feeling lightheaded from the spin and giddy with joy.

"Kimmy. She asked someone else out."

"Really? Who?"

"Who cares?" He laughed. "Anthony or Jerry, I think. It doesn't matter. What matters is that she's not going to slash my tires."

"Wait, what?"

"You know, the little scene in the library this afternoon."

Chloe raised an eyebrow as a pit formed in her stomach. "You mean the kiss?"

"Yeah. The one everyone is talking about."

He was so close that Chloe could feel the warmth from his body. As she felt the heat rise in her cheeks, she asked, "They are?"

"Of course, they are. You were perfect. I said it before and I'll say it again – you are my hero." He reached out his hand and ran it down her ponytail, twirling it through his fingers. "I love the fact that you went along with the plan like that, no questions asked."

"What plan?"

"The plan to keep Kimmy from slashing my tires."

Her heart dropped. "Wait. Back up just a second." Chloe's world started to tilt. Her mind racing to catch up. "I need to get this straight. You kissed me because Kimmy was going to ask you out? And if you said no, she was going to slash your tires?"

"That's it in a nutshell."

And just like that, Chloe's heart shattered.

TWO

-Ten years later-

Friday

Chloe Harris sat in the meeting, feeling nervous and slightly sick to her stomach. This was huge. Bigger than she could have ever imagined. She looked across the table at the Belov brothers, owners of Belov Productions.

Mattison Belov, his brother, Phillip, and their assistants lined the table in high-back leather chairs. They were all dressed impeccably in black suits, making Chloe wonder if there was a dress code. Opposite them, Eddie Lambert, one of her friends from high school, and herself.

She sold Eddie short with that kind of introduction. He was Eddie Lambert, literary agent, marketing guru, editor extraordinaire, and long-time friend, she silently corrected herself. Not that she would make any introductions or probably say anything at all. That's what Eddie was here for.

He was a man on a mission with the knowledge to make this whole thing happen. Working for months through connections he had previously established in the industries, essentially calling in every favor he could muster for this one meeting. Chloe knew emails had passed back and forth relentlessly to make this brief encounter happen. Something she didn't think was even remotely possible or even heard of in this day and age when a lot of deals like this were done completely through email.

But somehow, Eddie had done the unthinkable and secured an in-person meeting in their satellite office in Philadelphia, where Belov Productions started some twenty years earlier.

Chloe bounced her right leg in an attempt to funnel all her nervous energy.

Eddie's hand slipped under the table and firmly pressed on her leg. "Stop," he muttered under his breath. "You're making the water in the glasses ripple."

"Sorry," Chloe whispered back, trying not to fidget. She ran a thumb down her crystal glass and wiped at the condensation. Her glass wasn't the only thing that was perspiring.

Eddie sat to her right, dressed in a black three-piece business suit with a red tie. He called it his power tie. His lucky tie. He wore it when he wanted to impress, and he certainly did. He looked good. Classic. Professional. He'd come a long way from the lanky baseball player who'd always had his nose in a book in high school. He had filled out and grown into those stork-like legs and big feet. He had ditched his glasses for contacts and exchanged his mullet for a shorter, more professional style.

Chloe was dressed in a simple sundress the color of a lush green meadow. It was soft and flowing, dipping discreetly in the front. Her hair was swept up in a loose French twist, with wisps of hair framing her face, making her feel soft and feminine, the image Eddie wanted her to portray.

"Showcase your romantic side. You are a mystery romance writer, after all." Eddie had made her change three times this morning until he was finally satisfied. But now, seeing all the suits, she wasn't sure that the sundress had been the way to go.

She was uncomfortable; the men across from her were intimidating, and she felt like an imposter trying to swindle the deal of a lifetime.

"You never know when it will happen," Eddie liked to say. "You're already semi-famous. Now we must push you over the proverbial edge into fame and fortune."

"I'm not famous. Besides, it's the books they want, not me."

"That's where you're wrong," Eddie countered. "They want to meet the author behind the stories."

That thought made her insides turn. She was perfectly happy

staying behind the scenes.

Chloe had lost the thread of conversation and missed some of the introductions; needing to focus, she re-engaged.

She hadn't missed the fact that Phillip Belov hadn't spoken a word, though, or taken his eyes off of her. He was second in charge at Belov Productions and looked like he wanted to murder someone.

Phillip sat with his hands folded neatly on top of the table and looked directly at her with dark, intense eyes. He reclined slightly in his chair. His posture was meant to be casual, even relaxed, but Chloe didn't miss the fact that his hands were clasped together so tightly that his knuckles were white. His hair was cropped close to his head in a high, tight, military style, and the sizeable bump in the middle of his nose looked like a sign of a previous break.

Mattison Belov, the brother in charge, had the same broad build as Phillip. They shared the same brown hair, but that was all. For brothers, their facial features couldn't have been more different. Sitting next to one another, though, they gave off an aura of sheer masculine power held in check by the suits they wore.

Neither man looked a lot like the pictures she'd found online, but then again, most of the photos had been over ten years old. Nothing had been posted about them recently.

Chloe looked around the expensively furnished room, trying to keep from the gravitational pull that emanated from Phillip as his eyes locked on her.

On the far wall, elegantly framed movie posters depicting their recent blockbusters caught her eye.

A thought flicked through her mind, could hers be next? Her pulse skittered for a brief second.

Eddie lightly touched her arm as her name was mentioned, and she pulled her focus away from the wall and back to the meeting.

"Did you receive the papers my administrative assistant sent?" Mattison asked.

"We did," Eddie answered for both of them.

"And you've had time to review them?"

"Yes, we have."

Interrupting, Phillip directed his comment to Chloe. "You're not our usual choice." His eyes narrowed to a sharp and precise point that seemed to pierce her very soul, causing her to shrink into herself slightly.

"I think what my brother means to say is you're not quite as knowledgeable as our other writers," Mattison explained. "You don't have the experience yet. We tend to work with writers with whom we've established strong relationships over the years."

Chloe steeled herself, then answered in a calm and steady voice. "I can understand that. Connections are extremely important. Please let me assure you I may not have much experience in this particular part of the industry, but I know what makes an excellent story."

"No offense, doll, but you're insignificant in the realm of screenplays, production, and movies," Phillip continued as if she hadn't even spoken. His lips thinned, and in a sharp tone, he added, "A nobody. You have no connections or any understanding of what it takes in this business." He turned to his brother. "There's no draw here. Only a few hundred readers even know she exists. It'll be like starting from scratch."

"Thousands of readers," Eddie corrected. "She has hundreds of thousands of readers. With a little publicity and an epic story like this, it's sure to be another blockbuster for you."

Phillip flicked his wrist and brushed him off. He regarded Chloe for a brief moment. "Give me one good reason why we should take a chance on you."

Chloe looked him directly in the eye, lifted her chin slightly, and said, "Because I'm good at what I do. Whether I'm famous or not shouldn't matter. What matters most is the story, the characters, and the plot. This story is one of a kind, an epic love story that will leave you breathless and dying to have the slightest spark of what the two main characters have. The twisted plot will have you on the edge of your seat until the last scene."

The room was deadly quiet, so quiet that Chloe was acutely aware of the air conditioning kicking on. Had she said too much or not enough? "Did you read the book?" Chloe ventured.

"Yes," Phillip answered coolly.

"And what's your honest opinion?" Eddie asked, leaning forward.

"I've read worse."

Chloe raised both eyebrows. "Excuse me?"

"Phillip," Mattison warned. He looked apologetically at Chloe. "You'll have to excuse my brother. He doesn't travel well, and we just flew in last night. Long layover, and such, so he is extremely tired and confrontational."

Eddie was quick to intervene. "Of course. Traveling can be exhausting. If there's anything we can do to make this happen, please let me know."

"One of the things we need to ask ourselves is whether your novel is visual enough," Mattison said.

"I believe it is," Chloe answered without hesitation.

"That's something I think we can all agree on," Mattison replied. "The scenes are breathtaking." Sweeping his hand through the air, he said, "I can picture rolling hills covered in wildflowers rippling in the wind, the sun coming up over the vast horizon. . ."

Leaning forward, Phillip was quick to interrupt his brother. "Excuse me, Miss Harris," he said, locking eyes with her. "Have you ever written a screenplay before?"

"No, I haven't."

He smirked. "I thought not."

Chloe would be out of her league writing a screenplay, and Phillip Belov knew it. Imposter syndrome reared its ugly head, but she tamped the monster down. "I have been studying the process. I wrote an outline, kept the points to a couple of sentences each, and then broke it down into three acts to get it started."

Sliding the manuscript across the table, Eddie said, "Here's a printed version of what I previously emailed you."

Mattison picked it up.

"I was under the impression that I wouldn't be writing the screenplay by myself. That I would be working with a team," Chloe said, addressing Mattison.

"That's correct," Mattison agreed. "We have some of the finest screenplay writers on staff. Once we have signed papers, your input will be minimal. Our writers will do the heavy lifting, but we will guide you through our process. You'll be . . ."

"We will be holding your hand," Phillip grumbled, cutting him off.

Mattison gave his brother a piercing look. "I think you could use another cup of coffee." He looked at his assistant. "Would you be so kind as to get another for my brother?"

"Of course, sir."

"Would anyone else care for coffee?"

"No, we're fine," Eddie said, answering for both of them. "Please take some time, and look over it. Chloe would like to stay as involved as possible. Let us know how we can help and how we can move forward from here."

Mattison slid the hard copy to his assistant without looking at it. "From here, we will have to focus on the main conflict. The stakes have to be high. In your book, the main protagonist is relatable, endearing, and someone we want desperately to succeed. We have to maintain that in the screenplay, ultimately on the screen, and in the actors we select."

"I think that can easily be achieved," Eddie answered.

"Anything can be achieved if given enough time," Phillip grumbled. "But time is money. I'm not sure how much of either I want to waste on this project."

Avoiding his brother's comment, Mattison said, "To proceed with this project, we need to sign the papers I sent you." He opened a folder and pulled out a document. "Are you prepared to do that at this time?"

"We are," Eddie answered.

Chloe's stomach churned as she registered Phillip's hard stare. This didn't seem like the right fit no matter what Eddie said, or how much he tried to appease either side.

"Not quite." Chloe swallowed hard. "I can see that the opinions in this room are conflicting," she said, feeling like the meeting and the movie deal were slipping through her fingers. If she couldn't keep the deal, at least she could keep her pride. "But I assure you if you decide to go ahead with this project, my novel, I will work diligently to meet every expectation, meet every deadline, and manage every detail, no matter how trivial."

"I appreciate that, Miss Harris," Mattison said. "I'm sure you will be nothing but a pleasure to work with even though your part will be minimal as we move forward. I need you to sign the papers so we can get started." His assistant laid a copy in front of her along with a couple of ink pens.

Eddie reached for them and held out a pen for her to take.

"My part will be minimal?" Chloe questioned. "But Eddie assured me that I would be involved."

Phillip leaned forward holding her in place with his eyes. "We have been in this industry a long time and know first-hand that writers become very protective of their work once we begin dissecting the story. You should just sign the papers and let us worry about the rest."

Was he simply trying to intimidate her? She had read he was difficult to work with but this was beyond. He acted like he was doing her a favor, that she was beneath him. Her nerves were shot. This isn't the scenario Eddie had promised. There wasn't anything worth being talked down to by this man or any other. She was ready to cut her losses.

"I'm not sure what I have done to offend you, Mr. Belov. Clearly, this meeting was not your idea." Chloe stood, knocking over her purse and spilling the contents. Trying to keep her voice from shaking, she added, "If you don't want to move forward with this project, I understand. This is your business; you should be able to run it as you see fit. I hope that you can appreciate that I feel the same way about my writing."

"And there it is," Phillip smirked.

"If you are not interested, someone else definitely will be."

"Chloe," Eddie hissed through clenched teeth placing a hand on her arm.

For the first time, she ignored him.

"As far as I'm concerned, this meeting is over. I do hope that you will at least take the time to reconsider my involvement in the path forward. If at any time you wish to reopen discussions, I --" Chloe gestured to Eddie. "We would be more than willing to speak with you. Thank you for your time, Mr. Belov." Chloe reached for Mattison's hand, her own trembling. "It was a pleasure meeting you. Both of you."

"You as well," Mattison said. "I wish you wouldn't leave on this note. The terms of this meeting have yet to come to fruition."

Scooping up the contents of her purse hastily, Chloe tucked it under her arm and forced a small smile. "For me, they have. It's very apparent your interests are divided," she said, looking pointedly at Phillip.

"Chloe," Eddie muttered. "Don't do this."

Avoiding Eddie's gaze, she looked back at Mattison. "Please let us know if anything changes."

"Of course."

Her pulse drummed fast as she walked out of the conference room and made a beeline for the elevator. Luck was with her. It opened just as she reached for the button. After she stepped in, the doors started to close behind her. Eddie stuck his hand through and caught it in the nick of time.

The doors closed, and neither one spoke. Eddie simply turned to face her, briefcase in one hand, the other in his pants pocket.

"Don't look at me like that."

"I'm not looking at you any which way," he said with an edge to his voice.

"Yes, you are."

"How am I looking at you, then?"

"Like I just ruined the deal of the century."

Eddie pressed his lips together and stayed silent, which only made Chloe feel worse.

✳

The conference room cleared out fast. Mattison's suit jacket already discarded and draped over his vacant chair, he exhaled loudly. Standing at the window, squinting against the afternoon sun, he kept his back to Phillip and peered down at the street.

It took less than sixty seconds for Chloe Harris and Eddie Lambert to emerge from the building. Mattison loosened his tie and watched the agent hand the valet his ticket.

He noted that neither one of them spoke as they stood next to each other, pedestrians streaming by on either side. He could almost see the tension between them. She had guts; he'd give her that -- more than he'd anticipated. This was supposed to be simple. Straightforward.

The car came around. The valet got out, and Eddie Lambert tucked Chloe Harris neatly into the little sports car, got in himself, and pulled away from the curb.

The silver Jag stopped at a red light. When the light turned green it drove on. Only when he could no longer see the vehicle did Mattison turn back around and face his brother.

"The story was good."

"So?" Phillip shrugged as he flicked a look down at his suit jacket, brushing off an invisible speck. "What do we care? Money is money."

"You're right about that. But this time . . . it feels different. I don't feel good about it."

"Since when do you have a conscience? A job is a job."

"Maybe I'm just getting too old for this kind of thing." Mattison turned back around and looked down at the street, not really seeing it but still aware of a blur of cars passing a hundred feet below him. "Chloe Harris has talent. Real talent. She'll be famous, a household name one way or another, especially if Eddie Lambert has anything to say about it."

THREE

Saturday

The storm swept in fast through Central Pennsylvania. It blazed a path through the valley like a madman as it slammed its fists against the walls of Chloe's home. The trees swayed, the clouds burst, and the night turned pitch black, blotting out the full moon.

The only light in her bedroom was a red glow from the clock on the nightstand. Chloe huddled under the covers, unable to sleep.

I should get up and read, she thought. Better yet, I could write. She needed to do something besides lay here some twenty-four hours later, the meeting still replaying in her mind on an endless loop.

Multiple emotions reeled through her. She was angry with Phillip Belov and how he had dismissed her like she was second class. It was true she wasn't famous; she didn't have a lot of connections despite having a dozen books published, but everyone had to start somewhere.

That's when the insecurity set in. Maybe he was right, maybe she didn't have what it took, she needed more experience, and someone to believe in her. Other than Eddie, after all, she'd only really been in the industry for six years. It took a while to build your platform, make the connections, and establish a reputation.

Regret and self-loathing twisted in her gut. She had handled the meeting poorly, letting Phillip get the best of her. Walking out was unprofessional. Even though she knew this, she couldn't stop herself.

Eddie hadn't said anything on the way home, making the hour drive feel longer than it should have. As a result, she had just barricaded herself inside her house and had a good old-fashioned pity party. Once she'd gotten in anyway. For the life of her, she hadn't been able to find her keys, which she was certain she had when they left to go to the meeting. Just one more thing to make the terrible day complete. Thank goodness she had that spare key hidden outside.

She knew Eddie had hoped that someone from Belov Productions would try to contact them while they were driving but they hadn't. Chloe knew she had let him down, the farther they drove from Philadelphia, the more disappointment radiated from him.

Blinding white light ripped through the room, followed by a crack of thunder that shook the entire house. The clock blinked off, plunging her into complete darkness. The whir of the ceiling fan stopped, filling the room with silence.

"That's great," Chloe said into the eerily dark room. She turned, flipped her pillow over to the cool side, and laid her head back down. "Nothing to do now but sleep."

Lightning flashed and thunder rolled, making her jump.

She shivered and said into the empty room, "And pray the house is still intact in the morning."

✳

An eerie glow filled the space as a flash of lightning illuminated the book he held. It was heavier than it looked, a weighty feel in his palm. It was thick at the spine, the size the same width as the span of his thumb. The cover had a matte finish, smooth to the touch, with the image of a woman that was dark, mysterious, and seductive.

He traced the name that stood out in big, bold black letters, running an index finger over each. Chloe Harris.

He said her name out loud into the dark room. The vibration

of it surrounded him and echoed in the void that he was longing to fill.

Imagining the story inside, he placed his thumb on the front edge of the book and riffled through it, letting the pages vibrate under his thumb as they flipped quickly past. It was three hundred fifty-two pages, ninety-five thousand words.

A masterpiece.

From the moment he read her first words, she captivated him. Obsessed with her. Chloe Harris. He said her name like it was a mantra, over and over in his mind, until it played off the edges of his deepest fantasies.

Closing the book and turning it over to the back, he felt his mouth go dry as he stared at her picture. Long brown hair that flowed over her shoulders like silk and dark green eyes that seemed to pierce his very soul. What would he give to have her? Possess her. Own her. The answer to that was simple.

Everything.

FOUR

Monday

Tate stuck his hands in his front pockets and looked up at the old farmhouse that was nestled at the foothills of the Blue Ridge Mountains. Growing up he'd always loved this house as much as his own, with its wide front porch, high-pitched roof, and rambling addition. He hadn't been inside since he had done the remodeling a couple of years ago, turning the inside of a four-bedroom house meant for a family into a space suited for a single woman.

Now, it was time to update the outside.

Scanning the faded siding, he noted it was now more gray than white. The fieldstone of the original walls and foundation, which gave the house its old style and charm, still held like the day they were set. The windows were new, but the front porch had seen better days. The outside had weathered, but it still held that same appeal to him. Simply put, the house had character.

In the past, he imagined the huge porch could have served as a place to drop dirty boots on wet spring days, as a cool spot to sit on a hot summer's day, or as a place to stack firewood for the harsh Pennsylvania winters. But now, with its sagging middle and broken step, it looked more like an old man with a gaping smile and a missing tooth.

Tate went around to the truck's passenger side, scattering chickens, as he let his golden retriever out of the cab.

"There you go, old boy," he said, rubbing him. Completely uninterested in the hens, Bo retrieved his favorite baseball, dropped it at Tate's feet, and waited patiently. Tate grabbed his favorite bat with his initials carved in it out of the equipment bag in the cab, snagged the ball, tossed it in the air, and sent it sailing with a crack of the bat.

Bo leaped into the air and took off like a bolt of lightning, all paws and golden fur. Across the yard, racing past the horses that grazed in the nearby meadow, he skidded to a halt on the dirt lane and picked up the ball with his mouth. Bo trotted back, dropped the ball at Tate's feet, and they repeated the process. By the fifth hit, Bo was getting tired. When Bo came back this last time, he detoured to a nearby tree and laid down, panting.

Turning his attention back to the house, Tate stowed his bat and unhooked the ladder from the truck. They'd already been hired to update the siding and install shutters, but the storm bumped the work higher on his list of priorities despite his tight schedule. He had to maneuver a couple of other jobs and reroute the crews to fit this house into the schedule. Then he had added a few more items for this job, like removing the enormous tree that had fallen on it in the storm, replacing the broken windows, and updating the porch roof, and replacing the broken concrete with new.

As he carried the ladder, he ran through his mental list of things to do.

He envisioned how the house would look when it was done with the bright white beaded siding contrasting with the earth tones of the stone, black roof, trim, and shutters that had been selected. Adorned by those two mature red maples still standing on either side of the house, it would be as picturesque as a postcard when finished.

Construction was something Tate was born to do, from the minute he found a shiny nail on the ground or held a hammer in his hand, he had wanted to build things.

And he did, from birdhouses to sheds, dog houses to homes, and everything in between. He enjoyed the smell of sawdust from a precisely cut piece of wood, or the overwhelming sweet scent of a freshly painted room. Tate was completely comfortable with mindlessly hammering planks into place. On the flip side, he liked the intellectual challenge of determining the exact measurements required to hang a five-hundred-pound beam precisely at a forty-five-degree angle. Tate loved it all.

He accepted every challenge with enthusiasm. He embraced the day's work even when he knew it would be back-breaking stripping a one-hundred-year-old house to its bones to make it look brand new.

The agenda for the day: remove the fallen tree without damaging the house further, clean up the debris, and if time was on their side, get started on removing the siding.

He was a little surprised that Mr. Harris wasn't there to greet him, as the rest of the crew pulled in.

"'Bout time you guys showed up," Tate said to his brother Kurt and his best friend Neil as they hopped out of their trucks. "Thought I was going to have to do this all by myself. Can either of you drag your sorry butts out of bed before six?"

"I've been up since five," his brother replied dryly. "I thought we agreed to start at seven. If you wanted me earlier, you should have told me and brought donuts."

"It wasn't my turn, it was Neils."

Kurt looked at the man in question. "Well?"

"Never fear, I got 'em right here," Neil leaned into the cab of his old Chevy and pulled out a pink box.

Tate's mouth watered as the sweet scent of sugar and yeast wafted out of the container. Selecting a glazed donut, he sunk his teeth in, savoring the first bite.

"Neil," Kurt said, pointing a finger at him. "You're the man. Since you brought donuts, I'll forgive you for not stopping and picking me up this morning."

"I didn't know you wanted me to. Besides," Neil thought quickly. "If I did, you would have had to move all your tools into my truck, and I wouldn't have had room for the donuts."

"I could have held the box," Kurt said, licking the cream off of his thumb as it oozed out of his powdered confection. "And I could have used your tools."

"Not on your life," Neil said purposely, handing Kurt a

napkin. "You're too messy."

"You never have a problem letting the rest of the crew borrow something."

"That's because they know how to put things back."

"I put them back," Kurt answered, popping the rest of his donut in his mouth.

"Not in the right spots. And when you're done, my tools are always sticky."

Kurt chuckled as he licked his fingers. "That's fair. We know you're a little anal when it comes to your tools." He peered over the side as Neil raised the lid of his toolbox and saw the neatly arranged tools all in separate compartments.

"Nothin' wrong with being organized," Tate commented. "But when you start sleeping with them instead of women, that's when we need to start worrying."

Kurt let out a hoot.

"To hell with you both. That was one time. And I thought I explained that already."

"Something about being up all night, too tired, and sittin' down with a hammer in your hand . . . yadda, yadda." Kurt waved it off and snagged another donut.

"Alright, stop yapping you two, and let's get to work. This tree isn't going to remove itself."

"You don't need to tell me twice." With a grin, Kurt reached over the tailgate and grabbed his chainsaw. He made a show of stuffing the rest of his donut in his mouth and wiping his fingers on his jeans. With a quick upward jerk, Kurt pulled the cord and the chainsaw roared to life.

They worked steadily for a few hours as the sun rose. They stopped for lunch and reassessed the carnage from the tree. Branches, leaves, and logs littered the front yard.

With the tree completely removed from the house, Kurt continued to saw the trunk into smaller manageable pieces. Sawdust and the steady buzz of the machine filled the air.

Neil nudged Tate so he would be heard over the noise. "We have company," he shouted, pointing at a vehicle coming slowly down the road.

"Guess I'll go see who it is." Tate stretched, and shouted, "I'll be right back."

The black SUV pulled up to the house and a woman got out.

Tate walked toward her with the sun in his eyes and waved. "Hey, there. Can I help you?" he called over the noise.

She didn't answer, instead she greeted Bo as he trotted over wagging his tail happily. She patted him on the head obligingly.

Shading his eyes, Tate took in the quiet beauty standing in front of him, the afternoon sun behind her. She wore a pale green T-shirt and cut-offs showcasing long tan legs that stretched on forever. She was something so foreign and yet so familiar to him that his mouth went dry.

His stomach took an unexpected dip as he moved closer. Tate had to restrain himself from moving too fast. He was desperate to see her eyes hidden behind those dark sunglasses. Once he was close enough, it was all he could do not to reach out and remove them. He didn't have to, though; she did it for him.

She slipped her sunglasses down an inch and peered at him over the silver rims. A sense of déjà vu swamped him. Deep, intense green. Her eyes were shades of green so deep, so dark, that he imagined they only existed in the farthest recesses of a rainforest. He stood, struck dumb, for a second or two until she pushed the sunglasses back into place. He'd know her anywhere.

Finding his tongue, he asked jokingly, "Are you lost?"

"Now, why would you think that?" she asked in a cool even voice.

Tate stuck out his hand. "I'm Tate Becker," he said in a playful tone. "You usually avoid me at all costs."

She left his hand hanging in midair and took her sunglasses off completely, threading them through her coffee-colored hair.

"You're right, I usually do. Unfortunately, this time I wasn't able to," she said in the same cool tone, her demeanor frosty.

He couldn't help but crack a sly smile, he liked a challenge, sensing the steel behind the words. "Looks like it's my lucky day."

"You could say that."

Locked in the moment, Tate didn't realize his brother had shut off the chainsaw and walked over. Kurt pushed past him.

"Hey, Chloe."

Instantly, she smiled at his older brother, and the coolness melted like a crocus pushing through a layer of frost. That smile cut him in half, making him wish that she'd smiled at him like that. She had . . . once upon a time.

"Kurt Becker."

"I thought you were out of town?"

She laughed, which sent a spike of heat through Tate.

"I was. But now I'm not."

"The illusive Chloe Harris?" Tate said, teasing, vying for her attention.

Chloe put her hand on her hip. Looking directly at Tate with those eyes, a flash of heat in them, she asked, "Who were you expecting? The Queen of England? This is my house."

"I know it's your house, but . . ."

Neil walked over. "Hey, Chloe."

"Hey, yourself, Neil. Good to see you."

"When did you get back?" Kurt asked simply.

"Friday."

"So, you were here for the storm?" Tate asked.

"Yes."

"Looks like you were lucky," Tate commented. "Damage was minimal, considering."

"That's what my dad said."

"Where is he?" Tate asked. "I thought when he called yesterday that he was going to meet us here this morning. That I'd be dealing with him."

"Change of plans. My sister called. Chelsea's seven months pregnant. I'm sure you guys have heard. It's all my mom talks about lately."

All three nodded.

"She's very excited, and rightfully so." Chloe sucked in a breath and prepared to tell them the news. "Chelsea went to the emergency room yesterday in a lot of pain."

"Everything alright?"

"Not really. Long story short the baby and Chelsea are okay, but she will be on bed rest until the baby comes."

"I'm sorry to hear that, Chloe."

"Yeah, me too. This was completely unexpected. Everything had been going so well. My sister already has eighteen-month-old twin boys running around at home so staying in bed is going to be difficult for her." Chloe shrugged. "I'm sure you can guess what happened from there."

"Your parents agreed to fly out and help Chelsea with the twins," Kurt offered as a way of explanation.

"Exactly. My dad was hesitant to go with the damage from the storm, the tree removal, and the remodeling starting today, but I assured him I could handle it."

"Did you need to go with them?"

"No, I would just be in the way. Besides, someone has to take care of the animals."

Kurt looked down at her. "You know I can easily feed them; I've done it before."

She smiled up at him. "I know. Your name was even brought up, but none of us wanted to put you out, and I don't mind. I don't have any plans to travel. I'm trying to finish my current work in progress."

"My mom raves about your books," Neil said, "so much so that I even read a couple."

"Really?" Tate asked, clearly surprised.

"I read."

"And not just the back of a cereal box like you," Kurt chuckled. "Try picking up a book sometime."

"Go to hell, both of you."

Chloe looked at the house. "Looks like you are making progress, so I'll let you get back to it. Is it safe to use the front door, or should I go around back?"

"I'd continue to use the back for now. Even though the tree is off the porch, I wouldn't want to take any chances. We haven't had a chance to shore up the roof or take it off completely, and

I wouldn't want any movement to jeopardize its stability. I'll let you know when it's safe to use again," Tate answered.

"Okay, thanks. I'll talk to you guys later."

Chloe disappeared quickly around the back of the house, letting herself in through the mudroom.

Over the past couple of years, Tate Becker and Becker Construction had transformed the farmhouse's once boxy rooms into an open concept.

Chloe ran her hand over the cool, white granite countertops while admiring the sage green cabinets. Despite how she felt about Tate, she had to admit he always did a wonderful job. The eating nook just off the kitchen was one of her favorite spots in the house with its cozy bench piled high with pillows, surrounded by large windows, framing the outdoors in panes of glass.

She wandered into the living area, letting her eyes follow the angles of the vaulted ceiling with its exposed beams anchored in place by a stone fireplace on the far wall. The great room was decorated in soft earth tones pulling the outside in.

Chloe climbed the stairs that hugged the wall of the great room to her office in the loft, she smiled at the old familiar squeak of treads. But her smile faded as soon as she reached her desk, and she mentally prepared herself to write. She opened her laptop, pulled up her latest novel, and poised her fingers over the keyboard.

A second ticked by. Then ten. Another sixty passed and nothing happened. She blinked and tried to pull inspiration from the view. But nothing came.

Scolding herself she tried again. Closing her eyes, she took a deep breath. Clearing her mind, she began to type.

Blue eyes. Brown hair - the color of warm toffee. Chiseled jawline. Tate.

Her insides fluttered. After opening her eyes, she read what she wrote. "Fudge," she grumbled, hitting the backspace and deleted it.

Her mind wouldn't focus, at least not on writing. It only

wanted to think about Tate.

The minute she'd seen him her stomach had pitched. Of course, she'd been prepared to run into him at some point knowing that Becker Construction was handling the work. Her father always hired them. He insisted they were the best. Granted they had done an excellent job over the years but Chloe didn't want to hire them on principle. But every time she needed something done, her father hired Tate. So, she made herself scarce by scheduling events or meetings and then leaving town for work, thus avoiding Tate for the most part for the past ten years.

This time it was different though. This time she would have to stay, talk to him, and work with him. Her father wasn't here to run interference. Her shenanigans needed to stop. No more spotting him coming down the street and crossing to the other side before he saw her. No more going out a back door at the convenience store when she heard his voice. Chloe hadn't even realized how good a job she had done avoiding him until today - until the moment she was face-to-face with him and the hurt rushed back in.

Chloe decided right then she could do this. She could handle Tate Becker. Hopefully, a great deal better than she had handled the Belov Productions meeting.

That was a whole other situation, she sighed. She knew she needed to call Eddie, but not yet. She needed another day or two and assumed he did too or he would have called.

Her house was her priority. This was her home, she needed to be present to oversee the work and be here if they had questions, or needed anything. She straightened, this was where she lived and worked, Tate Becker was on her turf. She held the upper hand. His face filled her mind and her heart fluttered at the mere thought of him. Or did she?

FIVE

Tate loved the end of the day almost as much as he loved the beginning. There was just something about the quiet descending around him as the tools shut off and the sawdust settled. After surveying his crew's accomplishments and making a to-do list for the next day, Tate put his tools away. He enjoyed cleaning up the debris, even little pieces of wood that had been sawed off or a nail that had rolled away. In this case, though, it was branches, leaves, logs, and a scarred front porch held together by two-by-fours.

Taking his clipboard out of the cab, Tate stood in front of the house and ticked off what they had completed and the supplies they would need for tomorrow.

"Satisfied?" Kurt asked, loading his toolbox into the bed of the truck.

"Very. We accomplished a lot today."

"It's going to look damn good when we're done."

"Damn straight."

Neil wiped off his tools and placed them in the bed of the truck. "What time do you want to start tomorrow?"

"Originally, it was seven with Mr. Harris, but since Chloe's the one here now I guess I should check with her to see if it still works." Tate started for the house. "No need for you two to hang around. I'll text you the time after I've spoken with her."

"Sounds good. I have some errands to do," Kurt said, climbing into the cab. "Are we still on for dinner?"

"Yeah, by the time we get cleaned up it'll have to be at seven."

"Seven it is."

"Works for me too. Catch you later." Neil waved as he jumped in his truck and pulled out of the yard.

Tate threw the clipboard on the front seat and went to the side door. He knocked and when there was no answer, he opened the door and went in. "Chloe?" he called.

He found her easily in the great room with her back to him.

"Chloe," he said again but she didn't turn. He watched her for a minute taking things off the shelves and packing them in the boxes at her feet. That's when he noticed the phone in her back pocket and wondered if she had earbuds in. A sly smile crossed his face. He used to love to scare her when they were younger. He couldn't resist now. Tate crossed the room quickly and stood directly behind her.

She reached for a box.

He lunged. "Boo!"

Chloe screamed. Swung. Tate weaved.

"Tate William Becker!" she cursed at him pulling out her earbuds. "You scared the heck out of me!"

"You missed," he said with a laugh.

She punched him in the arm for good measure.

"Ouch!"

"That time I didn't," she said with some satisfaction. Putting one hand on her heart, the other on her hip, she asked, "Don't you knock?"

"I did." He stifled another laugh. "You just didn't hear me."

She glared at him, and once again he noticed her deep, dark, forest-green eyes. How had he forgotten those eyes?

"Did you need something?" Chloe asked, "Or just come in here to scare me?"

"I came in on official business, to ask you if you have a problem with us starting at seven tomorrow morning. Scaring you was a bonus."

She glared at him, but answered, "That should be fine. You're removing the siding, and installing the new windows here in the great room?"

"Yes."

"I'll be ready." She looked around the room. "I only need to remove anything that could fall off the walls, correct?"

"I would suggest taking anything breakable off these shelves too." He selected a book off the shelf. "You don't need to pack away books."

"I wasn't going to."

He turned the book over in his hand, and read the title and the author's name. "One of yours, I see." Then he eyed the spot from the shelf it had come from and noticed a whole row of her books. "Mystery romance, right?"

She tilted her head and watched him. "That's right."

If she was impressed that he knew, she didn't show it.

"How many books do you have out now?"

"Twelve. I'm just about a third of the way through the first draft of my thirteenth."

"Wow, that's impressive."

"Really?" she asked, sounding skeptical.

Tate looked at her . . . Chloe had been one of his very best friends in elementary and middle school. Somehow, their friendship had survived the awkward adolescent phase, and they'd come out on the other side unscathed. High school had been different. The first couple of years were good: riding in the truck with Kurt to and from school, studying together, staying late for practices, going to games, and cheering each other on.

But something had shifted their senior year. He couldn't quite put his finger on it. Somewhere amid everything, the lines had blurred. He felt their friendship become messy, and he privately wondered what it might be like to date the ever-popular but quiet, Chloe Harris. He knew those two characteristics were rarely put in the same sentences but somehow, with her, it worked. She wasn't the prettiest or the richest, she wasn't valedictorian or the trendiest, she was just simply Chloe. The kindest, fiercest friend anyone could ever ask for. He missed that. He missed her. Tate hadn't even realized how much until now.

He cleared his throat, all too aware that she was waiting for an answer. "It is." He looked her directly in the eye, and said as seriously as he could, "Very impressive." And he meant it.

"Have you read any of them?" she asked the question, barely audible.

"No," he said regretfully. "I haven't but mom has and says they're phenomenal."

The corners of her mouth flattened and turned into a straight line set firmly in place. The disappointment was written all over it. Lifting her chin slightly she took the book gently out of his hand.

He hated that he had disappointed her, but at the moment he didn't know how to fix it. Trying to change the subject, he asked, "Do you have some extra sheets?"

"I do. Why?"

"Well, it's bound to get dusty in here. I'll bring drop cloths to protect the floors from us coming and going while we replace these windows but I don't have enough to cover all the furniture in this room."

"I'll put it on my list of things to do before the morning."

"What else do you need to do?"

"Let's see," she held up her hand and ticked items off. "I need to finish packing the breakables, cover everything with sheets, feed the horses, lock up the chickens, get groceries, and . . . oh, yeah, somewhere in there I actually need to write."

"And eat."

"What?"

"You need to eat at some point," he stated.

"Hence, going to the grocery store." She put the book back on the shelf. "If I'm going to get to the store, I should probably get going."

"Can you wait?" Suddenly he didn't want the day to end without Chloe in it.

"What do you mean?"

"We, that is, Kurt, Neil, and I are going to the Taphouse to grab some dinner. Why don't you come?"

"I don't know. I have a lot to do."

"Look," Tate pulled out his phone. "It's five-thirty. I'm going home and showering. You can keep working until six-thirty. That's an hour."

Putting her hand on her hip, a gesture he was all too familiar with from her, she said dryly, "I can do the math."

He grinned and noticed her prickly attitude was back. He'd have to work at chipping it away. "Right. I'll pick you up, take you to dinner, and then take you to the grocery store before I bring you home. I'm sure you already made a list."

"I have but I certainly don't need your help buying groceries."

"Maybe not but I could make the trip faster for you."

"How exactly?"

Shrugging he said, "I know where everything is in the store."

"And you think I don't?"

He ignored her comment. "We can knock it out faster if there are two of us. And to sweeten the pot I'll even help you bring it in and put it away, or help you finish covering furniture. Whatever you need. How 'bout it?"

"I don't know. What's the catch?"

"No catch."

"That's surprising. Usually, there's something with you."

"Come on, you know you want to."

She didn't answer him directly. But when her stomach growled, she asked, "The Taphouse, huh?"

"Yep."

"I heard they just had some remodeling done. I've been wanting to go and check it out, but haven't had the chance."

"It's a trendy little bar and grill now with new ownership. It has a nice little deck that you can eat out on. Perfect on a night like this. The deck cantilevers out over the water. It has a great view of the river, and there are falls underneath, which gives it that relaxed sound. It's pretty cool if I do say so myself. You'll love it."

"Let me guess, you did the remodeling."

"Damn right, I did. Neil designed it, and Becker Construction made it come to life. It's our new favorite place to go and eat after a long day of work. You won't be disappointed with the atmosphere, the food, or the company."

"I am hungry," Chloe said.

"Of course you are. It's been a long day. And who wants to cook?"

"I don't, but I could have soup, and that doesn't take much effort on my part."

"That's not very filling. Besides, what kind of guy would I be if I let you eat alone?" Tate encouraged.

"It would be nice to have dinner with Neil and Kurt."

"But not me?"

She sniffed. "I guess I can tolerate your company."

"Wow," he said, shaking his head with a grin on his face. "And I always took you for a nice girl. Despite that, I'm still willing to take you."

She debated, "I need to bring in the chickens, and feed the horses."

"Do that while I go home and shower." He could see her hesitating. "You can't say no to me."

"I most certainly can."

"But you don't want to."

She sighed. "I'm only saying yes because I feel like you're not going to leave until I do. And then I'll never get anything done."

His smile was broad and instant. "That's the spirit!" He turned on his heel, before she could change her mind and said, "I'll be back in an hour."

What am I doing? She asked herself as she climbed up into Tate's truck. I've been around him for less than a day and I've already let him weasel his way back into my life.

It's just dinner, she reminded herself. Kurt and Neil will be there too. It's not like it's a date. Right, because you're never going back down that road with him, no matter how good-looking he is. Or fun. Or magnetic. He's still the same old Tate that broke your heart.

"Hey," he said as she closed the door. "Ready?"

"As I'll ever be," she answered stiffly. They rode in awkward silence as they drove down her lane and out onto the main road, the trees rolling by.

"I don't bite, you know."

"What?" Chloe asked, trying not to look at Tate.

"You're as far away from me as you can get and still be in the cab. What's the matter? Do I smell or something?"

The answer to that was yes. The whole cab smelled like him. It was a musky, seductive scent that made her insides feel like jelly. She'd forgotten how good he always smelled, especially in the truck's close quarters. The truck had changed since the last time she'd ridden with him, but neither the scent nor the man had.

Relief washed over her as they came around the curve and headed into town. The land covered in trees and pastures was free-flowing with a sprinkling of houses which gave way to more houses, and buildings containing small businesses. Structure replaced the organic, organized in small developments, sidewalks, and tree-lined streets.

"The way you're holding that purse looks like you might try to jump out at the first stoplight."

She wasn't even aware of how tense she was until Tate mentioned it. Chloe glanced down at her purse that was clutched to her chest like it was a floatation device. "Lucky for you, there's only two, and we already passed the first one," she said using all the sarcasm she could muster. She couldn't help but feel if she relaxed and let go, she would drown, swamped by the man next to her.

As they drove, they passed some cute shops, turned right at the beer distributor, and crossed the river just past the falls on a metal bridge that hummed as the tires rolled across.

"Here we are."

On the outside, the Taphouse was an old stone building that had once been a working mill. It stood four stories high, had a pitched shake roof, and small windows that glowed warmly within. A small roof jutted out, covering the front door.

"The new owner didn't want to change the exterior, so we left everything the same on three sides of the building. Simply repaired, restored, and painted."

"It's beautiful. I like the fact that you kept its original facade."

"Wait until you see the inside." Tate held the door for her.

The inside was everything Tate had promised. It had a high ceiling that was jet black with metal beams that gleamed as light reflected and bounced off the polished surfaces. The walls were made of the same river-rock as the outside, and a bar made of ebony granite ran the length of the room, reminding Chloe of a riverbed at midnight. Glass bottles with various shades of amber liquid were perched on shelves and reflected in the mirror behind the bar. At least a dozen stools were occupied at the bar. But the real focal point was the glass wall that looked out to the deck and the river beyond, where the large wheel moved slowly, water spilling off. The vast room was an eclectic mix of materials that contrasted and yet fit seamlessly together.

Chloe's breath caught. "It's gorgeous, Tate. You've outdone yourself."

He flashed her a grin. "Thanks. I knew you'd like it."

The hostess stand was near the front door, and immediately they were greeted by a petite woman about their age with a smile a mile wide and platinum blonde hair tucked into a perky ponytail. Her face was a perfect oval with painted bright red lips that drew up like a bow when she said, "Tate! So good to see you."

"Hey, Kimmy." He leaned over and gave her a quick peck on the cheek.

"I see you brought a friend." She winked at Chloe giving her the once over. "Oh. My. Gosh! Chloe Harris, is that you?"

Chloe narrowed her eyes trying to put the name Tate had said to the face before her. With all that perk and sass, she knew the head cheerleader from high school instantly. Kimmy Keller.

"It's me," Chloe said with a smile.

The woman squealed and wrapped Chloe in a hug. "I can't

believe it! I haven't seen you in years, and we live in the same town. How does that happen?"

Kimmy released her, holding her at arm's length. Chloe wasn't given a chance to reply.

"Look how pretty you are! You haven't changed a bit. Which makes me hate you all over again."

"What did you just say?" Chloe asked, taken back.

"Nothing, silly," Kimmy waved it off with a laugh.

"Tate didn't mention you worked here."

"I don't work here, silly. I own it."

"Tate didn't mention that either."

"Men!" Kimmy laughed. "They always leave out the important details. But I'm sure he told you he did the remodeling."

"Yes, he did." Both women gave him a sideways glance.

"I see."

"What?" Tate asked, all innocent.

"Regardless, the place is gorgeous, Kimmy."

"Thank you. I'm very proud of my little establishment." Kimmy beamed. "Are you home for a few days? I hear through the gossip chain that you travel a lot, attending book clubs and what-not."

The door opened behind them, a few more customers walked in, and once again Chloe didn't get the chance to respond.

Kimmy turned to Tate. "Look at me chatting when you came here to eat. And now I have a line. We need to get you to your table. Chloe, we will have to catch up later. You both must be starving."

"I know I am," Tate said.

Kimmy directed her attention to the new guests. "I'll be right back to get you seated." She turned back to Tate and Chloe. "Fiddle-dee-dee! Follow me! Your brother and Neil are already out on the deck at your regular table."

Chloe shot Tate a quick glance. "How often do you eat here?"

"Enough."

They threaded their way through the tables and out the large glass doors to the deck. There were lights strung from poles overhead, and in the center of it all, an open fire pit that snapped and popped.

The tables were made of dark wood, dotted with glass globes that glowed like soft yellow orbs. The deck itself was surrounded by water, edged in ferns and trees, making it the perfect little oasis.

"Here you go," Kimmy said, pulling out a chair for Chloe. "Promise me we can get together soon?"

"I'd like that."

"Great!" She clapped her hands together like the cheerleader she used to be. "Enjoy!" she said, trailing a hand over Tate's bicep as she walked away. A little more spring in her step than a moment earlier.

"Thank you, Kimmy."

"You didn't tell me Kimmy owned the Taphouse," Chloe said, picking up a menu.

"It didn't occur to me that it mattered." Tate shrugged.

"What's good here?" she asked.

"Everything," Kurt replied. "But I'm partial to the loaded nachos." Pointing them out on the menu, he added, "That's just the appetizer. For my meal, I get boneless wings with the sweet chili sauce."

Chloe scanned the menu, unable to decide. "And Neil, what about you?"

"I usually get the cheeseburger sliders with a side of beer batter onion rings."

"I get the Taphouse burger with the bacon-wrapped tater tots," Tate added. "Thanks for asking."

"I was getting to you," she said, rolling her eyes. "It all sounds great."

"You'd better decide because here comes the waitress to take our order."

The waitress, barely eighteen, came over, delivered water, took their order, and promised to be back soon, giving Tate a small smile.

THE FURTHER I FALL

Inside, the atmosphere hummed, but outside on the deck, it was more laid-back, lazy like the river that ran beside it. Chloe sat back and relaxed.

She was actually glad Tate had asked her to come along. She hadn't eaten anything since about ten, which consisted of a smushed granola bar she found in the bottom of her purse on the way to take her parents to the airport and a Diet Pepsi. Her stomach rumbled as the waitress brought the loaded nachos and set them on the table.

"I'm starving," Neil said, reaching for the plates and passing them out. "Don't be shy, Chloe. Help yourself."

"Thanks, I am hungry."

"Hungry? Your stomach is growling so loud I thought there was a bear sitting beside me," Tate said, pulling a nacho dripping in salsa off the top of the pile.

"You're hilarious," Chloe mumbled, doing the same.

Kurt reached for a chip. "Did your mom and dad make it to Arizona okay?"

Chloe nodded, breaking a chip in half. "Yes, they landed around five. I expect the pictures to start flooding in of the twins pretty soon. My parents haven't seen them since Easter, so they were pretty ecstatic to get the chance to go even if the conditions aren't the best for my sister."

"Now that they're there, I'm sure everything will be fine. Chelsea will get some rest, and your mom will handle everything."

"Does your mom still bake a lot?" Neil asked.

"Yes."

"She always made the best chocolate chip cookies."

"Still does," Tate said between bites. "She just made some last week when I was over."

"And you didn't think to bring me one?" Kurt asked.

"I was on official business, and she just happened to serve coffee and cookies." He shrugged. "I can't help it if you weren't there. It's the perks of being the project manager."

Their meals came, and they waited patiently for the server to distribute the entrees.

Chloe watched the waitress make eye contact with the men, but she lingered a little longer on Tate. Then she glanced at Chloe and realized she'd been caught. The waitress blushed a bright red.

Oh, brother, Chloe thought. Another woman who isn't immune to his charms.

"Can I get you anything else?" she asked, placing the ketchup on the table and directing the question to Tate.

"I think we're good. Thank you," Tate answered.

"You're welcome. I'll be back to check on you," the waitress said.

Kurt chuckled. "How many times have you dated that one?"

Picking up his burger, Tate spared Kurt a glance. "I haven't dated her once, and she's like eighteen."

"He does draw the line at robbing the cradle," Neil commented. He gulped his beer. Neil looked knowingly at Chloe and explained, "Tate has to be careful dating any of the waitresses from the Taphouse."

"Why is that?" Chloe wanted to know.

Neil grinned, dipping his onion ring in ketchup. "Because Kimmy has "dibs" on him," he answered using air quotes.

"Really?" Chloe asked.

"Yes."

"No, she doesn't," Tate protested.

"Then you're stupider than I thought," Kurt said to his younger brother. "She's liked you for years."

"I second that." Neil nodded.

"Kurt's right, she has," Chloe agreed softly, as a pang of hurt tore through her ripping open an old wound.

"That was in high school. This is now. We're adults. Let it go, you morons," Tate grumbled, concentrating on his burger.

"Yeah, but not for her lack of trying or hinting around," Neil said.

"You guys like to make shit up. It's nothing but professional between us."

"Keep telling yourself that," Kurt chided, stuffing in three fries at a time. "She's still into you even if she's able to hide it better than she did in high school."

Chloe felt her phone vibrate in her back pocket. She slipped it out and saw that it was from her parents. She smiled.

"What?" Tate asked, leaning over to look.

"It's pictures of the twins. I told you it wouldn't be long." She held the phone out so they could see. "Aren't they sweet?"

"May I?" Kurt asked, taking the phone from her.

"Of course."

Kurt swiped through the pictures, angling it so Neil could see. "Pretty cute kids. Looks like those boys adore your father."

Finished, he passed the phone to Tate.

"They look like your sister."

"They sure do."

"A message just popped up. Looks like your boyfriend misses you," Tate said with a smile in his voice.

Chloe stopped with her fork midway to her mouth. "What?"

"There's no way you don't have one," Kurt teased.

"Let me see that." She reached for her cell.

Tate moved it out of reach. "Looks like it's Eddie Lambert."

"Give me the phone, please."

"Is he your boyfriend?" Tate asked, teasing her like he used to.

"No, we sometimes work together. He's an agent. I thought you guys knew that."

"We do," Neil acknowledged.

"Please, give me the phone," she said sternly, holding out her hand.

Tate relented and moved the phone closer to her. He locked eyes with her. Without breaking eye contact, Chloe pried the phone out of his hand. "You're such a brat."

The text was four words.

Eddie: We need to talk.

Chloe: I'll call you tomorrow.

"Anything urgent?" Tate asked, leaning over her shoulder.

"Nope," she said casually, trying not to think about the

apology she needed to give over the botched meeting. She stuck her cell in her purse.

"Well, speak of the devil," Kurt said as he pointed toward the front door. "Here comes Eddie now."

"Hello," Eddie said as he walked up to the table. "I'm surprised to see you all here."

"Shouldn't be, we eat here every Monday night," Tate answered.

"So, it's not a special occasion?" he asked, as his eyes settled on Chloe.

"Nope."

"Then, do you mind if I join you?" Eddie asked.

"Not at all," Kurt said. "Pull up a chair."

Eddie snagged an empty chair from a nearby table and slid in between Tate and Chloe. "Don't mind if I do."

Chloe slid her chair over and made room. She could feel Eddie's eyes on her. She avoided his gaze, focusing on her meal, feeling completely awkward. Glancing up, she caught Tate's eye. It felt like Tate could see right through her. It seemed like he always could. Except for when it came to her heart. Chloe was the first to look away.

SIX

"Okay, spill it," Tate pressed as they carried groceries into the house.

"What?" Chloe asked, dropping her purse onto the kitchen counter.

"The text on your phone."

"I get a lot of texts on my phone. You'll have to be more specific." But she knew exactly what he referred to.

He held the door open for her, followed her back to his truck, and grabbed a couple more bags.

Once inside, he asked, "What did Eddie want? He was pretty cryptic at dinner."

"Nothing important."

"You could have fooled me. First, he texts, then he shows up and plops himself beside you."

Chloe ignored Tate as she took fresh fruit and vegetables from the bag, placed apples and oranges in the ceramic bowl on the table, and put the vegetables in the refrigerator.

Tate dug through a bag of canned goods. "Where do these go?"

She pointed. "Pantry."

He opened the door, disappeared inside, and let out a low whistle. "No wonder you needed groceries. When's the last time you went to the store?"

"It's been a while." Chloe snuck past him into the pantry and laid the bread on a shelf. Turning to go, Tate blocked her way. "Excuse me, please. I need to get the ice cream in the freezer."

"Then you had better answer my question before it melts."

She sighed.

"What did Eddie want?" Tate asked, putting his arm out and boxing her in the small space.

She was all too aware of how good he smelled, how big he was, and the heat radiating from his body. Chloe looked up into his eyes and almost melted.

"If this is about work, why won't you tell me?" He stared her down. "Is Eddie your boss?"

"I'm an indie author, Tate. I'm my own boss. I already told you that Eddie is an agent, I have worked with him, but only for certain things. I don't always deal with him on every project, but not for his lack of trying."

"Then why won't you tell me what he wanted? He certainly didn't say while he was wedged between us."

"Because it doesn't concern you. Why do you want to know so bad?"

"I'm curious by nature. Maybe there's more going on between the two of you than you let on. Is he your boyfriend?" Tate teased.

"Let it go."

"Not on your life. You have me intrigued now. I won't stop until I've figured it out."

Chloe ducked under his arm. "You won't guess it."

"Challenge accepted."

She shook her head, put the ice cream in the freezer, and sighed, "It wasn't a challenge."

"Not to you."

She had to laugh at that. "You always did like a challenge."

"You bet I do." He pulled a sleeve of bagels out of the bag. "Catch." And tossed it at her. She caught it on the fly and set it on the counter. "Let's see. We've covered the boyfriend angle. Past, present . . . maybe future?"

"No," she said simply. "It's not like that."

He opened the fridge and put the milk in, leaning on the door, looking perplexed. "You got me? I've got nothing. Tell me."

Ignoring him, she said, "I think that's everything." Chloe held the egg carton out to him since he still had the refrigerator door open.

Tate didn't take them. "Chloe, look at me."

"Can you put these in the fridge?" she asked, avoiding his gaze. "Please?"

"You're not going to tell me?"

"The eggs," she said, pressing them into his hand. "Tate, honestly. I don't know why you think this is important."

He stared at her.

She sighed. "We had a meeting that didn't go as planned."

"What kind of meeting?"

"We met with a production company about possibly turning my first book into a movie."

"Wow! That's exciting."

"The meeting didn't go well."

"I'm sorry to hear that. What happened? Did you roll your eyes at the guy in charge when he gave you too much attitude?"

"You're funny," she said sarcastically. "And why would you assume it was my fault?"

His smile was quick. "I could answer that, but then you'd probably be mad at me again, so I'll refrain from answering."

"Well, that's a surprise. Besides, it's not as big a deal as you were making it out to be." Keep telling yourself that, she chided.

He took the carton, put the eggs in the refrigerator, and closed the door. "I don't know. A movie deal sounds pretty big to me. Bet Eddie thinks so too."

Chloe entered the great room, avoiding the statement, and Tate followed.

"It looks like you're almost ready for tomorrow down here. How about I help you cover the furniture?" he said, pointing to the pile of sheets.

"I can do it."

"I know you can, but it will be faster if I help."

"Fine," she said, tossing him a sheet that she'd brought down earlier. They shook out the fabric and floated it easily over furniture, tucking the material in where necessary.

It only took a few minutes, and they had everything covered. "That should do it."

Chloe ushered Tate to the door. "Thanks for your help tonight, and thanks for dinner."

"So does that mean we're back on good terms?"

"What do you mean?"

"Well, you've been a little grouchy since this morning. I can't help but think you're mad at me for some reason."

Not mad, she thought. Just hurt. But it's been years now, so she should let it go. Needed to. He was a good guy, and she missed being around him. She'd forgotten how much fun he could be.

"I'm not mad, Tate; I'm just tired," she said, letting him off the hook. She'd forgive him — maybe, and maybe she wouldn't. She hadn't fully decided yet, but she wouldn't forget. "Good night, Tate."

"Good night. See you at seven sharp." He stepped off the porch.

She shut the door and turned the lock.

Wearily, she shut off the rest of the lights and climbed the creaky stairs in the dark. At the top, she paused and looked down over the great room, which had all the furniture covered. The faint moonlight gave the house an eerily quiet feel.

"Geeze," she whispered. "It looks like something right out of one of my books." She shivered despite herself unable to shake an unsettling feeling.

❋

Two-for-one specials always drew a crowd on Monday nights. Despite that, he saw her come in. With brown hair, dark eyes, and red lips, his interest peaked. He had an itch, and it needed to be scratched.

He stared straight ahead, pretending to drink his beer. Instead, he watched her through the strategically placed mirror behind the bar, taking her in. If he squinted just right, he could pretend she was someone else. She would do. She would have to.

He watched as the woman found an empty booth and slid in.

Spinning around on his stool, he stared. His gaze was so intense that he knew she felt it. The second she looked up, they made eye contact. He nodded and raised his glass as a salute to what was about to happen.

He signaled to the bartender, ordered a glass of champagne, and paid his tab in cash. When the bartender walked away to serve another customer, he slipped the crushed powder into the drink, watched it quickly dissolve, and picked up the glass.

He crossed the bar as if he owned it, cutting a direct path to her. He was in charge of the situation, and the prospect of controlling another person surged adrenaline through him. He needed the feel of domination to quench his thirst.

He cleared his throat. "Excuse me, I hope I'm not interrupting."

"Not at all."

He turned up the charm. "I couldn't help but notice you from across the room. I'm desperately hoping you're here to meet me."

Her smile was instant and a bit too toothy for his liking, but tonight, she was the closest thing in the room to what he wanted, what he craved.

"I believe I am. Please," she indicated from the other side of the booth, clearly delighted. "Have a seat."

He slid across from her. "I hoped you'd say that. I took the liberty of getting you a drink. Do you like champagne?"

"Wasn't that sweet," she said, accepting it. "Thank you. What's your name?"

"What would you prefer it to be, if given the choice?" he asked coyly.

She threw her head back and laughed. "So that's how you want to play." She lifted an eyebrow and contemplated him. "I think I'll call you Steve."

He raised his glass in salute. "Mind if I call you Chloe?"

"Not at all," she said returning the gesture.

He smirked as she took the first sip.

SEVEN

Tuesday

"You can do this," Chloe said, trying to convince herself when she could barely stay awake. She sat at her computer and tried to write, but it was difficult because her head kept hitting the keyboard, and her eyelids felt like lead. She was exhausted. Between the meeting, the storm and Tate, she'd barely slept the past three nights.

The windows were open, making being inside even more grueling, while the sunshine and warm air enticed her to come out. She looked out the window wistfully. With her chin on her hand, she wished she was outside instead of in, stuck behind a self-induced deadline.

It didn't help either that there was a steady pounding below her. The incessant hammering was quite the distraction, and in between, there were blasts from a drill, saw, or whatever that darn sound was. They were in and out, laughing, singing to 80's music, Disney theme songs, or pure country at the top of their lungs, completely and utterly out of tune. It made her wish she was working with them instead of writing. They sounded as if they were having a blast.

Shaking her head, she tried desperately to concentrate. After rereading what she wrote for the hundredth time, she deemed it good. Chloe decided it was time for a break. Standing up, she stretched and grabbed her water bottle.

Time to refill and go for a walk.

Maybe the fresh air would do her creative juices some good.

There was a lull in the hammering, filled with voices and the retreating of feet. Figures, they were taking a break as she was about to.

Chloe put her earbuds in her ears and her phone in her back pocket. Descending the stairs, she went to the mud room, shoving her feet into her sneakers.

Slipping out the door, she found Tate's golden retriever lying in the shade on her sagging front porch like he owned the place. Lifting his head, he wagged his tail, glad to see her. She couldn't help herself; Bo was just so sweet she had to stop and pet him.

"Hey there, Bo. How are you today?" she asked, scratching under his chin.

The deep voice came from behind her. "You'll talk to my dog, but not me?"

Chloe bristled slightly, but didn't turn around to look at him. "How exactly do you put up with him?" she asked Bo.

"I didn't so much as get a cup of coffee, a bagel, or good morning out of you so far today."

"Your dog is sweet." With one last rub, she stood and finally looked at him. "You, on the other hand, aren't."

"You're the only girl in town that doesn't think I'm sweet."

"That's because you're a habitual flirt with all the other girls. You can't help yourself. I've known you too long. I'm immune to your charm."

"So, I hear you saying that I am charming?"

"That's not what I said. More like annoying."

He laughed at that. "No one is complaining but you."

"I'm not complaining. I'm just stating the facts." She moved to go, but Tate stepped in front of her. Even though he was one step lower than she was, they stood eye to eye. He'd always been taller than her, and she wasn't short. She squared her shoulders and ensured she stood at her full five-foot-eight-inch height. Looking directly into his blue eyes, she tried to sound assertive. "Get out of my way, Tate."

"Make me." He grinned playfully, an easy smile spreading across his chiseled features.

"Make me?" she questioned. "You're so mature."

That comment only made his smile widen, and when it did, a dimple winked out on the left side of his face. Unfazed by his so-called charm, Chloe put her hand on her hip.

"Why so grouchy this morning?"

"If you must know. I didn't sleep well last night despite being exhausted."

"Oh?"

She shrugged. "Overly tired, I guess." Chloe wasn't going to elaborate more than that. He didn't need to know he was part of the problem; it would only inflate his ego more.

"Is it because you were home all alone?"

She raised an eyebrow at him. "Yes, I was alone. What's your point?"

"Well, if that's all, we can fix that. I'm available for sleepovers." He wiggled his eyebrows. "We used to do that once upon a time."

She rolled her eyes. "That's before I realized boys were gross."

"I thought girls were gross for a while, too, but then I grew up." He moved in closer. "Do you still think boys are gross?"

Chloe took a step back only because she wanted to step forward into him. "No."

"Then how about that sleepover? I could clear my schedule for tonight if you're afraid to be alone?"

"I'm not afraid to be alone. Besides, I'm not that desperate."

"But you are desperate?" he asked with a grin.

"I didn't say that."

"You implied it."

"I did not. Stop putting words in my mouth," she said, flustered. "Please move. I have things to do."

"What's on your agenda for today?" he asked cordially as he moved over.

"It's a beautiful day, so I'm going for a walk and then back to writing."

"You've been holed up in your room for hours. Aren't you done yet? How long could it possibly take to write one little book no thicker than the width of my thumb?" he asked with a smile in his voice.

Chloe bristled. She knew he was just trying to push her buttons. "Writing takes time, concentration, and inspiration." She brushed past him, adding, "And peace and quiet. Which has been hard to come by since you and your crew arrived this morning." Chloe snapped at him. Bo padded down the stairs, and stopped next to her, stretching.

Tate turned around and watched her for a second. "If we're bothering you that much, why don't you find a place to work outside or go into the bookstore?"

Standing, Chloe had a smart-aleck comment on the tip of her tongue, but she held it. Contemplating him for a hot second, she said, "That's a really good idea. Why didn't I think of that?"

Bo looked up at her with big eyes.

Tate opened his mouth to say something, but Chloe held up her hand.

"It was a rhetorical question. No need to give me your sarcastic comment that I know you have."

He laughed. "What makes you think I have a smart-ass comment to make?"

"I know you, Tate Becker. At this point, there's nothing you could do or say that would surprise me."

"I surprised you yesterday."

"That's only because I had headphones in and didn't hear you come in. Believe me, you won't surprise me again."

"Women," he said looking at Bo.

Not commenting, she stepped off the porch. Without looking over her shoulder, she called out, "You comin', Bo?"

The dog sprang after her.

"Traitor," he shouted, but the dog didn't even slow.

It wasn't long before they disappeared into the woods without looking back.

The sun was shining, the sky was a clear blue, and the trees that surrounded her were a green-gold. It was a perfect autumn day. Being out was already lifting her mood.

Trying to shake the irritation she felt, she took a deep cleansing breath as Bo trotted along beside her.

A flock of geese caught her eye as they flew over brushing the tips of the trees, heading south for the winter. They seemed to know that the days were growing shorter, the warmth more precious.

Her breath caught as a deer crossed her path not more than a hundred feet from her. Bo sensed the doe immediately.

"Bo, stay," Chloe commanded, stopping herself.

His body quivered with anticipation.

"Stay."

The doe watched them as they watched her. But the moment was fleeting as the wind shifted, and foliage swayed. The shift of branches put the doe on alert.

Bo crouched low, wanting to pounce.

"Bo," Chloe repeated.

The doe's white tail pointed as their scent drifted toward her. With a quick start, the white-tailed deer bound off the path, disappearing into the brush.

Looking down at Bo, she bent over and patted his head. "Good boy." She rubbed behind his ears enthusiastically, down his sides. "You're such a good dog. I know that was hard, but you did it. Good boy, Bo. Tate trained you well."

Bo barked once. Chloe laughed and fell in love with the dog despite the owner.

"Maybe you're the one who trained Tate. You have good manners and patience." She rubbed his head one last time. "Come on then, there's a lot more woods to explore."

Bo leaped into the air and darted off, raced straight ahead to a tree, picked up a stick in his mouth, and all but pranced back to her. Falling in step with her again, he proudly carried his prize. Chloe couldn't help but laugh at the dog.

"You're a character, just like Tate."

Tate. Tate Becker. Just the mere mention of his name was enough to start her heart pitter-pattering. She let out a sigh.

Why did she let him get to her? Chloe knew why, but she

didn't want to admit it. Like the dog, despite everything, he was easy to like. Just another thing she'd have to work on. She felt like her whole life was a work in progress.

As she walked, her muscles started to relax, getting out the soreness and kinks from lack of sleep and sitting at her computer too long. She had tossed and turned all night. Despising Tate Becker for breaking her heart their senior year wasn't easy, even when she kept him at bay. But it got increasingly harder when he was right up in her face every minute of the day.

Even after all these years, it still hurt, and yet he was so casual and fun to be around. She knew it was going to be a lot of extra work to keep her distance from him, let alone stay mad at him. Truth be told, she didn't want to be mad at him anymore. Ten years was a long time to hold on to something. She desperately wanted to forgive him, needed to for her own sake.

Chloe wasn't naive, though; she knew she'd have to keep her heart locked away in order to survive the next few weeks while he worked on the house, but she was confident she could do it. If it wasn't for those eyes and his lopsided, dorky smile, his fun-loving personality, and . . . Stop listing his good qualities, she scolded herself. Forgiving him was the only way to survive.

Making that decision, she felt lighter, inspired even. She hadn't found inspiration in the flock of geese that flew over or the deer that had just crossed her path. No, it had been letting go that had inspired her and the color of Tate's eyes that took her breath away. Darn. This wasn't going to be easy. Tate and those eyes. That smile. This was going to be harder than she thought.

Tate sat back on his haunches, pulled his shirt off, and wiped his brow.

"Starting to get pretty warm out here," Neil said, running his hand over his auburn hair, putting his ball cap back on, adjusting it to shade his face. "I didn't think it was supposed to get hot today."

Reaching for his water bottle, Tate chuckled. "Weathermen, it's the only job you can have that you can be completely wrong and still get paid."

"That's for damn sure," Neil agreed.

"Having said that, though, I want to get this half of the house done today if at all possible. Looks like rain for the weekend. It would be nice to get all the windows in by Thursday."

"I think we can get it done."

"Someone's coming back from her walk." Tate pointed in Chloe's direction as she and his dog emerged from the woods and headed up the dirt path toward the house.

"Looks like Bo enjoys being with her."

Tate took a long, slow drink of his water and wiped his mouth off with the back of his hand. "Looks that way," he agreed. "Hopefully, the walk did them both some good. Chloe's a little bristly today."

"What did you do?" Neil asked.

"Nothin'."

"You sure?"

Tate looked at his best friend and tilted his head in Chloe's direction. "With that one? I'm never sure." He thought about it for a moment. "Actually, that's not true. There, for the longest time, it was like we could read each other's minds. We always had a connection."

"What do you think happened?"

"Not sure," Tate said.

"You really don't know?" Neil questioned.

"I know why he doesn't know," Kurt said, coming over and getting a drink of his own.

"Do tell?" Tate asked curiously.

"Because you're stupid," Kurt answered matter-of-factly. "Of course, it's your fault."

Neil snorted, choking on his water. "If that ain't the truth."

"Okay, jackass. Why would you assume that I did something?" Tate demanded.

"Because you usually do," Neil replied.

"Exactly," Kurt said, wiping off the water that ran down his chin.

"Thanks. I appreciate the support. You know I can fire both of your asses, right?"

"I'm not worried," Kurt said. "My last name is on the truck, same as yours."

"And without my professionally designed floor plans and renderings, you wouldn't know what to do or where to install anything," Neil added.

Tate was only half listening to them. Instead, he was watching Chloe cross the yard with his dog. Bo dropped the stick he carried, exchanged it for his favorite ball, and ran back to her. Bo placed the baseball neatly at her feet and nudged it with his nose. She bent, picked up the ball, and gave him a good rub. Patting Bo on the head, she said something Tate couldn't quite hear. She chucked the ball, and Bo bolted after it with a leap of delight.

At the sight, a little twinge of desire lodged itself in Tate's gut as he watched the girl and his dog. Woman, he corrected himself. She was a woman, no longer the girl who had been his best friend.

It had been years since he had spoken to her for more than five minutes up until yesterday. Despite what these yahoos insinuated; he didn't know why. After graduation, she attended the University of Iowa, halfway across the country, and majored in English and Creative Writing. Iowa had one of the best programs in the world. And for Chloe, there had been no looking back. For him, he'd been lost, suddenly off balance without her.

Tate watched the golden retriever bring the ball back to her again, drop it at her feet, and hunch down, waiting eagerly for the next throw. She picked it up, faked a throw, tucking it behind her back, laughing as Bo took off.

Her laughter carried across the expanse of the lawn, and a slow curl of lust went up from that twinge.

Bo didn't get far when he realized he'd been tricked. He came back barking and wagging his tail at her, eager for her to really throw it. This time, she did. She wound up and sent it sailing. Bo took off like a rocket.

She disappeared for a few seconds as his dog ran after the ball. Chloe reappeared with her laptop and a folding chair about the same time Bo returned the ball. They both settled down under a tree, Chloe with her laptop and Bo with his baseball. The sight ripped open a longing in him, one he'd never felt before, making him a little uneasy. When he looked at her all he could think was once upon a time, his whole world had circled around her, even if he hadn't realized it then. He could see it easily happening again. Like a moth drawn to a flame . . .

Quickly pushing the feeling away, he focused on the folding chair. He couldn't wrap his mind around it. Was that all she had to sit on? Wasn't much of a place to work, he thought. She needed a table and a comfortable chair. He'd have to do something about that.

"I think our five has turned into fifteen," Kurt said, screwing the top back on his bottle.

"Yeah, that's a long enough break. We need to get back at it." Tate shook himself mentally and turned back to the task at hand. "Let's get it done. We have a baseball game tonight to get to."

"Yeah, tonight and Thursday. We still need a pitcher, though," Kurt reminded him.

"What happened to Eddie?"

"He's out of town for a business conference or something. Won't be back until at least six, maybe later," Neil said, picking up his hammer. "I'm pretty sure he told you."

"He did," Tate admitted. "It just slipped my mind."

"You could pitch at least until Eddie arrives."

"I could," Tate agreed. "But then, who would play shortstop? And what if he doesn't make it for the game at all? It would be better to have another pitcher."

"Sure, but who are you going to ask? Our usual backup is hurt," Kurt replied.

Tate glanced over his shoulder and said, "I might have just the person."

Kurt followed his gaze and chuckled. "That just might work if you can talk her into it."

Tate flashed an easy grin. "She can't say no to me."

"Wanna make a bet?" his brother asked and stuck out his hand.

EIGHT

Detective Rita Sorenson waited for her partner, Detective Marc Fulmer, to lift the yellow crime scene tape. They both ducked under and walked in silence down the dirty alley toward the officers standing guard.

She prepared herself for the first look, the first glimpse. Even after ten years on the force, this part never got any easier. Would she know the deceased, or would Jane Doe be some random stranger?

As they approached, the two officers recognized them and stepped away from the scene to let the detectives get a closer look. Rita got her first glimpse of long, tan legs and black sandals peeking out from behind the rusty dumpster. She braced herself inwardly for the face.

Pretty was her first thought, and she waited for her brain to trigger any sort of memory or recognition. When none came, relief washed over her, followed by guilt at that relief, quickly chased by disgust at a life cut short. This woman was someone's daughter, friend, or sister.

"Do you recognize her?" she asked her partner.

"No."

"Me either."

Mentally shaking herself, she took in the scene with her well-trained eye. The woman was propped against the brick wall, wedged between the dumpster and a precariously stacked assortment of boxes.

She looked to be in her mid to late twenties with long brown hair, wearing a red blouse tucked into a short black skirt. The victim's head lulled slightly to one side, and there was a small cut above her right eye.

Rita's eyes traveled slowly, taking in every detail. Squatting to get a closer look, she noticed dried blood had trickled down her neck.

"Thoughts?" Detective Fulmer asked, squatting beside her. "Drug overdose?"

Knowing the scene had already been photographed because they had been briefed upon arriving at the scene, she took out gloves from her jacket pocket and slipped them on. "I don't think so," she said, lifting the woman's hair, tilting the woman forward, following the blood trail. "My guess would be a blow to the back of the head. But we'll wait for the coroner's report to be sure. There also seems to be alcohol involved. She reeks of it."

"Think she fell?"

"Could be. Might explain that broken fingernail and the large contusion on her head." Rita lifted the woman's manicured hand and examined the bright red nails closely. "Where are those crime technicians?"

"They were out front. Why?"

"Get one back here ASAP. I want to make damn sure these hands were scraped for evidence." She grumbled, "I didn't see anything listed on the report about her hands."

Fulmer didn't comment, simply called for a technician.

Rita fired off a quick directive to the tech, then backed off and let him take over.

Pulling off her gloves, she ran a hand through her auburn hair, which she kept in a stylish pixie cut, and watched him work, keeping a close eye.

"I have a sample," the young tech said as he sealed it in a bag for safekeeping.

"Get it to the lab ASAP," Rita ordered.

"Yes, ma'am."

They watched him hurry away. Rita looked up and down the alley and noticed the lack of lighting and security cameras on the buildings that lined it. "No cameras or windows down this little strip."

"Unless someone saw her come into the alley of her own accord or with someone, we may be out of luck," Detective Fulmer commented.

"We will check the streets on either side leading to this alley. There has to be at least one security camera. Someone somewhere had to see something."

"Looks like we're going to have our work cut out for us," Detective Fulmer commented.

"I'm afraid so," Rita agreed.

NINE

The baseball diamond was located five miles from town, right where the hills met the old abandoned quarry. For years, the site had been a vast wasteland where large machines had dug, scraped, and robbed the area of limestone, sandstone, and dolomite. The area was left void of raw materials, the company had vacated, and the quarry closed. The county took possession and turned it into a recreational area, building the baseball diamond.

Large walls of rock surrounded three-quarters of the diamond, making it hard to see until they drove around the broken wall of stone. Inside, though, it was lush, green, and flat, perfect for a baseball field.

There were already a few cars by the diamond when Tate pulled into the parking lot and drove around behind the equipment shed.

"I can't believe I let you talk me into this," Chloe said, getting out of the truck. "I haven't played softball in years."

"Well, lucky for you, we're playing baseball," Tate said, lifting a bag of equipment from the bed.

"Like that helps," she said grimly. "I played softball in high school and pitched for a rec baseball league in college. I haven't played competitively since then."

"I saw you throw the ball to Bo earlier today; you still have a strong arm. Just so you know, we only play seven innings. Unless there's a tie at the bottom of the seventh."

"Why do you stop at seven?"

"Because we play during the week, and we have to get up for

work the next day." He shrugged. "Sucks being an adult."

Chloe smiled. "I'll say."

"I'll warm you up. See what you're capable of. Then, if you're uncomfortable, I will pitch, and you can play shortstop."

"And you think that's a good idea?"

He ignored her question. Tate had no intention of giving up shortstop. That was his spot. If she could just get the ball across the plate at a decent clip, he was confident the rest of the team could cover anything that was hit. "You're right-handed, correct?"

Chloe nodded.

He tossed her a baseball glove. "See if that one fits."

"It's a little big."

"Kurt's bringing a smaller one. When he arrives, we can switch it out if you need to." Tate slung the bag over his shoulder.

"This is coed, right?" Chloe asked, sounding nervous.

"Yep." Tate led her through the fence, dropped his bag, fished out a baseball, and slipped on his glove. "Relax. You know pretty much everyone on the team and probably a few on the other team. It'll be fine. You'll be fine. Let's get you warmed up with a little catch."

Chloe nodded and put the glove on. Walking out to the diamond together, they stopped a few feet apart and started playing catch. Every few throws, Tate made her take a step back until she ended up at the pitcher's mound sixty feet away from him and home plate.

Kurt arrived and got out of his SUV, grabbed his gear, and headed to the field. With a glove and T-shirt in hand, Kurt approached Tate.

"Take a break," Tate called to Chloe. "Get a drink of water and rest your arm, but keep it warm."

Shaking her head, Chloe glanced at Kurt as she went for water. "Is he always this bossy?"

"Absolutely. Why do you think we let him think he's in charge?"

"I am in charge," Tate shot back.

"That's what we let you think. Here," Kurt tossed her the navy T-shirt with Becker Construction on the back. "Now you're officially a part of the team."

"Thanks, I think." Chloe pulled on the T-shirt and smoothed her hair. She asked, "How does it look?"

Tate held his favorite bat in both hands, twisting it. He looked at her, and his mouth went dry. Her hair was pulled back in a sleek ponytail, and she had on tight little shorts that accented long legs. Wearing her white Nikes and now his T-shirt, she couldn't have looked cuter. His stomach dipped slightly to see his last name on her back. "All you need is a baseball cap, and you're good to go." Tate held out his hand to his brother. "I'm waiting."

Kurt dug out his wallet and slapped a twenty into his brother's hand.

"What is that for?" Chloe asked.

Tate's smile was wide and instant. "He bet me twenty bucks I couldn't get you to come and pitch tonight. And yet . . ." He bowed slightly. "Here you are."

Kurt shook his head in disgust. "I didn't think you'd cave so easily. What did it? His boyish charm? His persistence? His stupid grin? Tell me, please. I have to know."

"None of the above," Chloe answered seriously. "He promised me a glass of wine and dinner if I pitched."

Kurt roared with laughter. "So much for your charm."

Tate whipped the ball at his brother. Kurt snagged the baseball easily.

"She's here, isn't she?"

"Yes, she is." Kurt winked at her. "Have mercy, girl. I've missed you and the way you could always put him in his place." He leaned over and gave Chloe a side-arm hug.

"I've missed you too," she said, meaning it.

Switching gears, Kurt asked, "How did she do warming up?"

"Not bad. She can throw. Definitely rusty."

"Excuse me, I'm standing right here. Why not ask me?"

"This is business," Tate stated, purposely ignoring her. "I told you she has an arm."

"The question is, can she get the ball over the plate?" Kurt asked.

Tate nodded. "That's the hundred-dollar question."

Chloe put her hand on her hip and made a face at them. "Again, I'm standing right here."

"We know," they said in unison, and they both flashed that Becker smile.

Chloe watched the men converse and conspire right in front of her. It was easy to see they were brothers; both were tall, but Kurt was huskier than Tate. They had the same toffee brown hair, chiseled features, and that Becker dimple, but the eyes were where they differed immensely. Kurt's were a pale winter gray, and Tate's were an intense sea blue.

"Is this the poor girl you suckered into pitching?" a man asked as he walked toward them.

"I'm afraid so," Tate answered. "Jerry Gray, you remember Chloe Harris?"

"Sure, I do."

"Hello, Jerry." Chloe smiled politely at him then turned her attention back to Tate. Slightly irked at him, she said, "You know I can leave, right?"

"No, you can't. You came with me," Tate reminded her.

"Chloe?"

"Yes." Chloe turned around. "Lucy!" Chloe's face lit up as she saw her best friend. Lucy's sunny blonde hair was pulled back in a ponytail, tucked neatly under her baseball cap, and threaded through the back. Her fierce gray eyes shone.

"What are you doing here?" Lucy asked.

"I was bribed." Chloe pointed an accusatory finger at Tate.

Lucy smiled, looking directly at Tate. "That explains a lot."

"What?" he asked innocently. "I'm persuasive."

Shaking her head, Lucy asked Chloe, "How did the meeting go?"

"Not as we hoped."

"I'm sorry to hear that. You'll need to catch me up," Lucy said.

"I will." Chloe glanced at Tate and said, "When you said you were playing baseball this summer, I had no idea it was with these guys." Chloe hooked a thumb and indicated the Beckers. "I guess they finally woke up and realized they needed the best first baseman in the state on their team. You're probably the only thing holding this team together," Chloe commented.

"Some days, it feels like it." Lucy laughed. "How in the world did you really end up here tonight? I must have asked you at least a dozen times to come and play."

"I'm asking myself that very question." Chloe narrowed her eyes in Tate's direction.

"Ask as you keep your arm warm," Tate called after them.

"Wine and dinner," Kurt reminded her as he tossed her a ball. "That's why you're here. I'll make sure you get it."

"What's that supposed to mean?" Lucy asked.

"Tate promised me a glass of wine and dinner if I pitched. Kurt's going to make sure he follows through."

"I never got that kind of offer," Lucy sulked.

"I'll have to teach you to negotiate better," Chloe laughed.

Tate walked over to the opposing team to get things started. Dalton Turk, the other team captain, met him halfway.

"Are you guys ready to play?" Tate asked.

"Yep," Dalton answered. "Are you?"

"Always."

"Heard Eddie's out of town." Dalton raked his hand through his hair and readjusted his cap. "Thought maybe you guys would be a no-show."

"We have a backup."

"Who? You?" Dalton smirked. "Might as well forfeit now."

"Not me."

"Then it has to be the brunette with the legs that are a mile long. She's the only new addition I see." Dalton jerked his head in her direction.

Tate knew Dalton was looking straight at Chloe. "Yes," he said coolly, feeling protective of her.

Dalton laughed. "She's damn cute, I saw her warm up. Looks like she might be able to get the job done."

"Of course, she can. Chloe wouldn't be here if she couldn't," Tate answered.

"Is that so?" Dalton grinned. "Bet I can hit anything that pretty little thing can throw."

"Don't think you're going to walk away with an easy win."

"Wanna put your money where your mouth is, Becker?"

"What do you have in mind?" Tate asked.

"Loser buys the first round at the Taphouse and enough pizza to feed the winning team."

"You're on," Tate agreed.

"That beer's going to taste even better going down with a slice of pizza and a sweet victory." Dalton chuckled.

"Let's get this game started. You're up to bat first." They shook hands, and Tate jogged off to his dugout.

Tate gathered his team around. "What can I say? You all know this team. We've played them before. They're good but not better than us. Sometimes we win, and sometimes we lose. Tonight, I don't want to lose. There's beer and pizza on the line. Losing team buys. Are you ready?"

"We got this."

"Let's go out and do what we do best, one pitch, one hit, one out at a time. Hands in." He looked each player in the eye as he glanced around the circle. "We win, and Dalton's buying us beer and pizza. We lose, and we're buying."

"Then we'd better not lose," Kurt agreed.

"Team on two," Tate said. "One. Two."

The team shouted, "TEAM!"

Everyone grabbed their gloves and ran to their positions.

Tate gently held Chloe in place, one hand on her arm, while his brother stayed close, holding the baseball.

"You know to grip the ball along the seams with your index finger and middle, right?" Tate asked.

"I'm not an idiot, Tate," Chloe grumbled.

"No, but you're talking to one," Kurt answered for him. He

gave his brother a nudge. "She's got this."

Tate nodded and jogged over to shortstop as Kurt placed the baseball in Chloe's glove.

Dalton approached home plate swinging. He pointed the end of the bat at Chloe and said, "Let it rip, Legs."

Chloe took a deep breath, waited for Kurt's signal, and adjusted the ball in her hand. She wound up and released the first pitch - a fastball on the outside corner. Dalton swung at nothing but air.

The lights came on over the baseball diamond as Chloe was mentally preparing for the next batter. The air had cooled as the sun set, and the wind had died down. She was beyond exhausted. It was the top of the seventh with two outs, and Becker Construction was up six to four with two runners on base. If the ball was hit deep, both runners would score, and the game would be tied. She just had to get through this last batter. Chloe cringed when Dalton strutted up to the plate, swinging the bat.

"Give us a minute," Kurt said to Dalton. He removed his catcher's mask, then gestured for Tate to meet him at the pitcher's mound.

Both Becker men jogged toward Chloe.

"How are you holding up?" Tate asked.

"Not good," Chloe answered truthfully. "My arm is shot."

"You're doing great," Kurt said, clearly meaning it.

"We only need one more out," Tate reminded her.

"I know, but it's Dalton Turk. He's gotten two home runs off me tonight."

"That's because the jackass is swinging at literally everything."

Bright lights swept across the field as a car pulled into the lot and parked. The driver got out and headed toward the field.

"What the hell?" They heard Dalton curse. "No way in hell. It's not happening."

"What are you bellyaching about, Turk?" Kurt called over his shoulder.

"You guys are stalling, so Lambert," Dalton stabbed his bat in Eddie's direction, "can come in fresh at the last damn minute and save the day."

Eddie leaned on the fence and held up his hands. "I didn't come to play. I was on my way home and thought I'd stop and see what the score was. Besides," he held up his arms. "I'm not dressed to play. I'm in a suit."

"Damn right! Eddie's NOT playing," Dalton bellowed. "Quit stalling, Legs, and throw the damn ball."

"Simmer down, Turk," Tate answered. "We're not changing pitchers."

Chloe looked at Kurt and then Tate. "Any advice?"

"Listen, Tate said it before, Dalton's swinging at everything you throw. Good, bad, or ugly," Kurt commented.

Chloe made a face.

"Sorry, I didn't mean it as it sounded. What he prefers, though, is high and tight. That's what he's been sending deep. He likes to undercut the ball. If you put it low and away, he's likelier to hit a pop fly."

"You can do this." Tate put a hand on Chloe's shoulder and looked her directly in the eyes. "We have faith in you. And if you screw up," he shrugged, "no big deal. You can just walk home. And . . ." Tate flashed her a grin, making her pulse skip. "There will be no wine for you."

"Right," she said, rolling her eyes at Tate, as if wine were her concern right now.

"Don't worry about him. If he makes you walk, I'll . . ."

"Give me a ride?" Chloe finished for Kurt.

"I was going to say that I'd follow you at a safe distance so my headlights could light the road, and then you can see where you're walking."

"You guys are great. Just great. Tell me again why I'm here when I could be home writing?"

"Because you can't say no." Tate ran a hand down her ponytail and gave it a little tug like he used to do when they were growing up. He started to back away, hooked both thumbs in his own direction, and added, "To me."

"I most certainly can."

"But you didn't." He walked backward toward shortstop with a full-fledged grin. "My money's on you, Chloe Harris."

Kurt tossed her the ball. "Remember, low and away," he murmured as he pulled on his catcher's mask and jogged back to home plate.

She nodded and took the mound. "No pressure or anything," Chloe mumbled.

"I'm waiting, Legs," Dalton growled. He took a couple of practice swings and then tapped the base. "Put it right there," he said, swinging evenly as a sly smile spread slowly across his face. "You know exactly how I like it. There ain't nothin' you can throw that I can't hit. Besides, Legs, I know you're tired. Let's finish it right here. Right now."

Chloe sucked in a deep, cleansing breath. There was nothing she'd like more than to wipe that egotistical smirk off his face, except maybe a hot shower or to hit him hard in the head with the ball. That was it. She could aim right for his mouth and literally wipe that smug look off it. If he called her Legs one more time, so help her . . . Chloe glanced over her shoulder to the runners on first and third. Got a head-bob from Tate at shortstop. "Heaven help me," she muttered under her breath. "Here goes nothing."

Kurt held his glove down and outside, giving her a target. She put her fingers on the laces and let the ball fly.

The ball was low and wide. Dalton took the bait and swung. He clipped the underside of the ball, and it popped straight up. Kurt flung off his mask, adjusted, and got under the pop fly, catching the ball easily.

"Son of a . . ." Dalton threw the bat on the ground and kicked at the dirt, cursing.

A wave of relief washed over her and a spike of pride coursed through her veins as a chorus of cheers exploded, drowning Dalton out.

Tate came running at her, and her heart stopped. He howled as he picked Chloe up and swung her around. Her world spun with Tate as the axis. "I knew you could do it! There was never a doubt in my mind."

"Man, that beer and pizza are going to taste good," Neil shouted. "Way to go, Chloe!"

Thirty minutes later, they all gathered on the Taphouse deck. The beer flowed, and the pizza came out piping hot. Instead of sitting, people stood and mingled.

Chloe anchored herself near the railing, and Eddie approached her with two beers. "Did you get your congratulatory beer yet?"

She laughed. "Not yet."

"Well, then, let me be the first to give you one and as a peace offering as well. I'm sorry about the meeting." He held out a beer to her.

"Don't be. You're not the one who needs to apologize."

"Neither one of us should be. They just aren't the right fit for us, even though I would have bet both our careers that they were. I have no doubt we will find someone else."

"You're taking it rather well," Chloe commented, watching him for a minute.

"What can I say? You win some, you lose some. But I have a feeling they might be back sooner or later." Changing the subject, he asked, "Since when did you decide to play for our baseball team? I've been asking you to join for a couple of years."

"I got conned into it earlier today since you weren't going to be here."

"Let me guess . . . Tate?" Eddie asked.

"How did you know?"

"No surprise there. Cheers," he said, clicking the bottles together and taking a sip. "Sore?" Eddie asked, changing the subject and nodding toward her arm.

"How could you tell? Is it the awkward way I'm holding my beer?"

Eddie grinned. "That was the tip-off. You should really cover it. Keep it warm so it doesn't get too stiff. You need to be able to write."

"I didn't bring a jacket with me. It was hot when I left the house. I never expected to be out this long or for the evening to cool off this much."

"I can give you mine."

"It's a nice suit, Eddie. I'm all sweaty and gross. You don't want me to put that on."

"Don't worry about it. Right now, you need it." Eddie moved to take off his jacket when Tate walked toward her carrying a flannel shirt.

"Here. Put this on," Tate said, holding the shirt out to Chloe. "You want to keep your arm warm, or it will stiffen up."

"I literally just said that," Eddie grumbled.

Chloe shifted, rubbing her arm. "Too late. I can barely move."

"Then let me help you," Tate offered.

Eddie held out his hand. "Give me your beer so you can put on the shirt."

She did, and Eddie set the bottle down on the railing behind her while Tate helped her slip on the flannel. Instantly, she was engulfed in the seductive scent of Tate, making her weak in the knees.

Taking the time to help her button a few of the buttons, he asked, "Better?"

Chloe let out a breath and answered softly, "Much."

"You did good tonight. Didn't she, Lambert?"

Eddie nodded. "I didn't see much since I arrived late, but the last at-bat was perfect."

Kimmy bounced up beside them, cutting in. "Hey, Chloe. Heard you were the MVP. Congrats!"

"Thanks, Kimmy," Chloe said, taking a step back away from Tate and trying to hide the fact that he made her tremble, afraid everyone could see the reaction she had to him.

"You don't mind if I steal Tate for a second, do you? I have a wobbly shelf I need him to look at before it becomes a real problem."

"Not at all. He's all yours."

Kimmy gave Chloe a knowing look, looping her arm through Tate's before he could object. He glanced back at her, and their eyes locked as he was pulled away.

"I'm sorry I missed most of it. But I was glad I was there for the last pitch," Eddie said, bringing her back to the conversation.

"Had you been there earlier, you could have pitched."

"True, but then we would have missed the pure agony of defeat that we saw on Dalton's face. That was priceless." Eddie sipped his beer and asked, "How's the next book coming?"

"Pretty well, considering."

"Considering what?"

"I had some damage at my house because of the storm."

"How bad?"

"A tree fell on the front porch and broke a couple of windows in the great room."

"I'm sorry to hear that. You should have called me. I would have come out. Do you need me to call someone for you to remove the tree and replace the windows?"

"Already got it covered. Becker Construction is taking care of it," Chloe explained.

"I'm sure they will get it cleaned up quickly," Eddie agreed.

"So, where were you today?"

"I was in Baltimore. I had a meeting with a new author. And I purchased a boat. I got a great deal on a nice little twenty-five-footer that I had my eye on for quite some time."

"Oh?" Chloe questioned, shifting slightly against the railing. "What genre?"

He flashed a grin. "And here I thought I would impress you with my new boat. But of course, you'd rather hear about a fellow author."

"I like boats just fine and would love to see it," Chloe said truthfully.

"Maybe I'll take you out on it before the season is completely over."

"That would be nice." She tugged at her shirt, wrapping it a little tighter. "Now, back to this new author."

"He writes sci-fi. I read his first novel. It was good. The chapters I've read from his second book are even better. I see the books being very marketable."

"He's writing a series?" Chloe asked.

"Yes. He's set to make it a trilogy. We had already agreed to work together. We've had multiple phone calls, emails, and a Zoom meeting. I simply wanted to meet him in person and was able to tie the meeting in with the purchase of the boat."

"Well, congratulations," Chloe said. "That's exciting news on both accounts."

"Thank you." Eddie smiled at her.

"A little different than when you and I started, don't you think?"

"Times have changed, for sure. Now, it's not just about the book. Readers want to know the authors, too. They want them to attend book clubs -- virtually or in person -- have book signings, write blogs . . . Then, there are websites, social media presences, and email lists. Add in Zoom meetings, and you have to be partially an actor as well." Eddie took a breath and loosened his navy-blue tie. "I don't have to tell you. You already know all this. You're doing it all, living the dream."

A ghost of a smile played across her face. "Yes, living the dream. That's me."

"Now, if only I could get you to sign with me full-time."

She laughed. "You would tire of me if you had me full-time."

"Hardly. With your backlist and my marketing strategies and connections . . . the things we could do together." He held her gaze. "How about it?"

"Maybe," Chloe hesitated. She didn't want to commit. There was just something holding her back from signing with him completely. She liked their arrangement. She liked being a hybrid author, having the freedom to work both traditionally and be self-published.

"I'm sorry we haven't heard back from Belov Productions. I truly thought that even though we walked out, we would hear something. Are you disappointed?" Eddie asked.

She shrugged. "What author wouldn't want one of their books turned into a blockbuster? But it certainly won't define my career if I don't get a movie deal."

Eddie's head bobbed. "You're right, but it sure would be fun to be able to put that on your resume, wouldn't it? To see your name in lights."

"It would."

They both fell silent as Neil approached. "I'm supposed to deliver this to you." He held out a glass of wine. "I heard you were promised one."

"I was," she said, accepting the glass. "Thank you. Why didn't Tate deliver it himself?"

"He's still a little tied up at the moment." Neil jerked his head to the side. Chloe followed the movement and saw Tate across the room with Kimmy, a shelf in his hands.

"Oh, I see." A tickle of jealousy raced through her.

"I think Tate should have bought you the whole bottle after you struck out Dalton Turk."

"I agree with that statement," Eddie chimed in.

"Speaking of which, here he comes now," Neil said.

"Hey, Legs. Need a beer?" Dalton asked, strutting closer with his fingers wrapped around two bottles.

"My name is Chloe, and no, I don't need one. Thank you."

Dalton scanned Chloe, his intense gaze lingering as he slowly worked his way down her body. "I know what your name is. Your sister was in my class." He held out the beer to her anyway, like he hadn't heard her.

Chloe wrapped her arms a little tighter around herself, shrugging deeper into Tate's flannel. "I'm not much of a beer drinker. One's enough. Thanks anyway."

"Then what's your pleasure?" he asked, finally returning his eyes to hers. "I'm buying, Legs." He moved in closer, looking at the wine glass in her hand. "Tell me what you want. Another glass of red, maybe?"

"Hey, man, back off," Neil said, holding up his hand to stop Dalton's advance.

Chloe backed up and accidentally knocked her bottle of beer from the railing. Glass shattered, and the din of conversation softened as every head in the room turned. The heat rose in Chloe's face as she felt Tate's eyes on her from across the room.

Hearing the commotion, Kurt and Lucy walked over.

"How much have you had to drink?" Kurt asked Dalton.

"Not nearly enough to stand here talkin' to you."

"Be careful, Chloe, so you don't cut yourself," Neil said, flagging down a server. "You should step out of there." Shards of glass sparkled on the floor, and the amber liquid pooled at her feet.

"You must be exhausted, Chloe," Lucy said, coming to her rescue and stepping in front of Dalton. "Back up, Dalton. Here comes the waitress."

Dalton lifted his beer at Chloe in a silent salute and nodded. "Later, Legs," he said, slowly backing away from the group.

"That guy makes my skin crawl," Chloe murmured to Lucy, keeping one eye trained on him as he sauntered away.

"Dalton? He's harmless. He thinks he's God's gift to women, but I know what you mean. He's always looking at me like he can picture me naked."

"That's exactly it," Chloe agreed and shivered slightly.

"Now, if Kurt was looking at me like I was naked," she whispered conspiratorially, pulling Chloe away from the mess so the waitress could attend to the spill. "That would be a whole other story."

"Why, Lucy Roberts?" Chloe laughed. She followed her friend's eyes, which were locked on Kurt. "Now, who's picturing someone naked?"

TEN

The only sound inside the cab of the truck was the soft strains of a country song coming out of his speakers. As Tate drove down the backroads toward home, the dark night was all around them. Chloe leaned against the passenger's door, still wrapped in his flannel shirt.

"You're quiet." Tate took his eyes off the road for a second to look at Chloe. "Everything alright?"

"Yes, just tired and in pain."

"You're bound to be. I'm impressed, though. You pitched seven innings straight without any complaining." He glanced at her as he drove into the lane. "Except for that little pity party at the end."

Even in the darkness, he could see her glare at him. He laughed.

"Pity party? All I said was my arm was shot. Unbelievable. . ." Her voice trailed off.

"No other comment?" He raised an eyebrow as he stopped in front of the dark house and parked the truck. "That's not like you."

"Oh, I have a comment, but my mom always told me if I can't say anything nice, not to say anything at all." Chloe smiled demurely. "Believe me, what I'm thinking about you right now is not nice. Instead, I'm just filing it away to use the next time you beg me to do something."

Tate shut off the engine, draped one arm over the steering wheel and the other on the seat behind her, and smiled wide. "What makes you think there will be a next time?"

"I've known you a long time, Tate Becker. There will be a next time. I have no doubt."

"Fair enough. But for the record, I don't beg. I just . . ." He paused, choosing his words carefully. "Effectively persuade."

"More like manipulate."

He chuckled. "I'd agree with that comment, but I like how I worded it better, Miss Author. Let me get the door for you. It's the least I can do." He hopped out of the cab and came around to her side. After opening the door, he held out his hand to help her down. She hesitated. "You know I don't bite."

Chloe cocked her head. "That's not exactly true. You've bitten me before."

"When?"

"In first grade at the school picnic." She waited for him to remember. "We had ice cream sandwiches, and you dropped yours on the ground. I took pity on you like I usually do."

He snapped his fingers. "That's right! You offered me a bite of yours, and when I took the bite, I accidentally nibbled your finger instead."

"Nibbled? Really? You drew blood."

"In my defense, melted ice cream was all over your hand and running down your arm. It was impossible to tell where the ice cream sandwich ended, and your fingers began. I can still remember your face. That bottom lip trembled, and your eyes filled with tears, but you didn't cry." His eyes lingered on her lips.

"You bit me. So, forgive me if I'm a little cautious," she said.

"Believe me, Chloe." He leaned way in. So close she could feel the heat of his breath against her lips. "If I wanted to nibble on something, it most certainly wouldn't be your fingers." He placed his left hand under her left arm and guided her out of the cab. When her feet were firmly planted on the ground, and only inches separated them, he said, "And if I did, there wouldn't be tears in your eyes."

She pushed past him and whispered, "Don't be so sure about that."

"What is that supposed to mean?" Tate asked, following her

to the front door.

"Nothing. Forget it." Chloe tried to dig through her purse one-handed, but it was difficult.

"Here. Let me."

"My keys probably have dropped to the bottom."

"It doesn't take a genius to figure that out. It's sheer physics."

"You're clever. It's no wonder you were able to pull off a solid C in science."

"You know it." He unearthed her keys triumphantly from the depths of her purse. Inserting the key, he unlocked the door and flipped on the light.

"Thanks," she mumbled as he held it open for her.

He followed her in, put her keys on the kitchen island, and set her purse down.

"I guess you need this back." Chloe started to unbutton the flannel.

"Let me help you."

Shrugging out of it, she pursed her lips together, biting back a whimper, pain coursing through her as she removed her arm from the sleeve.

"That bad, huh?"

Chloe nodded. "I'm trying not to complain so you don't think I'm a wimp."

"Nonsense. You're not a wimp." He hung his long-sleeved flannel over the barstool. "Do you have any Icy Hot?"

"Yeah, in the bathroom off the mudroom."

"I'll be right back."

He disappeared behind her, and she said, "Look in the bottom drawer on the left-hand side of the vanity."

A couple of seconds of silence ticked by, and then he reappeared. "Found it." He unscrewed the cap and hesitated. "Wait, this won't work. Take off your shirt."

"I already did."

"Not that one, your T-shirt."

"Not on your life."

"Get your mind out of the gutter, Chloe. You still have a tank top under there, don't you?"

She laughed awkwardly. "Of course, I forgot. Sorry."

"You should be. I know you want me, but try to restrain yourself," he joked.

Rolling her eyes at him, she asked, "Pretty sure of yourself, aren't you?"

Tate didn't answer right away. Instead, he helped her out of the T-shirt, pulled it gently over her head, and discarded it on the counter. Squirting the Icy Hot into the palm of his hand, Tate said, "It's a gift. Women can't resist me."

Chloe rolled her eyes, and the image of Kimmy hanging on him at the Taphouse crept into her mind.

He flicked down the straps on her right shoulder. "Brace yourself. It's going to be cold."

When he put his hand on her, she flinched at the contact. Working the lotion into her shoulder blade, he rubbed in a circular motion and kneaded her shoulder with the palm of his hand. Relief washed over her as her muscles warmed and loosened, releasing some tension.

"And besides," he continued. "It's not like I haven't seen you without a shirt before."

"You most certainly have not. I think I would remember that."

"Then let me take you down memory lane." His hands worked efficiently, rubbing up and down her arm as he spoke. "We were twelve, and it was the year it rained and rained. Everything for miles around was flooded. The roads were washed out, and we were stuck here on our own little island. You wanted to go to town so bad. You'd been invited to Lucy's birthday party if I remember correctly. But we couldn't get there. The roads were closed in every direction. And you were devastated."

"I was," she agreed. "But you wouldn't let me stay that way."

"That's right. I couldn't stand to see you sad, but nothing I suggested seemed to work."

"Luckily, we had built that dam in the creek a couple of days before the rain started, and you insisted we go check it out," Chloe supplied.

"With all the rain, the water was high enough for us to have our very own swimming hole. Neither one of us wanted to go back to the house for our swimsuits because we knew we'd be found out, but we also knew if we got our clothes wet, our parents would know we had been playing in the flood water."

"Which we were forbidden to do," Chloe added.

"Exactly. So, we stripped down to our underwear, and you had that little white training bra on."

She cringed. "Oh . . . I'd forgotten about that."

"I nearly keeled over when you removed your shirt and hung it on that branch."

"Well, maybe you hadn't noticed, but I'm not twelve anymore."

"Believe me, I've noticed," Tate answered softly. They both fell silent as he continued to massage her shoulder. After a long moment, he cleared his throat and asked, "How does that feel?"

"Better . . . much better." She all but sighed, enjoying the feel of his sturdy hands moving over her skin. His thumb worked a knot in the center of her back, pushing, kneading.

His fingers trailed down her back, running his hands over her sore muscles.

Tate stopped abruptly. "I'm done," he declared, retracting his hands quickly. "You're going to want to put that flannel shirt back on. You want to keep this shoulder as warm as possible overnight." Reaching for the shirt and tossing it to her, he crossed to the sink to wash his hands. "Got any ibuprofen in this place?"

"Should be some in the upper cabinet next to the sink." She slipped the shirt on.

Tate found the bottle, located a glass, and turned on the tap. He shook out a couple of tablets and handed them to her.

"Thanks." She popped the pills and took a drink to chase them down.

"You're welcome. Do you need anything else?"

"No, I'm good," she said, glancing down, trying to button the flannel shirt. The fingers on her right hand were still stiff and were not functioning properly. It had been easier to unbutton than button.

Noticing, Tate took over helping her as he had at the restaurant. He took his time painstakingly fastening every button, avoiding her eyes.

"Thank you," she said softly.

"You're welcome." He cleared his throat. "I should probably go."

"Okay." Chloe walked him to the door. "Thank you for tonight. I had fun."

Tate leaned on the door and looked at her. "Yeah, me too." His lopsided grin was easy and fast. "It was like old times. I've missed that. I've missed you."

Before she could respond, he turned on his heel, ducked out the door, and pulled it closed behind him.

She sighed heavily as she watched him pull out of the lane. Flipping off the lights, she locked the door. She was exhausted, but it was a good kind of exhaustion. One she hadn't felt in a long time. The baseball game was fun.

What made the night was being with Tate, to have that again, just to be in each other's presence. She'd missed that and him, but she hadn't realized just how much until now.

Chloe climbed the stairs and, halfway up, heard the familiar creak like an old friend saying goodnight. She smiled at the sound, crossed into her bedroom, and lay on the bed, fully clothed. She fell asleep the minute her head touched the pillow. Wrapped in Tate's flannel shirt, she dreamed of him.

ELEVEN

Wednesday

The sun hadn't even peaked over the horizon yet. However, Tate didn't think the sun would make much difference even when it did rise. Rain was in the forecast for today, which would keep the sky dark and wet all day.

Despite the darkness and the relaxing sound of the rain, Tate couldn't sleep. Every time he closed his eyes, all he could see was Chloe. The way she looked on the pitcher's mound in his T-shirt and those little shorts that hugged every curve. The concentration on her face when she'd pitched that last ball just like Kurt had instructed her to. Tate hadn't even paid any attention to where the ball was hit or who would catch it because his eyes had been locked on her.

With his head under a pillow, he tried to block out her face, but his mind only wandered to other parts of her. Like how her skin felt as he rubbed her arm, the thin spaghetti strap lay loose against her shoulder. The softness of her skin on his palm or how her hair smelled as he leaned in close. All night long had been like that. If it wasn't her eyes, it was her legs or the sound of her laugh intruding on his thoughts. In the end, he'd chucked the pillow across the room. Giving up around four in the morning, he made his way out to the workshop.

The place was lit up like a ball field, lights streaming out of every opening. Music blared, and the sander wailed away as Tate worked. Despite all the noise, Bo lay at the threshold of the open door, curled up on a worn blanket, snoring softly.

Piles of maple, cedar, and oak boards were stacked to the

side. One whole wall was floor-to-ceiling shelving dedicated to hand tools, boxes of hardware, and mason jars filled with nails, screws, or bolts haphazardly sorted by size.

Bo opened his eyes and wagged his tail in greeting as Kurt walked into Tate's workshop. He squat down beside Bo and rubbed his head.

Coming to the edge of the piece, Tate shut off the sander and wiped his brow with the tail of his shirt.

"Good morning," Kurt called.

Tate glanced over as the dust settled around him, then turned down the radio so they didn't have to shout.

"Mornin'," Tate answered. "Not sure what's good about it."

Kurt strolled in, hands in his front pockets. "How long have you been out here?"

"A few hours. Couldn't sleep."

"So that's why you're grouchy."

"I'm not grouchy."

Kurt chuckled. "Could have fooled me." He wandered closer. "You make these chairs this morning?"

"Yep. Made those first. Then started the table." Tate ran a hand over the top, testing the smoothness. "Looks damn good, doesn't it?"

"Yes, it does," Kurt agreed, examining it.

"Just wait until I have it stained and sealed. It'll be gorgeous."

"What or who is it for?"

Tate sorted through his stains, looking for just the right shade of brown to bring out the wood grains. "It's for Chloe."

"I didn't realize she asked for a table set. I could have helped you build it."

"She didn't. I'm doing it on my own. Chloe needs a spot to write outside. All she has is that pitiful folding chair she was sitting in yesterday."

Kurt raised an eyebrow. "Is it a gift?"

"No, it's a place to write while we work on the house. She's trying to finish her thirteenth novel, and with all the construction noise inside the house, it's hard for her to concentrate."

"Gotcha. Not a gift."

"I thought I would take it over later today or maybe tomorrow if I finish it." Tate held the can of stain in his hand and looked at his brother. "What are you doing here?"

Kurt bent down and inspected the table closer, running his palm across the edge as he talked. "When I went outside this morning, I could see your place was lit up like a Christmas tree, so I thought I'd hop in the truck and see what was happening."

Tate nodded because this was nothing out of the ordinary. He and Kurt only lived about a half mile apart by road, less as the crow flew. Kurt had opted to build a home on the far end of their land while he had taken over the original farmhouse his family had inhabited for over a hundred years.

"Can you pick up cushions for these chairs?" Tate asked.

"Sure. I saw the outdoor store has an assortment of colors. How about red?"

"I was thinking green. That would go the best with this stain." Tate held up the can.

"Any other reason?"

Tate shrugged. "Green is also Chloe's favorite color."

"There it is. The real reason." Kurt gave a quick smirk.

"What?" Tate questioned. "So, I remember green was her favorite color. So what?"

Kurt held up his hands. "No need to get defensive."

"I'm not."

"That's right. You're not grouchy or defensive this morning."

"Bite me." Tate snarled.

"Chloe was something last night on that pitcher's mound, wasn't she?" Kurt asked, changing the subject.

"Yes, she was." Tate's grin was lightning fast. "She couldn't have been more perfect. The way she laid that pitch low and away had Dalton swinging before he even knew it."

"It popped up just like I said it would. The whole thing was so seamless. The pitch, the hit, and the pop-up. It landed right in my glove before Dalton could even blink." Kurt bent and pet Bo as the dog bumped against his leg.

"Never saw Dalton Turk that mad before over a single hit." That thought made Tate smirk, wishing he could have captured it with a camera. Dalton's cocky attitude had faded, even if only for a brief moment.

"He didn't stay mad at Chloe for too long, though."

"What's that supposed to mean?"

"Nothin', 'cept that he cozied up to her pretty quick at the Taphouse."

Scowling, Tate asked, "Where the hell was I when this was happening?"

"I think that's when Kimmy commandeered you to fix that shelf." Kurt walked over to the ten-foot ladder Tate had propped against the wall. "Can I borrow this?"

"Help yourself, as long as you put it back."

"Will do." Kurt hefted the ladder and moved toward the door with it just as Tate cracked open the can of stain. He paused inside the door and asked, "When are you going to put a stop to Kimmy's advances?"

"What do you mean?"

"She's clearly into you. Why? I have no idea."

"Screw you."

Kurt chuckled. "Are you into her?"

"Not at all." Tate searched the workbench for a paint stick. "I thought that was obvious."

"Maybe to someone like me, yet sometimes even I'm confused. Stop leading the poor girl on."

Tate stopped and looked directly at his older brother. "We're just friends. She knows that."

"Does she?" Kurt questioned again. "I'm not so sure."

"It's been handled. Don't worry about it."

"If you say so."

"I do." Changing the subject, Tate checked his cell phone. "Now it's saying the weather is supposed to clear this afternoon, but I already texted Chloe and told her not to expect us."

"What was Chloe's response?"

"Nothing yet. Bet she's still sleeping after the night she had pitching."

Kurt scratched his chin. "Think about what I said in regards to Kimmy. I think there's more there than she's letting on." Kurt dipped the ladder to clear the top of the door. "I'll let you get back to work."

＊

The pitter-patter on the roof roused Chloe from a deep sleep. Turning over, she let out a groan. Her body ached; every inch of her was stiff and sore. Groping for her cell phone on the nightstand, Chloe glanced at the time. It was past nine. She couldn't believe it was so late. She had only meant to lie down for just a minute after dealing with the animals.

She should have just stayed up. Her mind was so groggy she couldn't think straight. Where were the guys? She squinted at her phone again and saw the text. Tate's message said they weren't coming today due to the weather.

A sigh escaped her lips, relieved. Forcing herself to roll out of bed and stumble into the bathroom, she turned on the shower. She let the water warm as she retrieved ibuprofen from the medicine cabinet and took two tablets.

She eased into the shower and let the hot water run over her sore muscles. Why had she let Tate talk her into pitching last night? Eddie's comment from the previous night returned to her -- you never could say no to him. Maybe that really was true.

She wondered if she would have to pitch again tomorrow night. No. Not Thursday. That was her book signing. She was slightly relieved because there was no way she'd be able to pitch again so soon when she wasn't used to it. It took all her strength to wash her hair. If she had time after her book signing, maybe she could catch the end of the game.

After shutting off the water, she got out, wrapped herself in a towel, and dried herself.

The rain continued to fall.

When she was a kid, Chloe always enjoyed rainy days — the slow, steady drum of the rain, and lazy days spent in bed because it was dark and dreamy outside. But once she was up and dressed, Chloe couldn't wait to be out in the rain. Her sister never enjoyed wet weather, though. As a result, Chloe inevitably sought out Tate.

Tate had always been up for an adventure. He would come over, and they would find something to do outside, like jumping in puddles or riding their bikes in the rain. Eventually, they'd end up inside somewhere playing games or just lying around listening to the rain hit the barn's metal roof.

Dressed, Chloe pulled her damp hair into a hasty ponytail, stuck her cell phone in her back pocket, and made her way downstairs. The shower had helped immensely, loosening her muscles. The ibuprofen was kicking in, too. But ibuprofen on an empty stomach always made her a little queasy.

She needed breakfast. Lucy texted her while she was trying to decide what to eat.

Lucy: Are you alive?

Chloe: Just Barely.

Lucy: Come to the store. I'm going solo. Could use help if you are free. Have an interview coming in later.

Chloe: Coming!

Lucy: Bring Coffee!

Chloe: On it!

Settling for a granola bar to ease her stomach and eat on the way, Chloe grabbed her keys and purse and headed out the door.

TWELVE

The bookstore was located on the corner in an old brownstone in the heart of downtown Willow Falls. The front stoop was lined with white mums and sunshine yellow daisies in bright green pots that enticed Chloe closer. Carrying coffee and a brown bag labeled with golden arches, Chloe walked up the damp sidewalk. The rain took a short reprieve, but the sky was still overcast. Large gray clouds hung heavily in the sky and threatened more rain.

Water dripped off the purple sign that read Lucy's Corner; as Chloe ducked inside, the bell tinkled.

"Lucy?" Chloe called out.

"Back here!" Lucy answered.

Chloe heard the snarl of packing tape as she threaded her way through the stacks and found Lucy bent over a box.

"Good morning," Chloe said, sliding the coffee onto the counter and shaking the brown bag. "I brought coffee and breakfast."

"Thank goodness! I thought I might have to curl up underneath the counter and nap. Which one is mine?" Lucy asked, indicating the coffee.

"Doesn't matter, they're the same. Black and caffeinated."

Lucy twisted out a cup, popped the top to let steam escape, and took a sip. "You're a lifesaver."

Chloe laughed. "What's the deal? Are you out of coffee? You're usually on your third cup by now."

"I am, here and at home. I didn't have time to stop at the store and pick some up. I need to get all these books boxed and ready to be shipped." She patted the stack of boxes beside her. "They have to go out today."

"Anything I can do?"

"You did it by bringing me coffee. Without it, I was afraid the next person that came through those doors might get murdered." Lucy let out a little gasp and covered her mouth for a second with her hand. "Oh, no. I shouldn't have said that in light of what happened to that poor woman."

"What woman? What are you talking about?"

"It was on the news this morning. They found a woman dead on the west side of town. They haven't identified her yet, but it definitely sounds like they suspect foul play."

"How awful."

"I know. And right here in Willow Falls, of all places. It gives me the willies to talk about it. Forget I brought it up." Eyeing the bag, Lucy asked, "What else do you have there?"

"Your favorite, an apple pie."

"You know just how to spoil me."

"You're here by yourself?" Chloe asked as she opened the bag and the scent of warm apples and bacon escaped. She handed Lucy the pie and kept the breakfast sandwich for herself.

"Yeah, I have been for the last couple of days."

Chloe unwrapped her sandwich and asked, "Where is everybody?"

"I have one employee off on vacation, another sick with the flu, and one that just put in her two weeks and didn't show."

"That's three. What about the fourth?"

"Ayesha will be in later this afternoon," Lucy answered.

"Who's leaving?"

"Long story, but here's the short version. Cynthia decided that she needed to spend more time with her boyfriend. She put in her two weeks on Sunday, but already called off twice. Cynthia told me she was going to work in the office of her boyfriend's mechanic shop. They need more --" Lucy used her fingers and made air quotes, "quality time."

"Really?"

"Yeah," Lucy shrugged. "Word on the street is that her boyfriend is cheating on her, she wants to keep an eye on him."

"And there's your real reason."

"Yep. If it was me, I would kick his ass out and run him over with my car, but I digress."

Chloe giggled. "Not everyone has your moxie, Lucy."

"I know. I'm a rare breed."

"You certainly are."

"So . . ." Lucy wiggled her eyebrows at Chloe. "How did it go last night when Tate took you home?"

Chloe bit into her sandwich. Chewed. "It was fine."

Lucy raised her eyebrows. "Fine? That's all I get? Come on, there has to be some juicy details."

"Why would you think that?"

"Because it's you and Tate."

"It hasn't been me and Tate for quite a while now," Chloe reminded her.

"Believe me, I know. You've avoided him like the plague. And in a small town, that's hard to do. But somehow, for years, you've done the impossible."

The bell tinkled, and a woman walked in.

Lucy craned her neck to see who it was. "It's Mrs. Fritz."

"Want me to help her?"

"I got her. I have that interview coming in shortly and need you to cover the counter while I meet with her. This may be the only chance you have to finish your coffee."

"Whatever you say, boss." Chloe gave her a salute.

Lucy hesitated, pointing. "Those boxes are ready to go. Someone should be here shortly to pick them up."

"Got it," Chloe said as she sat behind the counter.

"Good morning, Mrs. Fritz. How can I help you today?" she heard Lucy ask as she walked toward the older woman.

"I need a gift for my granddaughter. And you know me, once a librarian, always a librarian. So, to me, there's nothing better than the gift of a book."

"Come right this way. I'm sure we will find something perfect for her."

Their voices drifted away as they went to the back of the store, headed for the children's section.

The front door chimed again. Chloe swept the crumbs off the counter from their quick breakfast and tossed everything in the trash when she heard, "Well, hello, Legs. Fancy meetin' you here."

Cringing, Chloe turned around to face Dalton Turk. He stood mere inches from the counter, leaning on a handcart full of boxes. "My name is Chloe."

"I know – the famous author Chloe Harris. You can tell me your name all you want, but I like Legs better. It fits you."

He leaned over the counter his eyes slowly trailed up her body. She fidgeted, mortified as he licked his lips, looking like he might jump the counter and devour her at any moment.

Crossing her arms in front of herself, she cleared her throat. "Is there something I can help you with?"

He smirked. "I have boxes to deliver, and I'm here to collect the ones behind you."

"Right," Chloe said, turning to look. "Do you want me to . . ." she didn't get to finish before Dalton was around the counter, standing beside her, with his handcart full of boxes.

"I got them, Legs. Don't hurt yourself trying to lift them." He leaned over, brushing against her as he unloaded. Her skin prickled with dread. Packages stacked to one side, he let go of the cart and moved toward her, boxing her in between the wall and the counter. Panic crept to the surface.

The bell tinkled.

"I always pictured writers as old, stuffy men, wearing tweed jackets with patches on their elbows and a pipe clenched between their teeth, smelling of tobacco. But not you." He placed one hand on the wall and the other on the counter. Stretching his neck, his face only inches from her, he inhaled deeply. "You smell good."

Chloe inched back away from him until her back was pressed flat against the wall. Cornered.

Dalton shifted, moving closer. "What's the matter, Legs? Are you afraid of me?"

Chloe's stomach took a dip. "You'd like that wouldn't you?" she asked, trying to keep the edge of fear out of her voice. She stood frozen in place even though every fiber in her being wanted to run.

"I like it when my women squirm a little." He trailed a finger down her neck. "How 'bout you and I . . ."

Someone cleared their throat. "Excuse me."

Both their heads turned simultaneously.

A pretty young woman with long tawny brown hair and a painted-on smile stood at the counter watching them.

Chloe pushed past Dalton, "Can I help you?"

"Sorry," she glanced from Dalton to Chloe. "I didn't mean to interrupt."

"Believe me, you're not." Relief was evident in her voice, "How can I help you?"

"I'm here to see Lucy Roberts. I have an interview with her for the sales associate position."

"Yes, she's expecting you. Lucy is with a customer right now, though. My name is Chloe." She held out her hand. "What's yours?"

"I'm Tara, Tara Zimm," the younger woman said, shaking Chloe's hand.

"Nice to meet you, Tara. It should only be a few minutes."

Chloe glanced at Dalton and saw that he had the boxes stacked on his cart and was already maneuvering his way out from behind the desk.

His gaze landed on the younger woman, then flicked back to Chloe. "Later, Legs."

Her eyes bore into the back of his head as if to will him out of the store as he carted the boxes to the door. Chloe shook her head and closed her eyes for a brief second, relief washing over her.

"Are you alright?"

"I'm fine," Chloe said, trying to keep her voice from hitching. "Here comes Lucy now." Forcing a bright smile, she greeted the older woman with her friend. "Hello, Mrs. Fritz."

"Hello, dear."

"If you don't mind, I would be more than glad to help you here at the register."

"That would be wonderful," Mrs. Fritz said.

Chloe directed her attention to Lucy. "This is Tara. She's here for the interview."

"Perfect timing," Lucy said, then turned back to the older woman. "If you'll excuse me? I have an appointment."

"Of course, dear."

Lucy and Tara walked back toward the office, and Chloe took over the sale.

"The princess and the frog, always a favorite," Chloe commented, wincing at the shaky sound of her voice, as she took the older woman's credit card. "And the drawings in this version are gorgeous."

"My granddaughter loves princesses. Walks around in her mother's heels and a tutu most days."

"That's so sweet." Keeping her hand steady, Chloe slipped the items in and handed her the bag. "I hope she enjoys the gift."

"I'm sure she will." Mrs. Fritz picked up the bag. "Looking forward to your next book coming out." She waved her fingers at Chloe. "Ta ta for now."

The moment the door closed, Chloe's legs buckled. Shaking, she slipped down behind the desk, the feel of Dalton's finger still on her neck.

＊

The sun peeked out late in the afternoon. Tate had kept busy in his workshop all day after checking the progress at the other jobsite. He was putting the last coat of stain on the outdoor set when Bo came bounding in, followed closely by Lucy.

"Well, well, looky what the cat drug in?" Tate remarked as he dropped the brush into the empty can and wiped his hands off on a rag. "Or, in this case, should I say the dog? Of what do I owe this great honor?"

"I thought I would stop out and just say hi."

"Really?" Tate raised an eyebrow. "That's out of character for you."

"Is it?"

"It is." Tate watched Lucy for a moment.

Lucy's eyes scanned the large room, but quickly honed in on the table. "That's beautiful, Tate."

"Thanks. I think it turned out pretty well." Tate stood back to admire his own work.

"Chloe's going to love it."

He stuck his hands in his front pockets. "How did you know it was for Chloe?"

"I ran into your brother while I was out running errands a little while ago. He was buying green cushions."

Tate nodded. "That explains it." He walked over to the mini fridge he always kept stocked with drinks. Pulled open the door and examined the contents. "Want a drink?" he offered.

"No, I'm good."

"Suit yourself." He pulled out a bottle of water, twisted the top, and downed half of it in one long gulp. He wiped the back of his hand across his mouth. "Now – do you want to tell me why you're really here?"

"Speaking of Chloe . . ." Lucy bit her bottom lip as if to stop herself.

"What about her?"

"I just thought you might want to know . . ."

"Just spit it out, Lucy. I've never known you to be one to hold back."

Lucy laughed awkwardly. "I guess not. Here goes -- Dalton Turk came into the bookstore today while Chloe was there and –"

He stiffened. "What did he do?"

Lucy clasped her hands together tightly. "He gave Chloe a scare. That's what."

His plastic water bottle crinkled under the pressure of his hand as he clenched the bottle tight, afraid of what Lucy would say. "How?"

"Seems that Dalton had Chloe cornered."

Tate narrowed his eyes and moved closer. "What do you mean cornered?"

"Just that. He came behind the counter where Chloe was working and had her pressed up against the wall. He only stopped because someone came into the bookstore."

"Did he touch her?" Tate asked as a curl of dread formed in his stomach.

"I'm not sure. Chloe didn't elaborate. She just said that when Tara came in, she was able to get away from him."

"You didn't see it happen?" Tate asked.

"No," she shook her head. "I didn't."

"Did she report it?"

"No. She said there was nothing to report."

"But you think there was?"

Lucy chewed on her lip. "The thing is, Dalton has always been a little creepy, even in high school."

Tate crossed his arms. "That didn't answer my question."

Lucy shrugged, her face still full of concern. "I'm sure it's because she didn't want anyone to worry or make a big deal about it. Chloe chalked it up to that last ball she pitched to him. Dalton had been pretty put out after. Even I noticed that."

"He was," Tate agreed. "Still doesn't give him a right to corner her."

"I just thought you should know. You're working at her house and around town in case you happen to see him near her again."

"I'll keep an eye out," Tate said. He wanted to kick Dalton's ass for scaring her. "I don't know who he thinks he is."

"God's gift is what," Lucy put in.

Dalton always seemed to skim right below the surface. He'd never been in any real trouble, at least that Tate knew of. Neither man liked each other overly well, but they'd managed to keep it civil all these years. But harassing Chloe? That was out of line, and Tate wasn't about to stay out of it.

THIRTEEN

Chloe was in the groove; the words were flowing effortlessly. Her fingers floated over her keyboard as fast as they possibly could.

. . . he stood tall and dark against the deepening night, poised and sophisticated. All business in his three-piece suit. One hand was in his suit pocket, and the other held a smoldering cigar; the scent was musky, like a worn leather jacket that had absorbed the aroma of cedar.

She couldn't see his face, but knew exactly who he was. Asher, the name whispered across her heart.

He took a long pull on the cigar, and the end glowed red. He released the smoke as he exhaled. It drifted feathery brown against the black night. It wafted up and circled his head like a slow, curling fog.

"What do you want?" she sobbed, choking back tears.

He flicked ashes to the ground. "You know what I want."

"If I knew, we wouldn't be here now." It was all she could do to keep from running to him, desperate to be engulfed in his arms.

He pushed off the wall, staying in the shadows. He walked toward her. "Whether you know or not," he laughed a deep, dark, seductive laugh, "it wouldn't have mattered. We were always going to meet . . . like this . . . eventually. It was inevitable, just like the sun will rise in the morning. You can't stop it. You can't stop this. I have to have you. You know this just as surely as you know your own heartbeat."

"Asher," she whispered breathlessly. "Why now? Why, after all this time?" Raquel swiped at a tear that threatened to fall. "You

know I can't possibly . . ." her voice trailed off as he came out of the darkness, emerging like a knight from battle, glorious and . . .

There was a rap downstairs. She almost didn't hear the knock, which didn't register at first. She was so into writing, but the pounding was persistent, became more intense, and slowly sunk into her subconscious.

Chloe looked up from her laptop and noticed that night had fallen fast as she had been enthralled with her writing. The house was completely dark now except for the glow from her screen. She rubbed her tired eyes and glanced at the time. It was only eight, but it felt like midnight.

A sharp knock came again from the front door, making her jump. She flipped on the lamp on her desk. Who could that be? Dalton Turk's face floated through her mind. Pushing it aside, she stood. When the pounding returned, she shouted, "I'm coming. I'm coming!"

Descending the stairs, Chloe quickly turned on both lamps in the great room as she passed them and flicked the switch by the front door that illuminated the porch. Peering out, she saw Tate's face, which didn't look overly happy.

"I should be the one who's not happy," she grumbled. Chloe flipped the lock on the door and opened it wide. Cool air and a grouchy man greeted her.

"This better be good. I was in the groove."

He moved past her.

"Come in and make yourself at home, why don't ya," she said sarcastically.

Tate scrunched up his eyebrows and asked, "The groove? What the hell is that supposed to mean?"

"Seriously?" she asked. "The groove means I had the flow going." She added when he still looked stumped, "I was writing, for heaven's sake. I was fully immersed in my characters and the scene, and you just ruined it, so this better be good."

"Believe me, it is."

"Then let's hear it." Chloe closed the front door, crossed her arms, and waited.

"Why don't you tell me?"

"Tell you what?" she asked, perplexed. "Tate, I really don't have time for this. I need to get back to my laptop." She moved to go around him.

He caught her gently by the arm.

"Tate."

"Chloe."

"Okay, you're going to have actually to say more than my name. Clearly, I don't have any clue as to why you showed up on my doorstep."

"Have you seen Dalton Turk recently?"

Chloe visibly shivered, peeled his hand off her arm, and took a step back from him. "That's not funny."

"It wasn't meant to be," Tate said coolly.

"Why in the world . . ." her voice trailed off. "Who told you?"

He waved her off. "Does it matter?"

"Yes."

Now, he crossed his arms. "Why?"

"Because it's private. It doesn't concern you."

"You concern me."

"Since when? I have barely spoken to you in years up until two days ago."

"We've spoken."

"If you want to call saying hello as you pass by in the store talking, then fine. But otherwise, as far as a real conversation before that, not since . . . never mind."

"No, let's hear it. Not since when?"

Chloe clamped down, sealing her lips.

"I want to know, Chloe."

She turned on her heel and walked into the kitchen, avoiding the subject and him. She needed to do something with her hands to keep herself steady. She didn't need this tonight or any night. Going to the cabinet, she pulled out a glass. Moving toward the refrigerator, he stepped in front of her.

"Move, please. I need some ice."

Tate reached out and took the glass from her hand. Setting it on the counter, he asked again, only softer, "Chloe, please . . . tell me. What happened? Why did we stop being friends? I need to know."

Looking up into those eyes, Chloe was swamped with emotion. She was overly sensitive tonight; the scene with Dalton and the emotional one in the story she had been writing, her emotions were rolling. And now this. She swallowed the lump in her throat. "I don't think I can, Tate. It hurt too much."

"I'm sorry." He took her hand and led her to the sheet-covered sofa. He indicated that she should have a seat.

She shook her head no. He was too close, and the house was suddenly too small. "I can't. I need to go outside. I need fresh air."

Tate didn't say anything, only took her hand and led her through the house, out the front door, down the steps, to the folding chair under the tree where the grass was damp. The night was cool and dark, but the stars shone brightly.

"Sit," he said, simply pointing at the folding chair.

So, she did.

He crouched down beside her; they were so close their knees brushed. "I want to know. Correction," he said, leaning forward. "I need to know. I can't stand this distance between us. Whatever I did, believe me when I say I'm sorry."

She looked away, out across the expanse of the dark yard, to the road, then the trees, and then up to the heavens. Anywhere, but directly at him. A coyote howled in the distance, sounding as forlorn as she felt.

"I can tell you're not ready to accept my apology."

"Why would I?" she questioned, her words barely audible. "You don't even know what you're apologizing for."

He placed both hands on either side of her chair and scooted forward. Closer. "I would if you just told me. What did I do?"

"I can't believe you don't know."

"Humor me, please?"

Chloe took a deep, cleansing breath. "Do you remember in high school?" Her voice trailed off, and she wondered if she could actually go through with telling him.

Tate only missed a beat. "You're going to have to be more specific than that."

She frowned at him.

Caught, he cleared his throat. "Sorry. Continue."

"Our senior year . . . we were in the library, and Kimmy was about to ask you out."

"She was going to slash my tires if I didn't go out with her," Tate finished for her. "How could I forget?" He waited. When she didn't continue, he asked, "What does that have to do with you? With us?"

"Seriously? I knew this was a mistake." She started to rise.

"Wait." He held her gently in place, his face inches from hers. "I don't understand why that's significant or what it has to do with you and me."

"Think about it for a second."

"Okay."

She hoped to heaven she wouldn't have to spell it out for him, but when the seconds ticked by, she knew she would. "Remember what happened that day in the library?"

His eyes flicked down to her lips. A smile spread wide across his face. "How could I or anyone forget? I kissed you in front of everyone, right there in the middle of the stacks. It was quite the scene. Eddie stood beside you practically drooling as he watched." His smile widened further, if that was even possible, etching every muscle in his face into that expression. "That kiss was perfect. I said it then, I'll say it again, you were perfect. And in that moment, you were my hero."

Her heart soared for a brief instant. It was perfect. But just as quickly, her heart plummeted. He still didn't see it. How that kiss - meant everything - to her.

"Our plan worked perfectly. Kimmy," he laughed, "fell for it. Hook, line, and sinker." Tate rocked back on his heels and stood. "Wait, is that what you're upset about? That she fell for it? That we deceived her? If so, don't worry about it. We're fine. Kimmy and I are friends now."

Exasperated, she flopped back in her chair. "If you have to ask, then you're missing the whole point."

"So . . ." he drew out the word. "This isn't about Kimmy?"

Could he really have been this clueless the whole time? She shook her head. In the darkness, she could see him suddenly connect the dots.

"This is about us, isn't it?"

She nodded. Finally.

"Were you mad because I kissed you?"

"No," she said simply.

"Is this because Eddie was standing there? Did you have a crush on him?"

"Certainly not."

"Then what?"

"On you!" There, she'd said it. She leaned forward. "Y-O-U." She jabbed a finger at him.

Tate was struck speechless.

She shook her head in disgust and stood. Tate rocked back on his heels, a blank look on his face.

Frustrated, Chloe unleashed. "You're such an idiot! I can't believe I have to spell it out for you. Clearly, you didn't feel the same." This time, when she moved, there was no stopping her. She pushed past him and marched back toward the house.

He stood stunned. "Wait. What?" He jogged to catch up, caught her arm, and spun her around to face him. "You had a crush on me?"

She stared at him in disbelief.

He said it again. "You had a crush on me." This time, he said it as a statement, not a question. "Hell." With his free hand, he all but surrendered. "I didn't know. I had no idea you felt that way. Had I known, things would have been different."

Shaking her arm free, furious, she questioned him, "How? Would you have kissed someone else instead?"

"No," he said seriously. "I would have kissed you again."

Her breath caught. "What did you just say?"

"I said I would have kissed you again . . . if I had known."

Her heart fell at his feet.

Her face flushed red. She was thankful it was dark, so he couldn't fully see her reaction. She pushed past her anxiety and asked, "Why?"

"Because," he waited, but she didn't say anything. "Now, I guess I have to spell it out for you. I had a major crush on you, but I was afraid."

"You were afraid of me?" Chloe crossed her arms. "I find that hard to believe. Now you're just making fun of me." She narrowed her eyes at him, daring him to deny it.

His face went stone cold serious. "I would never."

Chloe raised her eyebrows. "Really?"

"Okay, I might make fun of you, tease you, and I guess I have in the past, but it was all good-natured fun. Something like this, though, Chloe, you have to believe me when I say I wouldn't."

"I believed you before." She took a step back and needed a little more distance from him to say it. "You said you loved me and that turned out to be nothing. So why should I believe you now?"

"I said that?" He shook his head slightly, sealing his lips, not admitting or denying it.

"Do you think I'm lying?" her voice sounded shrill even to her own ears. "You said you loved me right after you kissed me breathless, even if you didn't mean it or don't remember. You whispered that in my ear mere seconds after that kiss – so you can bet that I believed you. Then when it turns out it was all a ploy to make sure -- you, my best friend of all people, didn't get asked out by the wrong cheerleader . . . I was devastated. Crushed."

"Back up a second." Unable to control a grin that slowly took hold of his face, he asked, "I kissed you breathless?"

"Out of all that, that's the part that you focus on? Unbelievable." She crossed the rest of the yard at a steady clip, stomping up the porch steps. Chloe flung open the front door and disappeared inside.

Tate heard the lock turn, and the front porch light went out a second later.

"I guess this concludes our conversation for tonight," he said to himself.

Standing alone in the dark, he berated himself. "That didn't go according to plan." And yet, a small smile spread across his face as his mind latched onto a tiny thread of hope. The night sounds poured in – the chirp of a cricket, the rustle of dry leaves, and the far-off sound of an owl surrounded him, but despite that, all he could think of was that once upon a time, he had kissed Chloe Harris breathless.

✻

The laser vibrated and whirred in the printer as it rocketed back and forth across the photo paper, producing the image he coveted. Slowly, line after line, the image of her face was produced. It slid slowly out and lay in the tray. He waited a beat to make sure the ink was dry before he picked it up and examined it. Her.

Desire coursed through him. It was growing stronger every day, and it was getting harder for him to control. He studied her pretty face, and a surge of yearning swamped him.

Over the years, he'd been able to handle his desires, his cravings, his lust. But lately, the intensity of his feelings overpowered him, leaving him feeling weak and out of control.

Every waking moment, thoughts of her consumed him. He'd been on edge lately, unable to handle some extra pressures that came with his demanding job. Everything was spiraling out of control. The bills were piling up, and the pressure to do more, have more, and have her escalated.

But the other night, in the bar with that woman, he'd forgotten it all. He'd been in control from the minute he sat down. He'd picked her out and made his move, fulfilling his fantasy -- manipulating the situation and her.

For a moment everything had been perfect, and then he'd looked at her face, and the illusion had shattered.

It hadn't been enough. She hadn't been enough.

He knew in the deep, dark recess of his heart he'd have to try again.

FOURTEEN

Thursday

Walking down the center aisle, glancing into the empty stalls, dust stirred as Chloe's boots scattered bits of loose hay over the concrete floor. When she was younger, every stall had been occupied. Now, only the ones at the far end held horses, the two her father hadn't been able to part with when they had moved into town.

"Good morning, girls," Chloe said, greeting the two mares. Both horses poked their heads over their respective gates.

Shelby was a white and brown paint and the older of the two. Chloe rubbed her hand across Shelby's neck as the horse nuzzled her shoulder. "How are you, old girl?" she asked affectionately. "Did you have a good night?" The horse nickered softly and nudged her arm playfully.

"That good, huh?" Chloe grabbed the scoop from the grain barrel and filled Shelby's bucket. She moved to the next stall and rubbed Star's nose. "And how about you, young lady?"

The quarter horse snorted, and Chloe repeated the process of filling Star's feed bucket.

"It's going to be a beautiful day. Let's get you fed and then out of those stalls into the fresh air so you can stretch your legs."

Chloe dropped the scoop in the barrel, then leaned on the wooden boards separating her from the horses and sighed with the simple pleasure of them. Enjoying the quiet, her ears registered that the only sounds in the barn were the soft crunch of grain and the occasional swish of a tail.

A wisp of anticipation raced over her bare arms as both

horses shifted in their stalls, acutely aware of someone approaching.

The dog entered before the man, barreling through the door, Tate not far behind.

"Well, hello there, Bo," she said, reaching over with one hand and giving him a quick rub.

"You're out here early," Tate said, strutting down the middle of the aisle.

Without taking her eyes off the mares, she forced herself to relax. It was only Tate. She was still so jumpy. Damn that, Dalton Turk.

"The horses do best when they stay on a schedule."

"I would agree with that statement."

"This is the time my dad always comes out to feed them and collect the eggs," she answered, trying to sound relaxed despite the fact that last night's conversation with Tate came rushing back. She'd have to face him sooner or later. Her choice was later, though. If she could put off the awkward conversation even for a few minutes, she would. "I don't think my dad would have moved to town if my mom hadn't let him keep these two beauties."

Tate nodded. "It's like my mom and her garden. She didn't want to give it up or start a new one. Plus, it's her excuse to come out and check on me. Same with your dad, I suspect." He walked closer. "Need any help?"

She turned away from the horses and him, avoiding eye contact, and placed an empty bucket beneath the spigot, filling the pail. "Can you take this one to Shelby?" She lifted the full pail and handed it to him. Their fingers brushed as the metal handle passed from one hand to the other. Retracting her hand quickly, she said, "Thanks." Keeping her eyes trained on the next water pail.

"No problem. Looks like it's going to be a beautiful day." He lifted the pail easily over the stall and placed it so the mare could drink. "What's on your agenda for the day?" he asked conversationally.

"I need to get the chores done, write, and get ready for the book signing tonight." Shutting off the faucet, Chloe carried over the second pail. Unable to help herself, she glanced at Tate. Noticing his grin, she asked, "What?"

"Nothin'." He laughed.

"There's something," she stated.

"I was just hoping I could talk you into coming to pitch for us again tonight since you did such an awesome job Tuesday."

Hand on her hip, she asked suspiciously, "Why can't Eddie pitch?"

"I heard he's stopping by a certain author's book signing."

"Right, of course."

"If I didn't already have a prior commitment, I would stop by, too. I'm interested in seeing you in action."

She continued to work, ignoring the comment. She wasn't sure if she could handle Tate being there; signings always made her a little nervous, and she didn't need Tate making it worse. Still, it was nice that he seemed interested. Shrugging, she said, "The only thing I can do is promise not to keep Eddie long. It's not like he needs to be there." Turning to face Tate, she asked, "Who's normally Eddie's backup?"

"You're looking at him."

Chloe gave a half laugh. "Hope I'm done in time to see that."

"Hey," he said, sounding offended. "I'm decent, just rusty."

"And I wasn't?" she asked, noticing the horses were just about finished.

"No one would have ever known it."

"I'm not sure that's true, but thanks." Chloe reached for the stall gate, lifting the latch. The door glided open, and Shelby clopped out. Tate followed suit with Star. The horses walked on autopilot, with Bo leaping ahead, leading the way out of the barn and into the pasture. Chloe grabbed her bucket of cleaning supplies and went out into the chilly morning air, wishing she'd grabbed a jacket.

Tate followed her to the large watering trough. She drained what was left of the dirty water from the day before and proceeded to spray the tank with the hose from the outdoor faucet. Tate grabbed a brush and started to scrub the algae off.

"Not that I don't appreciate the help, but don't you have work to do?" Chloe asked.

"I do."

"But?"

"We never finished our conversation from last night."

"As far as I'm concerned, the conversation is over," Chloe started to protest.

"It's far from it," Tate answered flatly.

"What do you want to discuss then?"

"Dalton Turk."

Chloe continued to spray the tank, resigned to having this conversation. "It's not a big deal. I'm perfectly capable of handling him."

"I didn't say you weren't."

Tate dropped the brush in the bucket and walked toward her. Despite Chloe's protest, he turned the water off and gently took the hose out of her hand. "We need to talk."

"I thought we were."

"Okay, Miss Sarcastic. You listen, and I'll talk."

Chloe crossed her arms and leaned back in the crook of the fence, waiting.

He cleared his throat. "We got sidetracked last night."

"Maybe you did, but I didn't." Resentment bubbled up in her like a fresh spring. "It's not something I want to discuss. It's an uncomfortable and embarrassing situation, but I handled it."

"From what I heard, the situation might have escalated if someone hadn't walked in." He waited a beat. "Is that correct?"

She lifted a shoulder. "He was just trying to push my buttons like you are now. It won't work."

He moved a step closer to her. "What won't work?"

"You. Pushing my buttons."

His face softened as he moved toward her. "I think I could push exactly the right buttons," he was within inches of her. He placed an arm on either side of her on the fence and watched her

THE FURTHER I FALL

suck in a shaky breath. She wanted so desperately to lean into him. Have him wrap his arms around her and hold her tight. But instead, she shifted back and away.

His smile faded. His eyebrows furrowed, creating a crease between them, full of concern. "But I won't, not today when you're still jumpy."

"I'm not jumpy."

"Let's see." He reached up and tucked a wisp of hair behind her ear, and she trembled. He dropped his hand, inched back, and tucked his hands into his front pockets. "I think I just proved my point. Listen, I want you to know should you need anything . . ."

She cut him off. "I don't."

He nodded. His eyes flicked down to her mouth but just as quickly returned to her eyes.

Chloe jumped, startled as someone cleared their throat.

"If I'm interrupting, I can come back later," Kurt commented, standing just inside the barn.

Putting her hand on Tate's arm, she moved him aside. "You're not," she said, sidestepping him. "Did you need something?"

"Nope. Just wanted to check and see when we were going to get started."

"I guess now," Tate said and gave Chloe one last glance. "We can talk later."

Lifting an eyebrow, she remained silent as Tate followed his brother out.

Safely out of hearing distance from Chloe, Kurt grinned at his younger brother. "You look like a kid with his hand in the cookie jar just now."

"I feel like it."

"Would you have kissed her had I not interrupted?"

"Truthfully?" Tate asked.

"Yeah."

"No. The timing was off." He raked a hand across the back of his neck. "But I sure as hell wanted to."

Kurt slugged his younger brother in the arm. "Well, that's a start."

❋

He threw the papers on the desk and scraped his hands through his hair. Sweating, he loosened his collar as the fabric rubbed against the deep scratches on his neck, that seemed to be getting worse. He peered at his faint reflection in the window, pulling his shirt back from his skin.

That damn bitch had raked him good with those blood-red nails. He could still hear that high-pitched drunken cackle she made when she had started to fall backward, making a grab for him to save herself and drug her nails down his neck, scraping the flesh clean off. No amount of antiseptic or Neosporin lessened the burn. But he'd been the one to have the last laugh as he brought the proverbial hammer down on her skull. The bitch probably never even knew what hit her.

That thought, and that thought alone, brightened his mood slightly. But it didn't fix his problem. He squinted at the stack of bills and picked up his phone.

He made the call.

The phone rang and he started to count as his pulse and his anger spiked again. He drummed his fingers on his desk, increasingly harder each time the phone rang and went unanswered, and with the vibration, the haphazard stack of books shifted slightly closer to the edge.

"Hello?" came the deep, polished voice on the other end.

"It's about damn time." He didn't say his name. There was no need for formalities.

"Sorry, I was . . ."

"I don't want your pathetic excuses. I want you to get this job done. You need to turn up the pressure. Make the deal."

"You told me this would be easy, that you were in control. I think that's far from the truth."

He slammed his fist onto the desk, and the books toppled. "I am in control."

There was a short pause on the other end, followed by a harsh laugh. "It doesn't seem like it."

He picked up a book and threw it across the room, rage coursing through him. "I don't give a damn how it seems or what you think. That's how it is. I am in charge." His voice rose to a high pitch. "Do your damn job. I'm paying you a ton of money to make this happen. Apply pressure and get this thing done. That's what I'm paying you for. Not to sit and think!"

He clicked off the phone before the man on the other end could say anything else.

He yanked open the bottom drawer and dug out a small box. Flipping it open, he plucked the small tracking device out of its protective wrappings. He held the circular device up to the light and examined it. It was time to take matters into his own hands.

FIFTEEN

From halfway down the block, Chloe could see a beautiful handwritten chalkboard sign announcing that she would be signing books today and a line of people already wrapped around the corner.

Instead of going in the front, she turned down the alley. Pulling a heavy wooden door open, she slipped into the back of the store.

Tickets had already been sold, books had been shipped, and were stacked on shelves throughout the space and displayed by the front door. She found Lucy in the back as she chatted away with the new sales associate, Tara, while the others set up another display.

Chloe cleared her throat. "Am I early?"

Lucy turned on her heel without missing a beat and said, "Not at all. You're right on time. Chloe Harris, this is my new sales associate, Tara."

Tara smiled brightly. "We met yesterday."

"You got the job! Congratulations!" Chloe said, shaking her hand.

"Thank you," Tara beamed, smoothing back her hair. "I can't believe I have a job. I just moved here less than a week ago. I haven't even completely unpacked."

"Your new boss made you start right away?"

"I don't mind. I'm excited to get started. Besides, Lucy said I could have the weekend off to finish unpacking if I would help her today with the signing."

"I see. It's just you, then?"

"Me and my dog, Bruno."

"Bruno?" Chloe questioned. "That sounds like a big dog's name."

"He thinks he's big. He's just a little black lab. Still a puppy. Can't get him to sleep through the night yet. House training is crazy. We're out walking at all hours of the night. Do you want to see a picture?"

"Of course." Chloe couldn't help but catch the other woman's enthusiasm.

Tara pulled out her phone and scrolled through her photos. "Here he is."

"Awe. What a cute little thing."

"Isn't he, though?" Not waiting for a response, Tara kept talking. "I never thought I'd get such a great job in such a short amount of time. Today is officially the first day of the rest of my life, and I can't believe I get to spend it setting up for a book signing." Tara draped a tablecloth over the table. "I'm so happy to be here in this beautiful bookstore and work with Lucy and the other women."

"Alright," Lucy chuckled. "You already got the job. You don't have to keep flattering me."

Chloe leaned in, nudging the young woman. "Although it never hurts to flatter the boss."

Tara flashed a brilliant smile. "I wanted to say something the other day, but I was so nervous. I've read all your books."

"Or the authors," Lucy added with a smirk.

Ignoring the comment, Chloe asked, "Which one is your favorite?"

"I think the fourth one." She held up the paperback with an ocean scene on the cover.

"Why is that?" Chloe asked, picking up a couple of books and stacking them on the end of the table, arranging them aesthetically.

"I like that particular one because of the setting. I always love a good beach romance."

A hint of a smile played over Chloe's face. "Me too."

"Have you ever fallen in love at the beach like in your book?" Tara asked wistfully as Lucy muscled over another larger chalkboard sign.

"I've never fallen in love with anyone I've met at the beach, but I did go to the beach with my family and friends. I spent two glorious weeks on the sand, in the sun, and completely in love."

The Beckers and her family had rented a house right on the beach in the Outer Banks the summer before her senior year. That's when she fell hard for Tate. Head over heels, completely in love. They swam in the water, lounged on the sand, and strolled down the beach just like every other cute couple Chloe had noticed. She had a crush on Tate before, but that summer had set the wheels in motion, and her heart had tumbled right toward him, falling further. She hadn't been able to stop it, no matter how hard she had tried.

There were several times in those two weeks when he had reached for her hand to pull her into the surf or helped her up from a beach chair, and his hand had held hers a little longer than necessary. But when they returned home and started back into their everyday routine, getting ready for their senior year, it seemed like he had lost interest. She had kept that feeling, tucking it away in the depths of her heart, cherishing those two precious weeks.

Chloe was suddenly aware that the conversation between her and Tara had stopped. She glanced up from her box of books and looked over. Both Lucy and Tara watched her.

"What?" Chloe asked.

"Wow," Tara replied, shaking her head. "I wish I could have just been a part of whatever memory you just replayed in your mind. Because the look on your face was one of pure bliss."

Lucy added, "You should have seen her that summer. She was floating on cloud nine."

Chloe blushed.

"Really?" Tara wiggled her eyebrows. "I'd love to hear that story sometime."

"It was obvious to everyone. Well, maybe not everyone, but I knew you were in love," Lucy said knowingly.

"I'm sure it would make for a great love story or romance."

Chloe put her palm on the side of her face and felt the heat there. Then, her smile faded slightly. "Well, it would have to be a love story because romances always end happily ever after. Love stories don't. That's the big difference between the two."

Tara frowned. "I guess I never really thought about that. I didn't realize there was a difference. That's sad when you think about it."

"Who says the story is over? Who says the ending has been written?" Lucy asked, concentrating on her sign.

"Oh, it's over."

"Maybe, maybe not." Lucy brushed her hands on her jeans as she dusted off the chalk. "What do you think of my sign?"

"It's wonderful!" Tara exclaimed.

"Beautiful," Chloe cooed, and it was. There were daisies in the corners, and her name was scripted in a decorative cursive.

"You're very artistic. I can't believe you just did that in a matter of a few minutes."

"It's her superpower," Chloe said.

Lucy shrugged. "If it's my superpower, it's the only one I have."

"I wish I had a superpower like that," Tara said wistfully.

"Me too," Chloe agreed.

"You have one. You write. That's your superpower." Tara continued to stack books on the little table. "I hope you don't think this is too presumptuous of me, but yesterday, when Lucy hired me and said our first major event would be the book signing, I bought a bunch of books to give as gifts and would love for you to sign them, if it's not too much trouble?"

"It's no trouble at all."

"Great! I have them in a box and labeled with the names I want in them. I figured it was never too early to start my Christmas shopping. I can put them in your car later, and you can get to them whenever it's convenient for you."

"Sounds good to me."

Delighted, Tara hugged her. "Thank you so much!"

"You're welcome," Chloe said with a smile.

Lucy jumped as Eddie emerged from the back of the store. "Look who finally showed up." She crossed her arms. "It's about time. Were you hiding in the back? We are ready to open the doors."

He gave her a smug grin. "I won't confirm or deny. But you have to admit my timing is impeccable, as always." He turned to Tara. "Hello, I'm Eddie Lambert, Chloe's agent."

"Not exactly," Chloe interjected.

Eddie continued as if he hadn't heard her. "And you are?"

Tara stood a little straighter. "I'm Tara Zimm."

"She's my new sales associate," Lucy explained.

"Nice to meet you," Eddie managed. "Are we going to get this party started? There's a line down the block."

"I think we're all set. Let's open the doors." Lucy went to the front door to unlock it. "Here we go."

✳

Chloe autographed books already purchased, signed new copies, and posed for selfies with her fans. At last, the line started to dwindle.

"I can see the end," Tara said to Chloe as she gave her a fresh bottle of water.

Chloe unscrewed the top and took a sip. Setting the bottle down, she smiled at the next two women in line. "Hello. Thank you so much for taking the time to come out tonight. I hope your wait wasn't too long."

"We waited over an hour, but it was totally worth it," a woman said.

"We are so excited to be here and finally be able to meet you." Chloe held out her hand. "So nice to meet both of you."

"As you can see, we are huge fans," she said, as she dug a small stack of books out of her bag and placed them in front of Chloe.

"We've read all of your books," the other woman added.

"I see that." Chloe smiled as she reached for the first book and tried to make small talk. "Are you from Willow Falls?"

"No Lancaster. We both work at the hospital."

"We're both RNs."

"I thought you might be."

They laughed. "What gave it away? Our scrubs?"

"Well, that was a big clue," Chloe acknowledged with a smile.

"Maybe someday you'll write a book about a nurse falling in love. We could be your inspiration."

Smiling, Chloe said, "Maybe I will." Signing the last book, she pushed the stack across the table. "There you are."

The woman pulled out her cell phone. "Would it be terribly obnoxious of us to ask to get a picture with you?"

"Not at all." Chloe looked around. "But it looks like the sales associate has stepped away for a moment."

The woman turned around to the man behind them and held out her phone. "Would you mind?"

Chloe's eyes locked with his. Mattison Belov. Chloe's stomach did a flip. What was he doing here?

"Of course not," he said casually. He took the phone, and the two women scurried behind the table to stand next to Chloe.

He snapped the pictures, angling it a couple of different ways. Chloe plastered on a smile and took him in. He was dressed in blue jeans and a white buttoned-down polo, looking casual yet sophisticated. He held out the phone. "Do you want to check the photos?"

The woman looked at Chloe. "You don't mind, do you?"

"Not at all. No one wants a bad photo."

She scrutinized the photos, showed them to her friend, and deemed them good. "Perfect. Thank you so much," she squealed. I can't wait to post these on social media." Then she turned to Chloe. "I guess I should ask. You don't mind if we post them?"

"Not at all. Make sure you tag me when you do."

"Oh, I will. Believe me." She gave Chloe a quick hug, and then her friend took her by the arm.

"We should go. He's waited long enough," she said with a

nod in Mattison's direction, scooping up their books and loading them into their bags.

The ladies waved as they walked away. "Thanks again!"

Mattison turned to watch them go and chuckled. "Looks like you made their night."

"I certainly hope so. They made mine."

He looked at Chloe as if it made perfect sense that he should be standing in her line. "You don't mind?"

"Not at all. Without people like them, I wouldn't sell very many books. Now," Chloe said, smoothing down her shirt. "What can I do for you?"

"I have a book for you to sign if you'd be so kind?"

"Of course."

He held out the book, and she took it from him. Their hands brushed briefly. "Mr. Belov, what brings you to Willow Falls?"

The ghost of a smile played on his lips. "You did."

Chloe blushed. Flustered, she opened the book. "Is this yours? Or am I signing it for someone else?"

"It's mine."

Chloe looked up at him, slightly surprised. She figured it was most likely for a wife, girlfriend, or at least a sister.

"Surprised?"

"Sort of."

He laughed. "If I wasn't standing here in your line with my book, what would you have assumed I would be reading?"

Chloe shifted slightly in her chair, really looking at him. "Well, that's not quite fair. I know what type of movies you produce."

"Ahh, yes. So, you think you know me. But what I read in my spare time and what I produce are two completely different things. Maybe I don't read at all," he said coyly. "Maybe I rely totally on what others recommend."

"I highly doubt that. I would definitely say you're a reader. You have that intelligent, academic look about you."

He folded his hands in front of him. "Go on."

"I would have pegged you for the thriller type. But not a

THE FURTHER I FALL

scary, out-of-your-mind kind of guy that reads Stephen King, even though you might pick one up once in a while. No, you're more of a Grisham or Clancy, maybe even a Patterson. You like the letter of the law and the little nuances around it. You like the mastermind of a criminal and the intensity of a good plot that they create." It was Chloe's turn to laugh. "Have I said too much? Was I right?"

She slid the autographed book across the table toward him.

His eyes glinted with amusement, holding hers captive. "What gave me away?"

"Just a feeling about you. A vibe you give off, if you will. Sorry," she waved her hand in front of her to break the connection between them but, more importantly, to stop herself from talking. "I usually don't go on like that. Please forgive me."

"There's nothing to forgive. I found the way your mind worked fascinating. But more importantly, you were correct. Grisham would be one of my favorite authors. So are the other two. Until recently, Grisham was number one."

"And now?"

"You are."

He said it so simply that Chloe's face flushed red. It's probably a line, she told herself. He's charismatic, and he knows it. She tried for casual, even flippant. "How recent?"

"Can I be candid?"

"Please."

"You moved to number one in the last hour."

"Wow, that is recent. And how exactly did you put me at the top of your ranking system in the last hour? More importantly, was I even on the list before today?"

He held up the book she had just signed. "Obviously. And you have had the chance to visit my office. Very few do."

"True."

"But I digress. Standing in line, you hear a lot if you listen."

"And did you?"

"Yes, I had nothing better to do," he joked.

She smiled at that. "What exactly did you learn in the last

hour that caused you to bump me to number one?"

"I heard everyone raving about your books – the little romances, the plot twists, the mystery that brings the characters together and keeps your readers glued to every word." He held her gaze. "Some even went as far as to say you were brilliant."

"This is all very flattering." Chloe smiled and bounced her leg under the table nervously. "You got all that from standing in line?"

"Yes."

Chloe was speechless for a brief moment. "I don't know what to say."

"You don't have to say anything. It was merely an observation. And one that I felt truly comfortable sharing with you."

Tara came over to help her tidy up. "I didn't mean to interrupt."

"You're not," he said kindly. "I've taken up enough of Miss Harris's time." He lifted the book. "Thanks for the autograph."

"You're very welcome."

"I will be in touch with Mr. Lambert. I know we can work out our differences." He gave a slight nod. "Have a good rest of your evening, ladies."

"You as well."

Tara turned to Chloe. "What was all that about?"

"He's a movie producer and would like to work together on a project," Chloe explained.

"Wow!" Tara exclaimed. "That's exciting."

"It is," Chloe said thoughtfully as she watched him thread his way through the store.

*

Turning into the alley that led to the small parking lot behind the store, his breath was shallow, and his nerves were jumping. His eyes scanned the mostly abandoned lot. He fingered the small magnetic device in his pocket, no bigger than a thumbtack, as his heart raced, the three-inch nail was in the other hand. All he needed to do was walk casually like he was cutting through, dip behind her car, place the nail strategically at the tire, then the device behind her license plate, and keep moving. It would only take a second, two tops.

Lengthening his stride, he covered the ground quickly. Glancing over his shoulder to ensure he was alone, he ducked behind the black SUV. Bent. The magnetic device stuck. The nail was placed perfectly. He straightened. Seeing no one, he continued on.

Too easy, he smirked as he passed under a pool of light and back out to the street.

SIXTEEN

The night was dark except for a waning moon and a sprinkling of stars that scattered over the black, velvet sky. Chloe rounded the corner, passing the outcropping of the rock wall, and drove into the lot, not wanting to go home just yet. She was still on an emotional high from the successful book signing and the brief encounter with Mattison Belov.

Realizing it was later than she had initially thought, she parked, acutely aware of the massive lights keeping the black sky at bay. The large LED flood lights rained down over the diamond, creating a little oasis inviting and enticing all kinds into it.

Like a moth drawn to a flame, she wandered to the fence, pulled by the sounds: cleats crunching on gravel, the rasp of a leather glove, and the crack of a bat as it echoed off the rock walls. A cheer rang out as the ball was hit deep.

Chloe looked up, followed the baseball, and lost it in the gigantic bulbs some fifty feet overhead, blinded. Her eyes adjusted and focused on the silent war going on above her as insects flew frantically toward the light and certain death. Like the corpse of an insect, the ball fell silently from the sky. The centerfielder back peddled through the grass toward the fence and raised his glove. Everyone held their collective breath. He jumped and stretched, but the ball sailed high over his head and the fence. The runner took an easy lap around the bases as the cheers echoed off the walls.

Chloe leaned on the metal fence and shivered slightly. Glancing at the scoreboard, she noticed it was the top of the seventh, and the score had just been tied.

Tate stood at the mound with a frown on his face as the next batter approached home plate. She could almost hear his mind working, cursing himself inwardly for that last pitch.

A new ball was dug out of the bag. Kurt tossed the baseball to Tate and he took his place back at home plate.

Tate's scowl left his face as he took his stance. He glanced over his shoulder to first, even though the bases were just cleared. He wound up. His form was perfect, his posture relaxed, and the tension of the last pitch was already forgotten. He released.

There's a split second of silence as the ball sails through the air. Then the distinct sound of the reverberation of wood as ball meets bat. It pops up high to left field. With a snap of leather, the glove seals around the three-inch ball. The player is out.

A murmur of curse words mingled with cheers drifted over the field. The third out. Her team... correction - Tate's team, runs in from the outfield.

"Hey, Chloe!" Kurt said, coming over to her. "I was wondering if you'd show up."

Before she could answer, others noticed her too.

"Are you here to play?" Neil asked.

"We could have used you earlier," Jerry said, nudging Tate with his shoulder as he pushed past. "The pitching hasn't been up to our usual standards tonight without you or Eddie."

"Screw you," Tate said good-naturedly stowing his glove. "Neil, you're up to bat."

"On it."

"Get us out of this mess," Tate muttered.

"I'll do my best."

"Better late than never, Chloe," Kurt said, draping an arm over her shoulder. "Wanna bat?"

She laughed. "No, thanks. I just came to see how it was going."

"It's been alright despite the pitching." Kurt rolled his eyes in his brother's direction. "Our batting average improved tonight, keeping us alive, even without Tate having his favorite bat."

"What happened to his bat?"

"He probably just left it at home."

"Like hell I did. I think it grew legs and walked off." Tate grumbled as he watched Neil grab a bat and walk casually out to home plate, swinging. "If you could do better pitchin', you could have stepped in anytime, big brother. No one was stopping you."

"Looks like you only need one run to win. Neil could be it." Chloe quickly assessed the situation.

"Let's hope," Tate said and looked directly at Chloe for the first time since she had arrived. He had seen her SUV pull in, but tried hard to block her out so he could concentrate on pitching. Knowing she was in the vicinity had caused him to falter, to throw that ball directly across the plate—a perfect pitch for the batter. He had practically served the ball to him on a silver platter.

He had managed the next batter better and got him out in one pitch. Looking at her now, though, he silently hoped Neil would hit a homerun so they wouldn't have to play another inning. He wasn't sure he could get her off his mind after seeing her standing there in her faded denim and pale green off-the-shoulder blouse that revealed delicate skin. Her dark brown hair was swept up into a sophisticated twist with a playful braid tucked into the low bun that elongated her neck, making her look sexy as hell.

"How did the book signing go?" Tate asked, trying to pull off sounding casual.

"Really well, thanks for asking."

"Sorry, I missed it," Tate said sincerely. "I would have liked to see you in action."

She laughed. "There's not much action."

"Still." Tate turned his attention back to the game. "Let's go, Neil. Let's finish this."

Neil nodded and stepped up to the plate. Everyone went quiet, and their attention shifted focus to Neil and the pitcher. The pitcher threw the first ball, and Neil swung. The bat connected with the ball; it sailed deep into right field and stayed fair. A cheer went up as the ball dropped over the fence. Neil took the bases easily.

"That's a wrap," Tate yelled.

"And just like that, we earned ourselves one more game," Kurt stated.

"What does that mean?" Chloe asked.

"That was our last regular season game. We start playoffs."

"And its single elimination. We better bring our A–game." Kurt turned to Chloe and pointed a finger at her. "Plan on being there."

"Okay. Who will we be playing?" Chloe asked, excited that she'd been included.

"We don't know yet. A couple more games need to be played. We should find out on Monday."

They all filed out onto the field, shook hands with the opposing team, and then wandered back to the dugout to collect their equipment, scattering to their vehicles.

"A few of us are headed to the Taphouse. You coming?" Kurt asked Chloe.

"I think I'll just head home. It's been a long day. Thanks, though."

"I don't think you'll be going anywhere," Neil said. "Not even home."

"What's that supposed to mean?"

"He's right." Tate pointed at Chloe's SUV. "Your rear tire is completely flat."

"Not again," Chloe grumbled.

Tate crouched down, pulled out his cell phone, and turned on his flashlight app. Shining it over the tire, he said, "There's a huge nail sticking out of it."

"That'll do it." Kurt clucked his tongue.

"I can change it quickly." Tate stood. "Unlock the vehicle, and I'll get out the spare."

Chloe didn't move.

"What are you waiting for?"

She fidgeted from one foot to the other. "I don't have a spare."

"What?" Kurt asked. "Why not?"

"Because this is my third flat in less than a month."

"So, you see the importance of having a spare," Tate said matter-of-factly.

Chloe put her hand on her hip. "I know the importance. The last time I went in to have my flat fixed, the guy who repaired the tire forgot to put the spare back in. I just haven't had a chance to return to the garage and pick it up."

Kurt smirked. "Women."

"Women?" Chloe questioned. "It's most definitely men. A man forgot to put it back in, not me." She crossed her arms defensively. "I'll have you know, I changed both those flat tires myself. I'm not some incompetent . . ."

Tate cut her off. "No one thinks you're incompetent. Give her a break, you guys. Three flat tires in less than a month is a lot."

"It certainly is," Kurt admitted.

Chloe put her hands back on her hips. "Great, so now how am I going to get home?"

"I can take you. It's not out of my way," Tate said.

"Thanks, but aren't you going to the Taphouse?"

"Not tonight. Call the tow truck. Have them come out and get your car. If they forgot to put in the spare, it's the least they can do."

"If you're sure?" Chloe questioned as she searched for the local garage's number on her cellphone.

"I am."

Chloe nodded. She dialed the number of the local garage, which had a twenty-four-hour towing service.

"Looks like that's settled then," Kurt said. "If you guys are good, we'll head out."

"Yep," Tate answered for both of them while Chloe spoke on the phone.

The others got in their vehicles and pulled out.

When she finished, Chloe clicked off the phone. "He said it would be a while before they could come out. We don't need to wait."

Tate bobbed his head. "Do you need anything from your car?"

"Just my purse." Chloe leaned in and snagged it off the front seat. "Thanks for taking me home."

"Not a problem," Tate told her.

They climbed into the truck, and Tate was all too aware of how it felt to have Chloe back in it.

As he started the truck, the radio pumped out country music. Tate quickly turned the dial, bringing down the volume. They drove in awkward silence for a little while as he tried to think of something to say.

"The book signing went well?"

"It did. It was my most attended signing yet."

"That's great," Tate said as he drove. "Next time you're going to have a book signing, try not to have it on a Tuesday or a Thursday night. I can't afford to lose three of my best players in one fell swoop."

Nodding, Chloe answered. "I'll try to remember that. But I only had Eddie and Lucy. Who else were you missing?"

"You," he said simply.

She turned and looked directly at him as he pulled into her lane, stopping in front of the house. He shifted the truck into park. Their eyes locked in the darkness.

"Me?" she asked hesitantly. "I didn't realize I was a part of the team."

"I gave you a shirt, didn't I?"

"Wow." She shook her head. "That's one heck of a recruiting system. I believe you gave me that shirt before I played. What if I hadn't been any good?"

"Then I would have taken it back," he said with an easy grin.

"I have no words," she said dryly.

He chuckled. "Look at that. I render you speechless."

"That wouldn't be the first time."

That comment stopped him cold. What was that supposed to mean? His first instinct was to make the situation light, crack another joke, and make her laugh, but he couldn't do it for some reason. There was just a vulnerability there that he had never sensed before. It made him want to reach out and comfort her. Tate went so far as to reach for her face, but at the last second, his stomach pitched, and he shifted in his seat quickly and put his extended arm on the back of the bench instead of reaching for her.

"We used to tell each other everything. What makes now any different?"

This time, she frowned a little. "That was a lifetime ago, Tate. A lot has changed since then."

"Like what?" he asked sincerely.

Chloe looked at him for a split second. "Really?"

He lifted his hand off the seat, indicating she should precede. "We're older. We've changed."

He waited for her to add more, but she didn't. "The only thing I hear that's different is our age." He turned the truck off, shifting further in his seat as he tried to convey his sincerity. "I don't think things have changed that much. I'm still the same old me. And you . . ." his voice faltered.

"And me what?" Chloe asked, her voice barely above a whisper.

"And you . . ." are just as beautiful as when you were in high school. But instead of saying exactly how he felt, he fumbled for the right words. "You're still you. A little more talkative, a little more assertive, and very successful, but underneath, you seem like the same girl I . . ."

Chloe sat straighter. "The same girl you what?"

He faltered. "The same girl that I gave rides to. The same girl that I teased." He reached out, tugged a strand of her hair, and smiled. "The same girl I studied with. The girl that lived next door. The girl all my family loved and still does. The girl that I considered my best friend and the only girl . . ." He swallowed hard, forcing down the lump in his throat. "I ever had a crush on."

Her eyes widened. "You said that once before."

Nodding slightly, he answered. "I did." He reached over, unhooked her seatbelt, gently wrapped an arm around her waist, and slid her across the bench. Everything about her appealed to him, like the soft scent surrounding her and the contour of her body as she fit neatly into his embrace.

"Tate," Chloe whispered.

"And still do." He had her close, so close he could see the small scar just below her right brow where she had cut her eye when he had pushed her off the swing when they were in middle school. Reaching up, he carefully ran a thumb over it, remembering how she had looked that day. Small and fragile as she crumpled to the ground. Dazed and confused when she came too. God, he had been scared. Remembering how sorry he was that he had hurt her, and how grateful he had been that she was alright, and terrified that he was going to be in trouble. But Chloe hadn't told on him. That was something he couldn't fathom at the time. She had every right to tattle, but she didn't. He had learned something about her that day.

Wanting to kiss her, his eyes slowly searched hers for a sign, any sign of whether he should proceed, kiss her like he so desperately wanted to, or if he should back off before he crossed a line he couldn't uncross.

Her warm body felt good in his hands, too good. Her lips were perfect and close, and the seductive scent that whispered across her skin drove him crazy. Before he could overthink it, he moved tentatively, placing his lips on hers. When she didn't pull away, Tate fused his mouth to hers.

A small whimper escaped her lips as they parted for him. She was sweet and sexy all at once. A feeling of déjà vu overtook him as the memory of their first kiss swamped him, dragging him under. His world blurred between the past and the present. As good as it was the first time, this was better.

There weren't any library stacks brimming with books to push her against or gasps from curious classmates. There was no audience, only her and him. The night, and the casual caress of the breeze from the open windows that slipped through the truck.

His hand slid from her face to cover hers, which was pressed lightly against his chest. It was warm and soft under his. Their fingers entwined while his lips tempted hers, and his tongue teased, begging her for more.

She eased back as they slowly broke apart. He watched her for a moment, wishing he knew exactly what was going through her mind.

"Chloe?" he questioned as he drug in a haggard breath. "Say something."

Her free hand covered her heart, the other still in his. "I need a minute."

Her eyes were wide, dark, and beautiful.

"I've been waiting to kiss you like that for a very long time." He reached for her again, but she scooted back across the truck, out of reach.

"Tate, please."

"Please, what?" he could see she was unsteady.

"I need another minute."

Not wanting the moment to pass or the feelings, he couldn't stay quiet. "Do you know I couldn't step into the library at school or even walk by without thinking of you and that first kiss?"

"I find that hard to believe."

"It's true. My grades suffered because of it."

"Lucky for you, there were only a few weeks of school left."

"I think I might have flunked that entire semester if it had been any longer. I barely passed as it was."

"Don't try to blame your grades on me. You're the one who never picked up a book."

"That's not true. I carried them every day, just like you. Homework was the bane of my existence unless I was doing it with you."

A ghost of a smile whispered across her face. "It was more like I was doing your homework. You just happened to be the one signing your name to it."

He shrugged. "I thought we were simply comparing answers."

"That's right. I remember now." She gave him a sideways glance that made his heart skip. "You just always had the wrong answer."

He gave a quick laugh. Now that he had kissed her, the floodgates had opened, and he wanted more than anything to kiss her again. The distance between them was too much for this small of a space with her just out of reach. Needing to remedy the situation quickly, he said, "Come on. I'll walk you to the front door." Before she could protest, he hopped out and skirted the hood of the truck.

"I can walk by myself," she said as he opened her door.

"You are the most frustratingly independent woman I have ever met." He locked eyes with her, moving in close so she was efficiently wedged between him and the seat. "I know you are capable, but it wouldn't hurt for you to allow me to help you out or walk you to the door just because I want to, would it?"

Their bodies brushed against each other, and she relented. "I guess not."

Holding out a hand, he grinned at her. "I know it's hard, but you can trust me to help you down."

Reluctantly, Chloe placed her hand in his. "I know I can trust you with the small things."

"Good," he said, feeling a small victory.

"It's my heart I don't trust you with."

"Ouch," he said, stepping aside and letting go of her hand as he followed her up the sidewalk to the front porch. "That hurt."

Opening the door, she turned to face him.

Before she disappeared inside, he tugged her back over the threshold and pinned her against the door frame.

Her breath caught, and she looked up at him wide-eyed.

"I'm going to fix that, I promise."

"Don't make promises you can't keep, Tate Becker."

The words were barely out, and it had him completely undone. He wanted to kiss her again, but the look in her eyes told him to take it easy. Instead, he leaned forward and placed a kiss tenderly on her forehead. Lingering for a moment, his lips pressed gently against her soft skin as he murmured, "I promise not to break your heart." He reluctantly released her, but not before he noticed tears threatening to fall.

Chloe slipped inside, closed the door, and turned the lock. Once again, effectively shutting him out.

SEVENTEEN

He drove through the dark night as a test and followed the GPS tracker that he had carefully placed on her SUV. He smirked as the app did its magic and honed in on her.

His forehead scrunched up as he realized he was driving out of town, down a gravel road, and into the quarry. The lot was dark and empty except for a lone SUV. It was hers. He recognized it immediately.

He glanced around out of precaution but knew he wouldn't be caught. No one was out here at this time of night.

Without hesitation, he pulled up beside the SUV and parked. He noticed the flat on the vehicle's passenger-side rear tire. It had worked. And yet – it didn't. She wasn't here. He was too late.

He wondered how she had gotten home and who had taken her. The thought of her getting in the car with someone else made his blood boil. Relax, he told himself. Anyone could have given her a ride. It was all probably innocent enough. But damn, if she wasn't hard to control and hard to predict. He needed something tonight that would be a sure thing. No guessing, no complications. His nerves jittered. His hands itched. The need to be in control consumed him.

Then the thought crept into his mind before he could stop it -- like a spider scurrying across the floor undetected until it was - big, black, and unavoidable. Did she even go home, or was she somewhere else altogether? He put the car in reverse and backed out.

Just like a spider, the thought needed to be squashed. And there was only one way to do that.

❋

The puppy whined at the door, needing to go out. Tara yawned and rubbed her eyes; she must have fallen asleep on the couch when she got home. She stretched and eyed the little dog. "Seriously, Bruno? It's late. Can't you hold it until the morning? These nighttime outings are killing me."

He came running over and licked her hand.

She laughed and threw back the Afghan she had draped on the couch. "Oh, alright. Let's make it quick."

Tara grabbed the puppy's leash and clipped it to his collar. She then grabbed a sweatshirt off the hook and slipped it on. They went out the door and down the steep stairs, the puppy pulling urgently.

Outside, they walked down the block to the little park at the end of the street. The park was one of the main reasons she'd picked this apartment; she knew she needed space for Bruno to run around and do his business.

The apartment building itself was a little run down, but the street was nice with the well-maintained older homes on the other side.

Once at the park, Tara stopped under a pool of light and squatted down. "Now, if I let you off the leash so you can run, you promise to come back when I call, right?"

Bruno licked her hand frantically, lavishing it with puppy kisses. "Alright. Here you go." She unclipped, and stood, holding the leash in her hand, waving him off. "Go. Do your thing. Like last night, I'll be right here on the bench."

Bruno gave a little bark and raced off into the dark. The night air swirled around her, and she shrugged deeper into her sweatshirt, pulling it closer. She sat on the park bench, laid the leash on her lap, and waited.

The hair on the back of her neck prickled with anticipation.

"It's a little late to be out here alone, isn't it?"

Startled, Tara jerked in the direction of the voice. He stood just on the edge of the pool of eerie yellow, his face in shadow.

"I'm not alone. My dog is with me."

"That little pup?" he questioned.

The voice was familiar, but she couldn't quite place it. She'd met so many people this week. Trying to sound more confident than she felt, she said, "He's pretty fierce. I wouldn't mess with him."

He stepped from the shadows, and she tensed.

"Is it wise to let him run around in the dark?"

"Bruno's fine. He just needs to release some pent-up energy before he turns in for the night." He took a step closer, and she recognized him. "But it's late, and we should probably go. Bruno!" she called.

"Here, now," the man knelt at her feet. "It looks like you dropped something."

"Bruno's leash." Tara laughed nervously. Forcing herself to relax, she said, "We won't get far without that."

He stood. The leash was stretched out between both hands.

She froze, trying to figure out what was off about his hands.

"You're right." For a split second, his face was washed with light, and the sneer on it petrified her. "You won't get far."

EIGHTEEN

Friday

The sound of vehicles turning into her lane woke her before six. Doors slammed, voices carried, and tools scraped as they were unearthed from truck beds and toolboxes.

The thought of Tate already outside her house at six o'clock in the morning made her stomach flutter. Her fingers brushed over her lips where his had been only hours earlier. If she used her imagination, she could still feel the sensation of his lips on hers. She closed her eyes and snuggled into her blankets.

Stop it, she scolded herself. That's how she had gotten into this situation. Despite the comfortable bed, Chloe was stiff from a night of tossing and turning, her thoughts consumed with Tate. Would a relationship with him inevitably end in heartbreak?

He promised not. But as she'd learned the hard way, men's promises were fleeting and fickle. No, she wouldn't trust him -- at least not yet, not completely.

Her phone rang. Recognizing the number, she answered on the second ring. "Hello, Eddie."

"Chloe?" he asked.

"Who else would it be?"

He chuckled. "Sorry. Dumb question. Did I wake you?"

"No, I've been awake." Practically all night. "What's up?"

"I have news, and I couldn't wait until a more respectable hour to tell you."

"What news?" Chloe asked as she threw back the covers and got out of bed.

"You didn't tell me you had a visitor yesterday at your book signing."

"I had a great turnout, but you already knew that," Chloe answered, slightly distracted as she peered out the window, peeking from behind the curtains, and saw Tate. Just the sight of him made her knees weak. "You'll need to be more specific."

"Well, this visitor was not only a fan but a movie producer as well. The one and only Mattison Belov. Of Belov Productions." He waited a beat. "Am I right?"

That got her attention. "Yes, of course." How could she have forgotten?

"Why didn't you tell me?"

"You'd already left," she said dismissively. "Why didn't you just ask that outright?"

"I thought I was being coy," Eddie replied with a laugh. "Apparently, it's too early for that."

"I'd say. How did you know? I hadn't had a chance to call or text."

"I noticed that." He sounded slightly peeved but seemed to let it slide. "His assistant emailed me late last night. He wants to move on this project quickly."

"What about his brother?" she asked.

"He didn't mention Phillip."

"Okay," she thought of the book she'd autographed for him yesterday. He seemed genuine with his compliments. Why should she be concerned about his brother if he wasn't? A spike of excitement shot through her. "Why? When? And how are we going to proceed?"

"Whoa," Eddie said with a laugh. "I can only handle one question at a time. As soon as possible, and because he loves your book and watching you in action."

"Really?" Chloe asked again, sinking onto the corner of her bed.

"Yes, really. How many times are you going to ask that question?"

"Probably at least a dozen more." Chloe ran a hand through

her tangled hair. "So," she drew out the word. "When?"

"He wants to meet tonight if you're available. And Chloe?"

"Yes?"

"Before I ask if you are available, I would advise you to simply make yourself available and just say yes, no matter what."

"Then the answer, before you ask it, is yes. Anytime, anywhere."

"That's what I like to hear."

Chloe could hear him shuffle papers on the other end of the phone as she padded down the stairs to the kitchen to start some coffee.

"Mr. Belov has some appointments already scheduled for the day, a couple of Zoom meetings, I think he said. He said he would be available for dinner. Of course, I proposed the Taphouse for the food. Which is excellent yet casual, and the atmosphere, which is relaxed and inviting. And I know Kimmy will treat us right while we're there. I figured the extra attention to detail wouldn't hurt our chances of impressing him."

"Sounds perfect to me," Chloe said. "Eddie?"

"Yes?"

"If you don't mind. Could you pick me up?"

"Of course, but why?"

"My SUV had a flat last night. I had it towed to the garage. They said they would have it done this afternoon. Could you drop me off at the garage to get my car before the meeting?"

"No problem."

"Thanks."

"I'll pick you up at six. Oh, and Chloe?"

"Yes?"

"Wear that little black dress of yours."

She sighed, thinking of the classic pantsuit she'd bought a couple of weeks ago for just such an occasion. "That's not my first choice."

"But it's the right one. Trust me."

NINETEEN

Being an older brother meant sometimes knowing your siblings better than they knew themselves. Living under the same roof for eighteen years, watching him grow didn't make Kurt an expert when it came to Tate, but he was damn close, as close as anyone could be.

They worked later than they anticipated on a Friday, which he knew didn't sit well with Tate. Tate loved his job, his chosen career, and the business they had built together more than most. He lived and breathed it Monday through Friday, but when five o'clock on Friday hit, Tate was always ready to take a break.

They were so close to being done with the siding and the whole project that no one wanted to stop, especially after the setbacks they had this morning at another jobsite, splitting the three of them up, and monopolizing most of their day.

Without acknowledging the time, they just kept working. Kurt was acutely aware that Tate had one eye trained on the clock and the other on Chloe's front door.

Tate was in a mood. Good, bad, or indifferent, Kurt was still undecided, but he knew it was more than just working late on a Friday. Something else was stuck in his brother's craw, and Kurt was sure as hell going to find out what it was.

He imagined asking would be like finding a snake curled up in a corner. All Kurt had to do was pick up a stick and poke it to get the reaction he wanted.

The front door opened and all three of their heads turned as Chloe came out and headed straight for the barn without so much as a glance in their direction. Kurt watched Tate follow her to the barn with his eyes. When she disappeared inside, Kurt decided it was time to figuratively pick up a stick to poke at the snake.

"You've hardly said two words today, Loverboy. What gives?"

Tate didn't take his eyes off the barn, just grumbled something inaudible.

Kurt poked again. "Trouble in paradise?"

Tate's head looked like it was on a swivel as it swung around quickly. "What the hell is that supposed to mean?" he demanded.

Kurt held up his hands. "Nothin', little brother. Just making an observation."

"Well, don't."

Though he thought he already knew the answer, Kurt still asked, "Did you ever get to finish that move you were making yesterday?"

"It's none of your business."

Kurt exchanged a look with Neil behind Tate's back. "That's a no."

"Like hell, it is," Tate swore.

"So, it's a, yes?" Kurt asked, raising one eyebrow.

"I kissed her, okay?"

"And?" Neil asked, interested too.

"And what?" Tate scowled at both of them.

"What happened? Were there sparks?"

"Yes," Tate said flatly.

"For her or you? Or both?"

"Me. I don't know about her."

"Why?" Kurt asked, lifting a piece of siding. Neil silently took the other end. "Haven't you had a chance to ask, or been afraid too?"

"Haven't had a chance," Tate grumbled, reaching for the next piece of material.

"No time like the present," Kurt reminded him.

"Maybe I could if you'd quit yappin'. Then we could just finish this damn siding and call it a day."

Stick-snake. Kurt had to get in one last poke. "Do you have

plans with Chloe for tonight?"

Tate glared at his brother. "If you say one more word before we're done, I'm going to fire your ass."

Neil grinned at Kurt. "Didn't he already threaten that earlier this week?"

"He did, and yet I'm still here." Kurt shrugged. "Go figure."

"I'll fire both of you," Tate pointed a finger at Neil. "Don't think I won't." Not taking his eyes off either one of them, Tate reached over and cranked the radio, efficiently drowning out the possibility of more conversation.

Kurt chuckled to himself, rolled his eyes at Neil, and grabbed his hammer.

They worked for a solid hour without talking, but all bets were off when the last piece was in place.

"Phew," Kurt said, shutting off the radio. "I think that's the longest I've ever gone without talking."

"It's probably a record," Neil acknowledged.

"Since you've been stewing all day about knocking on that front door, why don't you?" Kurt directed his comment to Tate.

"The scaffolding needs to be dismantled, packed up, and put on the truck," Tate grumbled.

"Neil and I can manage. Go." Kurt pointed to the door.

"Right." Tate nodded at his brother, and without further discussion, he walked away.

It had been a pisser of a day, first getting pulled away to go to the other jobsite to deal with the electrician, the plumber, and then the building inspector. All of it had cost him time on both projects, and time was money.

Tate climbed the porch steps and greeted his dog. "There you are, Bo." The golden retriever lifted his head and snuffed, his way of greeting. "I haven't seen much of you all day."

Bo blinked at him.

"Wish me luck," Tate said as he wiped his sweaty palms on his jeans before he knocked. "Here goes nothin'."

Tate knocked nervously on the door and waited his heart

racing. He had gone from zero to sixty with Chloe so quickly that his heart was off balance. He'd handle his heart, he thought. He'd have to.

Chloe opened the door, and his heart dropped.

"Hey, Tate."

Momentarily struck speechless, he simply stared at her. He mentally kicked himself. This wasn't handling his heart or the situation. "Hey, yourself." He grinned. He couldn't help it. She just made him smile. "Well, look at you." And he did. She took his breath away. Her hair was loose, in waves framing her face and caressing her shoulders. Those green eyes, deep and dangerous as the rain forest, surrounded by dark lashes, blinked back at him. The little black dress brushed her knees, with a slit halfway up her thigh, the silky material hugging every curve. He nearly drooled.

She stood just inside the door and held it wide, inviting him in, but he couldn't move.

"You guys have been busy today," she said breezily. "Come in a second while I put on earrings."

His mouth was dry. All he could utter was, "Sure." He followed her like a puppy on a string into the kitchen. Watching her with fascination as she picked up an earring, put one small silver hoop in her ear, and fastened it without so much as a glance in a mirror. Then the other.

She reached for a delicate chain that was lying on the counter, held it out to him, and asked, "Can you help me?"

He gulped, forcing down the lump that had lodged in his throat. "That's why I'm here."

She turned around, swept her hair up in her hands, and stepped back towards him. Tate took the delicate chain, leaning in, slipping it around her neck as the soft scent that floated around her filled his senses. It was all he could do to clasp the silver chain and step back. "There," he said quietly.

When she released her hair, it fell neatly into place, whispering across her shoulders. As she turned around, she adjusted the chain. "How do I look?"

You're gorgeous. Tate had to control his heart, and the only way he knew how to do that was to resort to off-the-cuff casual flirting. "You clean up pretty good, Chloe Harris."

"Thank you, Tate Becker." She looked around the kitchen. "I have my lucky necklace. All I need is my purse," she said, fingering the chain.

"Your lucky necklace? Let me see that."

He leaned in close, knowing he might regret it, as her seductive scent surrounded him. Lifting the delicate silver cross off her bare skin, he asked, "Is this the necklace I gave you for your sixteenth birthday?"

She acknowledged him shyly. "That's the one."

He looked into those eyes and thought he would drown. "After all these years you consider it your lucky necklace?"

A hint of a smile tugged at the corners of her mouth. "Who would have thought? But I have had it on for all my big moments, so I thought tonight would be appropriate, too."

Realizing how close he was to her, his eyes trailed over her face and lingered on those perfectly kissable lips. Then, he pulled himself together and locked eyes with her. "You shouldn't have gotten all dressed up for little old me."

Her eyes held his. "I didn't."

"Then what's the special occasion? What's the big moment?" Mischief played at the corners of his mouth. "Were you going to ask me out to dinner?" He prayed that was the plan. "Because I would probably say yes, even if you were in your pj's."

"I'll have to keep that in mind if I ever want to ask you for dinner. Unfortunately, for you, I already have plans."

"With who?"

"Me."

The voice came from behind him, catching him off guard. He stepped back from Chloe, caught with his heart on his sleeve, and turned. "Eddie?" he questioned, taking in his friend dressed in his black suit.

"Wow," Eddie put a hand on his heart. "You look breathtaking." He reached out and took Chloe's hand. Lifting it, he gave her a little twirl. "Absolutely gorgeous."

Tate could kick himself. Those were his thoughts exactly. Why hadn't he said it out loud?

Blushing, Chloe gave a shy little smile. "Why, thank you. You look pretty good yourself. I'm surprised you're not wearing a tie tonight. You always wear a tie."

"I cut myself shaving and didn't want it to rub."

"Let me see." She reached up. "I might have something to put on it."

Eddie caught her hand in midair. "It's fine. Leave it."

"Oh, okay," Chloe said, pulling her hand back like she'd been slapped.

Still standing there in disbelief, Tate jerked a finger at Eddie. "You're going out with him?"

"Yes," she said, separating herself from Eddie.

"Why?" Tate asked, confused.

"We have a very important date."

"A date?" Tate pointed directly at Eddie. "With you?"

"Wow, Tate. I appreciate your confidence in me to get a date." Eddie shook his head incredulously.

"Tate was kidding," Chloe soothed.

"That's debatable," Eddie retorted in a clipped tone.

Chloe patted Eddie on the arm. "I'll be right back. I need to grab my purse." She quickly ascended the stairs as both men watched her go.

"I didn't mean it like that," Tate said, trying to diffuse the situation, but crossed his arms, feeling the surge of an ugly green monster lodged in his stomach.

"Didn't you?" Eddie took a step toward Tate. "What's the matter? Still can't picture anyone with Chloe but yourself?"

"I never said that." Tate's blood spiked. The green monster grew a little larger.

"You didn't have to. It's written all over your face." Eddie leaned in toward Tate, his voice barely audible. "You've had years to make her yours, and you haven't. Why is that?"

"I'm ready," Chloe called.

Tate never got the chance to answer as Chloe came down the stairs.

She ushered both men to the front door and out, locking it behind them. Chloe hesitated. "Tate, did you need something? I never got around to asking why you came in."

Tate stuck his hands in his front pockets, simmering. "It was nothing." He gave it one last shot. "What are you two really up to?"

"Didn't Eddie tell you?" she asked innocently. "We have a second meeting with Belov Productions -- or at least with Mattison Belov." She all but chirped with delight.

Tate's eyebrows rose. So that was it. "No, he didn't."

"We'd like to keep it quiet for now, at least until the papers are signed. So don't say anything," Eddie informed him.

"I won't."

"Wish us luck." Chloe smiled at Tate.

Looking directly at Chloe, he said. "Good luck," and truly meant it.

"We need to go." Eddie put his hand on the small of Chloe's back, guiding her to the little sports car. He opened her door, she slipped inside, and he closed it.

Eddie walked casually around the Jag and opened his door, shooting Tate one last parting comment, "Don't wait up."

TWENTY

Kimmy thought the Taphouse was hopping even for a Friday night as she carried a large, steaming pizza to table ten. Young families had come in early, but as the evening grew later, the families became fewer, and the couples became more plentiful. She reached over and dimmed the lights, wanting to make the atmosphere more romantic.

The large wall of windows that looked out over the river and the waterfall were open. The cool air poured in as the music and patrons flowed out onto the deck. Dishes clinked, laughter carried, and the smell of good food enticed. The place was thick with an electric atmosphere.

Kimmy enjoyed Friday nights. It was a night well spent at her own establishment; business was good, and there was always such an energy about the restaurant.

She never assigned herself a specific job on Fridays. She just floated wherever she was needed. Sometimes, that meant she was an extra set of hands as a large order came out piping hot, or she might be needed behind the bar serving drinks, maybe even bussing tables. But more often than not, it was an opportunity for her to work the hostess stand, drop by tables and check on new customers, or catch up on gossip with the regulars.

Tonight was a typical Friday night, except it wasn't. She'd seen him come in alone about thirty minutes ago and cozy up to the bar. That was the first thing. Tate Becker never traveled alone. If he had a date, they came together. So, it was definitely not a date night for him. Maybe he was meeting one of the guys.

She waited, keeping her eye trained on him, but no one

officially joined him. Sure, plenty of women flocked around him, like bees to honey. That was Tate Becker. He simply attracted the opposite sex wherever he was. He was cordial, she noted, as the women flirted, but his heart wasn't in it

Something was off, and she was determined to find out what. "Hiya, handsome. All alone?"

Tate glanced up at her. His smile was quick but didn't reach his eyes like usual. "Hey, Kimmy. And yeah, is it that obvious?"

"Only to me," she responded. "I'm used to seeing you with a small entourage." She gave the woman in the next chair a glance. She allowed the woman a half smile, but the message was clear – move along.

He barely noticed as the woman picked up her drink and moved further down the bar.

"What's up?" she asked.

Shrugging, he deliberately rolled his tense shoulders. "Everyone else had plans. It seems I was the only one that forgot it was Friday."

Nodding knowingly, she asked, "Busy week?"

"Somethin' like that."

"Mind if I sit down?"

"Not at all. It's your bar."

Sliding into the empty seat that the woman had just vacated, Kimmy brushed lightly against him. "So, where is everyone?"

"Neil had a family thing. Kurt, Jerry, and the other guys went bowling."

"You weren't up for bowling?"

"Not tonight."

Kimmy laid her hand on his bicep. "Did you eat?" she asked, eyeing the half-empty bottle of beer he'd been holding onto.

"Not yet."

"Let's get some food in you and see if we can improve your mood." She waved over one of her waitresses and placed an order for Tate's usual.

"Thanks, Kimmy."

"Of course." She giggled despite herself. Being around Tate

always made her giddy. She ran a delicate hand up his arm, "You didn't want to go bowling with the guys, and there wasn't one pretty girl out there that you could have asked for a date?"

"You were busy." It was quick and said with a flash of a smile. "So was everyone else worth spending time with." He glanced over his shoulder.

She followed his eyes to the far corner of the huge room, spotted Chloe, Eddie, and some mystery man, and wondered if he was really upset about that. She had seen Chloe come in over an hour ago, all dressed up and looking fantastic. With the door open behind her, she held her breath desperately, not wanting it to be Tate who followed Chloe in. She hated to admit to even herself how relieved she was when Eddie walked through the door a second later.

She wasn't stupid, though; there was something between Tate and Chloe. What, no one could ever be quite sure. She didn't think they knew either. Not wanting to spiral down that path of what ifs or what could be, she turned her attention back to Tate, pushing Chloe out of her mind.

"What a shame. For what it's worth, I would have said yes if you had asked." She shifted in her chair and decided to go for it, even though it was like rubbing salt in an open wound. "What's with Eddie and Chloe? Is something going on there? And who is that other big handsome guy?"

Tate drained the last of his beer, set the bottle on the counter, and swiveled in his chair to face her directly, leaning in close. "I can't say."

"Can't or won't?"

"I can't." Tate leaned back on his barstool. The moment was gone, the connection broken.

The waitress skirted down the bar toward them, smiling brightly, plate in hand. "Sorry to interrupt, but I have an order of boneless wings just for you." Lingering, she placed the hot plate on the bar in front of Tate. "Can I get you anything else right now? Another beer?"

"Nope, just the one, I'm driving. How about just a glass of ice water," Tate responded.

"One glass of ice water coming right up." She turned around, filled a tumbler with ice and water, and then set it beside his appetizer. "FYI, Kimmy, you're needed at the hostess stand."

"Okay, thanks." Directing her attention back to Tate, Kimmy patted him on the arm. She hated to leave him like this, but work called. Giving his arm a little squeeze, she stood. "You need anything, anything at all. You let me know."

"Thanks."

Without looking back, she threaded her way through the restaurant, desperately hoping he would need her.

TWENTY-ONE

Chloe drove home with the windows down thankful that Eddie had dropped her off at the garage to pick up her SUV after the meeting. The cool night air caressed her skin as it drifted through the vehicle, playing with the ends of her hair. She took the long way home because she wanted to. Savoring the moment, the little victory of getting the movie deal, she told herself this was her way of celebrating.

Enjoying the night, the vast ebony sky, and the sprinkling of stars, she turned off the highway, passing a parked vehicle on the side of the road, barely giving it a thought. The second she passed it, the lights flicked on, and the car pulled out behind her.

The vehicle followed her out of town, tailing her too close. The lights blazing in her rearview mirror were so bright she had to lift her hand to shield her eyes. The car sped up, swerving back and forth behind her. Chloe's heart hammered as the driver laid on the horn and swerved out into the other lane, flying past her. Chloe slammed on her brakes as the vehicle jerked back into her lane and sped off. She sat for a moment, shaken, watching the red taillights diminish.

Was that some random jerk, or was it Dalton Turk? The memory of his breath on her neck and the pressure of his body against hers had goosebumps skittering up her arms. Chloe pushed the image of Dalton away, trying to keep those thoughts at bay. But like a match struck, producing a tiny flame, the thought of him took hold and grew.

The red taillights vanished, and she was all alone on the highway. The landscape rolling out, making the dark seem even darker. Suddenly, the night didn't seem quite so enchanting. Her mood was not so happy as she turned onto the road that would take her home. The thought of a big empty house made her cringe. Nerves skittered across her bare skin. She didn't want to go home. Not yet. She didn't want to be there alone. Not with her thoughts now tainted with images of Dalton and what might lurk just beyond the shadows.

What if she stopped by Tate's instead? She could put off going home alone by telling him the good news. She could talk to him until she was tired, until the fear of being alone subsided. She wasn't sure if he would be up. Maybe she should call or just drive by. If the lights were on, she'd stop.

Her mind was made up. She passed her house and continued to his.

She saw the light almost at the same time she heard the music. Every light in the house was on, and every window was open, letting the night air in and the music out. The house shone like a beacon against the darkness, keeping shadows at a distance, warm and inviting.

Chloe had expected Bo to come out and greet her when she pulled into the yard, but with the backbeat of a hard rock song so loud it vibrated her sunglasses on the dash. She was sure Bo would have no idea she had arrived, and neither would Tate.

She heard the whir of a saw as the quiet came rushing back as one song ended and another began. This time, it was a slow country song, with the twang of a fiddle filling the air. Chloe climbed the short set of stairs and let herself in the front door. She wandered through the sprawling house, following the whine of the bandsaw, noticing the once tiny rooms had been replaced with wide open spaces.

She wandered for a minute, stopping to take it all in. Beams supported the large expanse of the main hall, while plank interior barn doors could be rolled shut to divide off a dining room. Large craftsman-style moldings framed new windows, adding to the farmhouse decor. Chloe ran a hand over the square newel post on the banister as her eyes followed the angle of the staircase and marveled at the magnificent craftsmanship.

Coming into the kitchen, Chloe lifted a sheet of plastic, spotted Bo asleep in the corner, and stood in awe as Tate bent over a piece of wood. His bare chest glistened gold in the incandescent light. Her mouth went dry when she noticed jeans that hugged his hips. Muscles across his chest and abs rippled naturally as he lifted, shifted, and adjusted the board. Chloe swallowed hard, mesmerized by him in action.

Suddenly, Tate stopped and looked straight at her. One eyebrow raised slowly, pulled up by an invisible string, slow and enticing. He cut the saw and placed the board on a makeshift work table. His eyes went wide. His smile was instant and deep -- so deep that a dimple creased his cheek. He removed his work gloves, one by one, throwing them down beside the board. Sawdust rose and filtered down around him like tiny snowflakes trapped in the light.

Caught, she stood where she was. He only hesitated a moment and then moved toward her. It was like a dream: dust floating, a guitar wailing, cool air caressing. In three easy strides, he was in front of her. In four, his arms reached out and encircled her waist with one hand and her face with the other. Testing, his thumb ran lightly over her bottom lip, and then he brushed her mouth with his.

"You are real." His voice was husky in her ear. Her breath caught just before his lips sealed hers.

It was hot, intense, passionate, and not nearly long enough. The smile that escaped his lips, breaking the connection, was sly and knowing. That's when it shifted.

She felt it in his kiss, in his body pressed against hers. Slow, lazy, and seductive. Her body hummed as the kiss lingered on, attacking all her senses, overpowering every feeling and thought until she could think of nothing but Tate. His hand that caressed her face slid pleasantly down her arm, snaked behind her back, and linked with his other hand at the small of her back. He pulled her in closer yet, until even the night air couldn't pass between them. The warmth from his body pressed to hers and spread a delicious sensation over her skin and into every fiber of her being.

He drew back again, this time his eyes dark with desire. The music died, and the house fell silent so quickly that her ears rang.

"I'd been thinking about you, wishing you were here . . . Imagine my surprise when I looked up, and there you were." He ran a rough thumb over her tender lips. "I thought I'd wished so hard that I'd only imagined you, that my mind was playing tricks, but you're real."

She didn't say anything. She couldn't. She was still reeling from his kiss.

"I just want to savor this moment." He ran his hands across her bare skin. Her body warmed to his touch. In a voice laced with desire, hot and sultry, he murmured in her ear, "You look beautiful. I don't know why I didn't say anything earlier tonight. I wanted to." His fingers traced lightly over her, seemingly taking in every inch, like a blind man reading Braille.

She tried to focus, but his hands were distracting her. "I love what you've done with the place."

He smirked. "I think the tarp gives the place a nice cozy feel."

"I meant the entryway, the larger rooms, the trim, and the rolling barn door. Everything."

"Thank you. It's coming along. Do you want the five-cent tour? You think this is nice, you'll love what I did to the main bedroom." He linked his fingers with hers and brought them to his lips. "I think that should be the first stop on our tour." A smile tugged at the corner of his mouth as he lifted his eyebrows. "Maybe the only stop."

"You wish," she whispered breathlessly.

"I do. Why don't you make my wish come true?" he asked playfully, his dimple winking out, making him all the more tempting.

Her pulse skidded to a halt. She turned to the only tools she had in her arsenal. Sarcasm and disdain. "I'm not in the habit of granting wishes to half-naked men."

Tate raised an eyebrow. "What if I was completely naked? I bet you would grant my wish then."

She gave a weak half-laugh as she tried desperately to keep that image out of her mind. "I wouldn't bet your life on it."

"I like to gamble." He stepped closer to her and said, "Twenty bucks says I can get you in my bed before the week is out."

She stepped back and released his hand. Retreating. "As if, but I'll take that bet."

"You're on. This is going to be fun." His smile faded, his brow furrowed, and a look of concern passed over his face. His voice lowered. "That doesn't answer my original question. Why are you here? Did something happen?"

Finding her voice, completely charmed by him and his sudden concern, she responded benevolently, "I wanted to tell you my news."

She could have simply gone home and called her parents. After all, it wasn't late yet in Arizona. They would have been thrilled for her, but she hadn't. Her first instinct was to come here -- to him.

"Your news?" he questioned, his voice still raspy with concern. "The movie producer?"

She nodded. "I'm in. He wants to go ahead with the project."

He let out a whoop. Circled his hands around her waist and lifted her into the air, giving her a quick spin. "That's awesome, Chloe! I'm so proud of you."

A bubble of laughter emerged. "I can hardly believe it myself. Or won't let myself until we have papers signed."

"When will that be?"

"Eddie said he would have the papers ready tomorrow."

He placed a hand tenderly on her face. He looked into her eyes, and with all seriousness, he said, "We need to celebrate. I don't have any champagne, but . . ." he linked his fingers with hers again like it was the most natural thing in the world, pulling her through the disheveled kitchen to where the fridge stood alone. "I have beer. Want a congratulatory drink?" he asked, opening the dusty appliance and peering in.

She giggled. "I think I'm good."

"I wish I had something else." He closed it then. "When the papers are signed, we will celebrate. I'll take you out to dinner any place you like. Until then . . ." He tugged her against him. "This will have to do." His smile was lazy as his eyes slid slowly down to her mouth, and his hands cupped her face. The anticipation of what he was about to do had her trembling.

It was slow at first. Just a nip. He tempted, then tasted, and teased. Pressing in, his mouth plundered hers. She felt light like a feather floating under his touch, drifting out of control. His fingers trailed down her neck and across her collarbone. Her brain became foggy as his name floated through her mind. She sighed into him, letting her defenses down.

Suddenly, it registered -- like a snap of fingers. This was Tate, the one who had broken her heart. You won't survive a second time, her heart shouted.

She stiffened and wiggled out of his grasp. "Tate, stop. That's enough."

His smile was quick and seductive. "I was just getting started."

"That's what I'm afraid of."

"Chloe, what's so bad about us being together? I won't pressure you into the bedroom if that's what you think. That was only a joke." He reached for her, but she stepped back, away from his outstretched hand.

"I just can't. Not yet."

He tucked his hands in his front pockets. "When you're ready, I'll be here. I'm not going anywhere. I want you. I've wanted you for what feels like forever. I made the mistake of playing it cool before, taking you for granted that you'd always be around, that we would always be together. I learned my lesson. Chloe, please," he all but begged.

Desperately wanting to believe and dying to stay, she dragged in a shaky breath, stealing herself to get out the words. "I can't . . . not yet." Jerking a thumb over her shoulder, she indicated the door. "I'm going to go. Need to."

Tate followed her under the tarp to the front door with Bo padding beside him. "I'm falling for you all over again."

Those words pierced her heart and had her hesitating. She nodded but continued out of the house and down the porch stairs.

"Chloe?"

"Yes?"

"I'll be here when you're ready."

Safely tucked in her SUV, she saw him and his dog framed in the open door, the light streaming out behind him. Tears bubbled to the surface. For once, she was thankful she was in the dark so he couldn't see her.

She was so focused on Tate that she didn't notice the car hidden behind a hedgerow as she drove away.

TWENTY-TWO

Saturday

Parking on Pine Street, down from the city park, Chloe examined the address on the slip of paper, eyeing the old two-story brick building. She hadn't been to this side of town in years, but finding the small wooden door with the number painted on it wedged between two others wasn't hard. Shifting the box of books in her arms, she twisted the knob.

A streak of black fur came racing toward her, yipping and jumping.

"Hey there, little one," Chloe said, setting the box on the sidewalk. "Where did you come from?"

She fumbled for the dog tag on his collar as he lavished her hands with puppy kisses. "Ah, so you're Bruno. Nice to meet you." She rubbed his belly as he flopped down on the sidewalk. "You're as cute as your picture. But what on earth are you doing outside? And where is your owner?" Chloe glanced down the sidewalk, half expecting Tara to come running up the street to chase after him, but there was no one in sight.

"Did you slip out while she was in the shower or something?" she asked as he continued to lick her hand. "Well, let's go see." Giving him one last rub, she opened the door, picked up the box, and stepped inside.

The stairs were steep and narrow. Maneuvering the box, Chloe climbed to the second floor as the puppy dashed ahead.

At the top, she had to stop to catch her breath. Bruno let out a soft whimper. Chloe smiled down at him. "What's wrong? Afraid you're going to be in trouble for sneaking out?" She laughed.

"Don't worry. As cute as you are, Tara can't possibly be mad at you."

She knocked, and Bruno scratched the door, but there was no answer. Chloe called out, "Tara? It's me, Chloe Harris. I have your books and your dog." She waited a beat, but there was still no answer.

"Tara? Everything okay?" Chloe's voice sounded hollow even to her own ears as it died quickly in the narrow space. A pit formed in her stomach as she tried the handle, which turned easily in her hand. "Tara? We're coming in."

The second the door opened a crack, a stale, sickly odor of decay, and soiled clothing wafted out. Bruno squeezed through the opening, racing into the tiny kitchen and his water bowl. The only sound in the apartment was the lap of water. Otherwise, all was quiet. Too quiet.

Chloe covered her nose, calling out as she walked further in. "Tara?" Chloe gasped, swallowing back the bile that rose in her throat. Tara was sprawled across the couch at a weird angle with a leash wrapped around her neck.

❋

Four days, two bodies, and a compromised crime scene. Rita had her hands full, to say the least.

The crime scene had been jeopardized the minute Chloe Harris, and the little black lab crossed the threshold of the apartment. Regardless, Rita looked around at the buzz of activity in the flat and had confidence in her team that they would piece the evidence together despite that.

Sealed in its plastic bag, she held up the leash to the light, her mouth set in a grim line of dismay. What sicko would do such a thing?

Rita shook her head and slipped the leash into the container marked evidence. "Fulmer," Rita called to her partner. "Let's go down and talk to our witness."

He nodded and followed her out.

They emerged from the dimly lit stairwell. Rita slipped on her sunglasses and adjusted her blazer as they walked down the block to the park.

"Miss Harris," Rita said, her eyes taking in every detail of Chloe Harris as they approached the woman sitting on the park bench. She thought she was pretty but not drop-dead gorgeous or heavily made up with excessive makeup. She had more of a quiet, natural beauty. Her face was almost flawless except for the small scar at the edge of her eyebrow.

Rita exchanged a look with her partner as she noticed the dilated pupils, the pale complexion, and the tremble in her hands as Chloe Harris stroked the puppy. And in shock. "Miss Harris?" She cleared her throat. "I'm Detective Rita Sorenson. This is my partner, Detective Marc Fulmer. We want to ask you a few questions."

Chloe straightened, shifting the sleepy puppy in her lap. "Yes, of course."

Rita sat beside her, and Detective Fulmer stayed standing, gazing down at the young woman. Rita pulled out a notepad, flipped it open, and asked, "Cute puppy. Is he yours?"

Shaking her head, Chloe lifted her watery eyes and looked at Rita. "No, he's Tara's."

"The woman from the apartment?"

"Yes." Chloe swiped at a tear that escaped.

In a soothing voice, Rita asked, "If you're comfortable here, can you walk me through what happened, and we can make this your official statement? That way, you won't have to go down to the station."

Chloe nodded.

"Detective Fulmer will be recording your statement." Rita nodded at her partner, who pressed the button on his phone.

"When you're ready," he said.

"There's not much to tell." In a monotone, she ran through it for Rita, from the moment she arrived and found Bruno outside to climbing the stairs and discovering the body.

Rita sat quietly, jotting down notes while listening to Chloe

Harris, observing her body language, looking for clues or signs that anything was off.

When Miss Harris was finished, Rita let the silence hang between them for a couple of seconds, digesting the information.

Even though Rita had been on the force for fifteen years now, ten as a detective, she never got used to the fact that the world could be normal. Like now, to the casual observer, they were just three people in a park on a nice fall day. The sun shining, the birds chirping, and people going about their business. And yet, not more than a hundred yards away, up a steep flight of stairs, death lurked, laced with remnants of a deranged killer.

Rita forced herself back to the task at hand. "When did you say you met the deceased?"

"Two days ago, on Thursday. Wait," Chloe shifted on the bench. "No, I'm wrong. It was Wednesday. She came to the bookstore for an interview."

"The bookstore here in town?"

"Yes, Lucy's Corner. Lucy Roberts, my best friend, owns it," Chloe explained.

"And Tara Zimm, the deceased, came in on Wednesday for an interview, correct?"

Chloe nodded.

"And you were there. Why?" Rita questioned.

"Lucy asked me to come in and cover while she had the interview."

"Do you help at the bookstore frequently?"

"I do."

"Are you a paid employee?"

"I used to be, but not anymore."

Rita casually draped an arm over the back of the bench. "Care to explain?"

"When Lucy first opened the bookstore and I was a struggling author, I worked there four days a week to help pay the bills."

"And now?"

"Financially, I don't need a part-time job, but I'm happy to help Lucy out whenever she needs it. I enjoy working in the bookstore, and Lucy does a lot to help support me as an author."

Nodding, Rita asked, "And business is good?"

"I think so, but I don't handle anything financially for Lucy."

"Are there any other employees?"

"Yes." Chloe gave the detectives their names and the reasons they were unavailable on Wednesday.

Rita made a note and then asked, "Did anything out of the ordinary happen at the bookstore while Miss Zimm was there, on Wednesday or Thursday?"

"We had the book signing Thursday night."

"And Miss Zimm helped with that?"

"Yes."

"How did she seem? Was she nervous or distraught in any way?"

"She was thrilled to be there, excited that she'd found such a great job so quickly," a ghost of a smile played across Chloe's face.

"The night went well?"

"Yes, extremely."

"No incidents? No irate customers?"

"Not that I'm aware of. The line was long, but everyone waited patiently."

"What about Wednesday?" Rita noticed the shift in Chloe's body language as she remained silent. The avoidance in Chloe's eyes, the tension in her shoulders, and her mouth drawn out in a firm line. Rita exchanged a look with her partner. "Did anyone come in while she was at the store?"

"A . . . delivery man."

Rita could hear the hesitation in Chloe's voice and leaned in closer, "How long was he there?"

"A couple of minutes. Maybe ten. I'm not sure."

"Did something happen between them? Was there an exchange of any kind?"

"Not between them. He left when she came in."

"Did you know him?" Rita noticed that Chloe's eyes still avoided hers.

"Miss Harris, Detective Sorenson asked you a question," Detective Fulmer said firmly.

"I'll ask again. Did you know the delivery driver?"

"Yes, his name is Dalton Turk."

"Is there something we need to know about him? What was he doing there? Was he invited?"

"Lucy was expecting him."

Rita jotted his name down, intending to have him checked out. "Is there anything else we need to know about him?" Rita waited a beat. When Chloe didn't seem to want to elaborate, she decided to move on. Mentally, she switched gears. "Can you explain to me what you are doing at Tara's apartment if you only met her on Wednesday?"

"She asked me to autograph her books. I was just dropping them off."

Rita had investigated the carton of books dropped just inside the door of the apartment. "When did the deceased give you those books to sign?"

"Thursday at the event. I didn't have time to autograph them for her then. There were quite a few, and she wanted them personalized. I told her I would drop them off as soon as possible. She needed one soon for a birthday present."

"Miss Harris, this is going to get out. Another murder in such a short amount of time, it's inevitable. We will try to keep your name out of it, but you have to promise you won't seek out the press either."

"Believe me, I won't. That's not something I want to talk about to a reporter."

"If it does get out, and the press approaches you by chance, I would advise you to avoid talking to them and simply use the phrase - no comment. Do you understand?"

Chloe's head bobbed.

"Is there someone we can call for you? Someone who can take you home?" Rita asked, closing her notebook. "After the shock you've had, I don't think it's safe for you to drive."

"I'm fine. Besides," Chloe said, "my parents are out of town."

"I can have an officer drive you home."

"No, I don't want to come back here for my car." Chloe trembled.

"That's understandable. What about a friend or a neighbor?" Detective Fulmer asked.

Hesitating, Chloe said shakily, "I guess there is one person I could call."

"All right, go ahead and make the call."

Both detectives stood. "We will give you a minute."

They stepped away to give Chloe some privacy. Slowly scanning the area, Rita took in the immediate vicinity.

It was an older part of town, an old apartment building on one side of the street and a sprinkling of houses on large lots on the other. The street itself dead-ended at the park, so there was only one way in and out for a vehicle. On foot, that was a different story.

Noticing Chloe was off the phone, they walked back over to her.

"They're on their way."

"Glad to hear it. I want you to go home and try to relax. If anything else comes to you by chance, please call me." Rita pulled out her business card and handed it to Chloe. "We may have some more questions for you in the next few days as evidence rolls in."

With a shaky hand, Chloe took the card.

Rita saw that the van from the animal shelter had arrived. She signaled for one of her officers to come over and get the black lab. "Miss Harris, this officer will be taking the puppy now."

Chloe shifted and helped lift the puppy into the air. Bruno woke up and started to protest, wiggling in his arms.

"Where will they take him?" she asked with a small hitch to her voice.

"To the shelter," Detective Fulmer answered. We have a vet who will thoroughly examine him, ensure he hasn't been mistreated, and observe him for a few days."

"And then?" Chloe's voice cracked.

"If everything checks out, they will try to find him a new home."

"Would I . . . could I adopt him?" Chloe swiped at a tear as she watched them carry away the puppy.

"I don't make those kinds of arrangements." Rita straightened, trying not to feel anything about the heartbreaking situation. It would have been better if she stayed neutral and emotionally distant. But she couldn't. Instead, she took out another business card and jotted down the number of the animal shelter on the back. Handing it to Chloe, she managed, "If you give them a call and inquire about the puppy, they can give you more information."

"Thank you," Chloe said softly.

A truck with Becker Construction in big black letters pulled onto the street and parked behind Chloe's SUV.

"Would that be your ride?" Rita asked, noting the truck and the two men inside.

Chloe nodded and stood but was a little unsteady on her feet.

A man got out of the passenger side and waited for her.

"Take care of yourself, Miss Harris," Rita said.

Chloe nodded and walked toward him. He met her halfway, draped an arm protectively around her, and escorted her to the vehicle, tucking her into the SUV. Once he was in the driver's seat of her vehicle, he pulled out, and the truck followed.

Both detectives watched the vehicles turn the corner and drive out of sight.

Hands on her hips, Rita adjusted her holster. Feeling as if she was being watched, she did a slow one-eighty. Her eyes roamed behind the dark sunglasses. Movement caught Rita's eye. She nudged Fulmer. "Time to go see what the neighbors know." She indicated the little house directly across the street.

TWENTY-THREE

Tate didn't take her back to her place like she asked. He took her to his house despite her feeble comments that she needed to be alone. He suspected she didn't really want to be alone, and he was banking on it as he turned Chloe's SUV into his yard.

"This isn't my house."

"Nope. It's mine."

"Clearly," Chloe said with a smidge of disdain. "Why are we here?"

"For starters, if I take you home, then I need a way home. I thought it easier to stop at my house and let myself out." Tate parked in front of his house, turned off the vehicle, and got out, pocketing the keys.

He wasn't quite sure how to handle her in this situation. Chloe wasn't fragile, or at least she didn't seem to be. The fact that she had even called him at all was a complete surprise. But anyone, even he, would have been shaken and in shock after finding a dead body.

The real problem was that they had only just started to reconnect. He didn't want to mess up this time around, so he knew he needed to tread lightly.

Chloe waited in the vehicle for only a beat, and then she hopped out and followed him to the house. Holding out her hand, she asked, "Can I have my keys, please?"

Bo padded down the stairs toward them, tail swishing. Tate patted him on the head and took the steps easily. "Yep."

"Tate," Chloe said firmly, planting her feet on the dirt. "My keys, please. I would like to go home."

"You can and you will, but you should eat something first," he said over his shoulder, not looking directly at her because he knew if he did, he might cave. Disappearing inside the house, he left the front door open for her.

She followed him in, and so did Bo. "I'm not hungry."

"Maybe you aren't, but I am, and I don't want to eat alone." He ducked under the tarp and went into the makeshift kitchen. "I don't have a lot, but I can grill up some hamburgers or open a can of soup."

He heard the tarp rattle and crinkle behind him as she passed underneath.

"Tate," she said softly.

This time, he did look at her. She stood just inside the plastic, one hand on her hip and the other stretched out for her keys, his dog sitting obediently beside her. His heart pitched. What was he thinking? He didn't have any idea how to handle her, not Chloe Harris. He never did.

Wanting nothing more than to treat her like everything was normal, he did the only thing he could think of, falling back on what he knew. He turned on the charm.

He dug the keys out of his pocket and laid them on the makeshift counter. Softening his voice to match hers, he answered, "Look, I just don't think I should be alone right now. I'm feeling a little faint, and after what you found . . ." He took a deep sigh, laying it on thick, "I feel like we're better together. I feel safer with you here."

"So now you're the damsel in distress?" she asked in disbelief. "I'm here because you're uncomfortable after what I found? That's rich. Even for you."

She eyed the keys on the counter, looking at him like he might have laid out a trap for her. That he would snatch away the keys at any moment. He expected her to reach for them immediately, but she didn't.

He knew he was pissing her off just enough to have an effect. Her color was almost normal, and there was a small twitch at the corner of her mouth. When he had first helped her into the SUV, she'd been as white as a sheet. It had gone against every fiber in his being not to wrap his arms around her and hold her tight, but he hadn't only because Tate knew that he wasn't back to that comfort level with her yet. But he'd be damned if he wouldn't get there with her eventually.

He nudged the keys with a finger toward her. She was free to take them if she wanted, but he prayed she'd stay anyway. "I have a beer if you need a drink. Something to calm your nerves."

She wrinkled her nose, scooped up her keys, and clutched them in her hand. But she didn't run for the door. That was one small step in the right direction.

"How about food?" he asked. "Hamburgers or soup."

"You're the one that's hungry. Why don't you decide?"

He considered that a victory. "I think I will. I vote for hamburgers. Let's go out back."

She sighed heavily, relenting. "I need to call Lucy and tell her about Tara."

"The police may have already spoken to her."

"I still need to call her and ensure she's okay."

"Go ahead. I'll start the grill."

Death was a dreadfully sad occurrence, but when the shock of it wore off, it usually brought out the best in people: their compassion and their concern for the family of the deceased. But murder ... murder brought out the curious, which was good for business. Kimmy knew how that sounded -- morbid and selfish, but it was true.

Families, friends, and neighbors gathered on every street corner, speculating. They stopped each other in the store, on the sidewalk, or in the bank. Death, even murder, brought out human nature for good old-fashioned gossip and comfort food.

Fortunately, the Taphouse had both.

It was standing room only at the bar and the wait was out the door. It had been all day, ever since the news broke of finding another body.

Kimmy felt light on her feet, and despite the unusual circumstances, her heart bounced unexpectedly. Everyone who walked in wanted an update, to compare notes, and to rehash the few details they had already heard.

Kimmy noticed Judith Fritz, the old busybody who used to be the librarian at school until a few years ago, and half the women who made up her Tuesday night card club waiting for a table.

"Hello, ladies," Kimmy said with a genuine smile. "It's a few days early to play bridge."

"We're not here to play cards, dear."

"You're not?" Kimmy asked sweetly, knowing full well what they were here for. "What brings you in then?"

"Those poor women," Mrs. Fritz tsked, leaning in.

Kimmy caught a hint of lavender surrounding her.

"The ones that were murdered. It's so awful."

"It is," Kimmy agreed sincerely.

"Dreadful," another woman cooed.

"It's all everyone is talking about."

"That's true," Kimmy acknowledged as she straightened her shirt. "It's on everyone's mind."

Mrs. Fritz laid her hand on Kimmy's arm and patted it. "We just couldn't stand to be cooped up in our homes alone with a murderer on the loose."

Kimmy's eyes went wide. "Oh, dear! Of course not. What is that saying? Safety in numbers?"

"That's exactly right, dear. Better to be here where everyone's at than home . . . alone." Mrs. Fritz let the word hang in the air.

"Well, lucky for you, I have a large table in the back."

"What about something in the middle?" Mrs. Fritz asked, looking about. "Something in the thick of things."

"Oh, fiddle-de-dee!" Kimmy exclaimed. "You're right. I can't put you lovely ladies in a corner. I have the perfect table. It was just cleared." She nipped menus off the hostess stand. "Follow me."

Threading their way through tables, they made it to the

center, to the heart of the restaurant and the action.

"How is this?" Kimmy asked.

"Perfect," Mrs. Fritz all but purred.

She waited until they were all situated, then handed out the menus. "What's the word on the street? Any suspects? Or motives that you've heard?" She couldn't imagine that they'd heard anything new.

Mrs. Fritz pulled her in close. "I don't know about a motive or suspects, but," she glanced around the table carefully, making eye contact with each woman, making sure she had their full attention. "I know who found the body."

"Really?" Kimmy asked, intrigued. This was new information.

"Do tell, Judith."

"Well," Mrs. Fritz started. "You all know I live on Pine. The lady that they found today, Tara Zimm, lives on Pine in the old apartment building across the street."

"That used to be so nice when we were growing up. My sister lived there for a while," one of the women said.

"Yes, it was a lovely building at one time but the landlord has been doing very few repairs or maintenance on the building recently. It's become quite run down. Anyway," Mrs. Fritz said pointedly, looking at her, "I saw Chloe Harris this morning going into the apartment building across the street carrying a large box, and there was a little black puppy with her."

"Are you sure it was Chloe?"

"Of course, I'm sure," Mrs. Fritz stated. "I'm positive. I just saw her a few days ago at the bookstore and I taught her for years in high school. I never forget a student. I never forgot you, did I, Kimmy? You and your perky little pep squad parading around the building."

Kimmy gave a quick laugh. "That was us!"

"Like I was saying, not more than twenty minutes after Chloe Harris went into the apartment building, the police arrived. She's the one who found the body. I'm positive."

They all spoke at once.

"Oh, how awful!"

"The author? Is that who we're talking about?"

"Yes, keep up, Agnus."

"Maybe she could include that in one of her books."

All four women, including Kimmy, looked at her.

Mrs. Fritz shrugged. "I'm only stating the obvious. Chloe Harris writes mysteries. Maybe the whole experience gave her some new material."

That sparked another round of comments.

"I can't believe you said that!"

"The audacity."

"I love her books, but I think you went too far."

"The poor girl is probably in shock."

"I would be. I can't even imagine."

Kimmy stifled a giggle at their forced outrage for Chloe and secretly wondered if they all didn't hold that same opinion. She couldn't imagine what it must have been like to discover a dead body. Kimmy shuddered at the thought. "This is all quite fascinating, ladies. I would love to stand here and talk to you some more, but I have a line out the door waiting to be seated."

"We understand. You run along then and send the waitress over," Mrs. Fritz suggested.

"I will," Kimmy said.

"I hope that Chloe didn't try to drive herself home after such a shock," Agnus said.

Kimmy started to walk away.

"I should say not." Mrs. Fritz tsked. "The Becker boys took her home."

Pulse spiking, Kimmy hesitated. "What did you just say?"

"What, dear?" Mrs. Fritz blinked up at her.

Kimmy stepped back toward the table. "Who did you say took Chloe home?"

"The Becker boys—you know, Kurt and Tate Becker -- drove up in one of their construction vehicles. Tate put Chloe in her SUV and drove off."

"Those guys are so sweet, aren't they?"

"And handsome, don't you think, Kimmy?"

Tate took Chloe home? She didn't like that, not one bit. Kimmy gave a reserved smile. "I won't argue with that." Kimmy walked away, picturing Tate and Chloe together, not quite as cheerful as before.

TWENTY-FOUR

His body tingled with anticipation as he slipped through the darkness, keeping to the shadows. He hesitated for a moment, his body in tune with the night sounds, the rustle of trees, the chirp of a lone cricket, and the nesting of chickens. Everything else was quiet. He smirked as he let himself in.

The house was dark and eerily silent, even for him. The hair on his forearms prickled with electricity. He was in her space. Her home.

He pictured her upstairs asleep and couldn't wait to go up. He could almost smell her scent lingering in the air, tempting him. His heart quickened as he thought of her all curled up and cozy above him. Forcing himself to wait, to savor the moment, he boldly walked through the main portion of the house.

He'd wandered, enjoying the rush of being alone in the quiet house, her safely tucked in bed.

The longer he stayed, the more the anticipation of being caught bubbled in his veins, and daring himself to do more, to stay longer. He almost wanted to be caught by her to see her reaction, but then the game would be over, and he had only just begun to play.

The smile tugged at his lips. What if he just crawled into bed with her? A delicious shiver raced up his spine. No, he couldn't. It was too soon. She didn't even know she was being watched. A sneer twisted his lips. She would after tonight.

It had been almost too perfect that she'd been the one to find the second body. He couldn't have planned that better if he had tried. He pictured her face when she opened the door and saw the woman that closely resembled her sprawled on the couch, dead and unseeing, staring at the ceiling.

Had she made the connection? Did she see the resemblance? Probably not. In the end, there hadn't been much except the brown hair, her height, and the little mark he'd left.

Looking up toward the loft, wondering how sound she slept, he decided to go find out.

Before he approached the stairs, he made a vow to himself, he would only look, not touch. Because the minute he crossed that line, everything would change. This moment was about control -- his and hers. And every moment after, he would be in control of her. It was only a matter of time before he made her his own and controlled everything.

He made his way upstairs like a panther stalking his prey. His heart pounding in his chest, cringing when the stairs creaked under his weight, careful not to be caught. Adrenaline surged through his veins as he conquered the last step.

At the top of the stairs, in the ghostly darkness, he could see the open bedroom door. That was odd, he noted. Didn't most people close their bedroom door at night? He snickered like that could keep him out.

Crossing the loft boldly, he went to the bedroom. Standing at the threshold he could see the bed was empty, untouched. He clenched his jaw, instantly pissed. Where the hell was she? She sure as hell wasn't home in bed where she should be. He cursed himself for not using the tracker; he'd been too caught up, too zealous.

Emboldened, he went into her room, crossed to the dresser, and examined the bottles on top. Opening drawers, he fingered her things and touched her intimate items.

"How dare she not be home at this hour," he hissed into the dark room. "Where the hell are you? And who are you with?" That comment shifted something in him. Like a switch being flipped, his hand plunged into the top drawer and clutched her panties. "I'll teach you a lesson, you little bitch!" His roar echoed through the empty house. He spun on his heel and flung what he possessed, sending her things flying. He pulled out every drawer, overturning them and dumping the contents.

With his gloved hand, he swept the dresser clean. Bottles crashed to the floor and shattered on the hardwood. He selected a tube from the debris, pulled off the cap, and twisted it until the red stick emerged. He stood at the dresser and caught sight of himself in the mirror. Power coursed through him. Lifting his hand, he wrote her name in blood-red lipstick.

TWENTY-FIVE

Filling the sink, Tate squirted blue liquid soap into the stainless-steel bowl.

"Are you sure you don't want me to help?" Chloe asked, hovering. "It'll be faster if we wash the dishes together."

"If you want to do something together, I have a much better idea," he said, plunging his hands into the soapy water.

"Oh? What would that be?" Chloe asked, coming closer and grabbing a towel.

"There's always a matter of that bet we have going."

"Of you getting me up to your bedroom?"

"That'd be the one." Handing her a plate, he gave her a mischievous grin.

After drying the plate thoroughly, she set it on the thin slice of plywood and then accepted another one from him. "You really think I would give up so easily? Twenty dollars is twenty dollars."

"A big-time author like you? Twenty bucks is chump change."

She gave him a laugh. "I'm not a big-time author. I'm a small fish in a very big pond. Besides, even if I was making a lot, I have this very expensive contractor working on my house." She set a pan down and reached for the glass he held out, not meeting his gaze. "Personally, I think he's taking advantage of me with his outrageous prices."

Tate pulled the plug out of the drain, wiped his hands on the end of her towel, and tugged her forward against him. Her breath caught.

"Too expensive, huh? I bet he'd be willing to take payment in other forms."

"Like what?" she asked innocently as her heart galloped in her chest. "Cash or credit?"

"I was thinking of a completely different type of currency."

Acutely aware of what he was about to do, Chloe squelched the protest on the tip of her tongue. In truth, she wanted him to kiss her again like he had last night. This is what she wanted. No, needed, she corrected.

He tilted her face up to his, angled his head just so, and dove down deep. Mouth on mouth. Lips warm and teasing. Her heart couldn't keep up, and neither could the rest of her body. Unsure what to do with her hands, Chloe clutched the towel to her chest, shielding her heart as her mouth raced in time with his. The tips of his fingers caressed her face and trailed down her arms. He moved her back, pressing her up against the newly installed drywall while exploring her mouth.

She inhaled sharply, and he smiled against her lips. Her mind begged for more, but her heart screamed, too fast, too much, too soon! She pushed him back gently, breaking the connection. "I should probably go." She gulped in a breath of air, trying to steady herself and calm her racing heart. "It's really late."

"If you ask me, that's a good reason to stay." He brushed a strand of hair off of her flushed face. "It's late and cold outside. That big house of yours is all the way down the road, dark and empty."

"It's tempting," she answered slowly.

"Really?" he asked, genuinely surprised.

She figured this was her best time to escape before she caved. Pressing the towel into his hands, Chloe said, "Thanks for dinner, Tate. For . . ." she hesitated, "everything. I don't know if I would have survived today without you. In your weird, sadistic ways, you always know just how to make me feel better." Her voice softened. "You always have."

He flashed a grin. "I think that's the best compliment you've ever given me."

"Don't get cocky."

"I can't. At least not with you." He moved closer. "Stay with me."

She stepped back even though she desperately wanted to step forward into him. "I'm going to go. It's been a long day, and I really am tired." She turned on her heel and ducked underneath the tarp, aware that he was only a step behind her.

"That's understandable. But Chloe?"

"Yes?"

"All kidding aside. Are you alright?"

"I'm as good as can be despite the circumstances." A faint smile flitted over her face.

"Can I at least take you home?"

"There's no need, I'll be fine. Good night, Tate."

"Good night, Chloe."

Before he could say anything else, she slipped out the door, jumped in her SUV, and pulled out of the yard.

TWENTY-SIX

Tate stood at his bedroom window, still damp from his shower, and stared out into the dark night in the direction of Chloe's house. He could see her lights were still on and wondered if she was having as hard of a time crawling into bed as he was.

Red and blue lights approaching from the south caught his eye. He watched curiously as they came closer. A pit formed in his stomach when they turned onto his road into their little valley.

Chloe. His heart dropped. He cursed himself for not taking her home.

He whistled, and Bo's head popped out of his cozy bed. Tate slipped on a pair of jeans and grabbed a shirt, his boots, and his cell phone. Noticing two missed calls from her, he took the stairs two at a time and pressed her number. It went straight to voicemail as he jumped into the cab of his truck.

"Damn it," he hissed, his heart slamming into his chest. "Let's go, Bo!" he hollered.

If Bo was confused about going for a ride this late at night, he didn't show it. The golden retriever jumped into the bed without hesitation.

It took Tate less than two minutes to cover the distance between houses. He fishtailed into the drive, skidding on the gravel, arriving only seconds behind the police. Stomping on the brakes, he jumped out of the truck with Bo right beside him. Spotting Chloe sitting on the porch steps, he ran to her.

"Chloe! What happened?" Tate demanded, pulling her up off the steps. "Are you alright?"

THE FURTHER I FALL

"I'm okay," she said shakily.

Not wanting to be left out, Bo sniffed around her, too.

Tate ran his hands over her just to be sure. "Nothing's hurt?" He could feel her tremble, but everything seemed to be intact. "You aren't hurt?" he repeated.

Shaking her head, she said again, "I'm fine."

He held her head in place and lifted her chin. Her eyes met his. They were glassy, and she was as white as a sheet. This was the second time he'd seen her this way, and he didn't like it -- not one bit.

"I promise I'm alright. Just shaken up."

Detective Rita Sorenson cleared her throat. "Now, Miss Harris, Detective Fulmer, and I are going to take a look inside. The officers who arrived before us have already cleared the house and secured the perimeter. Tell me where the damage was done."

Chloe's voice cracked when she spoke, "Up the stairs and to the left. My . . . my bedroom. That's where . . ."

Detective Sorenson gave Tate the once over. "Where did you come from?"

"My house."

"Did you call him?" she addressed Chloe this time.

Before she could answer, Tate did. "I missed her call, but I saw the flashing lights. Chloe had been at my house only a half an hour to forty-five minutes before."

If Detective Sorenson thought anything of this she didn't say. She simply dipped her head slightly. "Very well. Take her to your house." She signaled for a couple of her men. "I have two officers who will escort you and stay with you until we can get your statement."

Both Detectives disappeared inside the house.

Tate put an arm around Chloe, guiding her toward the truck as Bo followed obediently.

Tate kept quiet on the short drive, sensing that Chloe wasn't prepared to talk just yet. He parked the truck, jumped out, and skirted the hood, opening the door for her.

He held out his hand, and much to his surprise, she took it.

"Come inside," he said, tugging her along. "I'll get us something to drink."

"Like what?" she asked, following him. "You don't have anything. I was just here, remember?"

Looking at her he decided that some of the shock must be wearing off, as her color was returning. "I still have that beer."

"Great – beer."

He heard the sarcasm in her voice as he led her to the couch and had to smile. "Maybe if you're lucky, I can find some brandy, and we can really have you humming in time for the Detective to come back. Sit. I'll be right back with -- something."

"I'm not a dog, you know."

He glanced back at her, still standing by his couch while his dog sat where he was, tail thumping. He flashed her a grin. "Maybe I was talking to Bo." But they both knew he wasn't. "Please have a seat, Chloe." He said a little softer. "I'll be right back."

"Promise?"

That stopped him in his tracks. She said it in such a small, reedy voice that it pulled at his heartstrings. Even Bo felt it. He moved closer and lay down by her feet.

"I promise."

He disappeared under the tarp.

Crossing to the pantry, he muscled the old pantry door open and vowed to finish the kitchen sooner. He eyed the contents, or lack of it, gave up, and went to the fridge. Leaning in, he spotted the lone beer he had tried to bribe her to stay with before and shrugged. If that's all he had, so be it. Then he spotted the box on the bottom shelf and smiled. He'd forgotten he had bought those. He checked the expiration date and deemed them good, grabbed two, and closed the door.

He ducked back under the tarp and stopped cold. Chloe sat curled up on the couch, her legs tucked under her, and his dog protectively by her side. Bo's head was in her lap. She stroked him softly, and both heads turned in his direction.

His whole world shifted when two pairs of forlorn eyes

looked at him. He needed to make the situation, the atmosphere – light. He couldn't stand to see her looking frightened and alone.

Chloe lifted both eyebrows. "What exactly do you have there?"

His grin was fast and wide. "Juice boxes."

"Juice boxes?" she questioned. "What are you eight?"

"Apparently in my food and beverage choices, I am. I have some goldfish, too, if you're hungry?"

She laughed. "No, I'm good. I had a burger earlier, remember?"

"Bo, down," Tate commanded gently.

Obediently, Bo jumped off the couch and went to his spot in the corner, circled and curled up in his comfy bed.

Tate plopped down beside her, handing her a juice box. "I assure you, though, my taste is the only thing that is."

She eyed the square container curiously. "Strawberry kiwi. That's my favorite."

Nudging her playfully with his shoulder, he said, "Mine too." He peeled off his straw and poked a hole in the top. Held it out for her. "Switch."

So, she did.

He repeated the process. Tate took a small suck from the tiny straw. "Ahh, refreshing."

She gave him a small smile.

Better, he thought. "Now," he let out a breath and prepared himself mentally to hear what she had to say. "Tell me what happened."

"I'd prefer to wait until Detective Sorenson gets here so I only have to go through it once."

"I get that. So, we will wait."

As if on cue, there was a knock at the front door. Tate headed to the door, and let Detective Sorenson in, followed closely by Detective Fulmer.

Not dispensing with the formalities. He blurted out, "Anything?"

Rita was slow to answer. "That depends on what you mean by

anything."

"Point of entry, fingerprints, clues of any kind." Tate's mind was racing. "Do you think this was some random break-in?"

Without answering, Rita asked, "Do you mind?" She indicated the straight-back chair near the sofa.

"Please," Tate said, trying to control himself. He sat back down next to Chloe, and Detective Fulmer pulled another chair closer.

Settling in, Detective Sorenson looked at Chloe. "Can you run through it for us?"

So, Chloe did, from the minute she got home until she went upstairs and found her room torn apart. "My room is a disaster, and the mirror . . ." she shuddered.

"What's on the mirror?" Tate questioned.

"He wrote my name in red across my mirror."

Tate was silent for a moment. The realization that it wasn't random and that the intruder knew exactly who he was targeting hit home hard.

"The point of entry is yet to be determined. It almost seems he or she could have walked right in the front door. Nothing has been forced. Is it possible you left a door unlocked?" Detective Sorenson asked, leaning forward.

"I guess it is."

"Does anyone have a key besides you?" Detective Fulmer asked.

"My parents, but they're in Arizona."

It was Detective Sorenson's turn. "Is there a key hidden outside anywhere?"

"There used to be, but not anymore."

Detective Sorenson tilted her head, angling it in Chloe's direction. "What's the reasoning behind that?"

"I lost my keys a couple of days ago."

"Your house keys?"

"Yes, everything. House keys, car keys, and a key to my parents' home. Luckily, I had an extra set of car keys at home, but they didn't have a house key on them, so I took the spare from outside and used it to get in. I need to go to the hardware store and get another copy made. That's why I haven't put one back out."

"When did you remember seeing or using your keys last?"

"Friday morning. I locked the door before we left to drive to Philly for a meeting. When I came back, I didn't have my keys."

Detective Sorenson exchanged a look with Detective Fulmer.

"Was your purse in your possession the entire time?"

"Yes, it was."

"Is it possible someone reached into your purse when you weren't looking?"

"No, I had my purse with me the entire time. In the car, it was at my feet. I carried it into the building for the meeting."

"Did you stop anywhere after the meeting?" Detective Sorenson asked.

"No, we didn't. We came straight home."

"And yet your keys are missing," Detective Fulmer stated.

"Which could be why there is no forced entry," Tate added.

Chloe was silent for a long time

"Miss Harris?" Detective Sorenson questioned.

"How can I have been so stupid? I feel so dumb. I should have changed the locks."

Detective Sorenson shifted her body slightly, turning further in her chair. She unbuttoned the single button, holding the blazer closed, and the handle of her gun winked out. "No need to feel stupid. It could happen to any of us. But now that we know, we can better handle the situation. And we aren't positive that anyone has keys at this point. It's just speculation."

Chloe nodded and looked down at her juice box.

"I can change out the locks for you," Tate said. "It's not hard."

"Maybe you could install a couple of deadbolts as well," Chloe asked hopefully.

"I will, first thing tomorrow."

"What about my car?"

"It can be rekeyed. It might cost you a few hundred dollars, but it would be worth it," Sorenson said. In the meantime, I don't want you to stay at the house until the locks have been changed. Do you have somewhere else you feel safe staying?"

"She can stay here," Tate said without hesitation. There was no way he was letting her out of his sight. He could kick himself for letting her go home alone earlier. Come hell or high water, or a furious woman, it was not happening again. Chloe started to protest, but he cut her off with a look. He placed his hand on her to keep her from objecting and reassure her that he was there for her. "We can talk about the sleeping arrangements later," he murmured softly.

Their eyes met in a silent understanding. She turned her palm up, linked her fingers in his, and gently squeezed them. A silent truce was formed.

Looking back at Detective Sorenson, Chloe asked, "Do you think this break-in has anything to do with Tara Zimm or the other woman being murdered?"

"I'm not at liberty to discuss those cases as they are still ongoing. But it is a possibility."

"We don't usually handle a small break-in when no one was hurt, and only minor damage was done. If it weren't for the fact that you found Tara Zimm only hours before, we wouldn't have been called in tonight unless they found something major," Rita explained. She stood.

"Is that everything?" Tate asked.

"At this point? Yes." Rita directed her attention to Tate. "Since Miss Harris will be staying here, do you have a cell phone number that you could give us, Mr. Becker?"

"I do." Tate rattled off his number, and Rita added it to her contacts.

"Miss Harris, do you still have my card?"

"Yes."

"Excellent." Rita tugged at her blazer, buttoning the single button so it covered her gun. Sticking out her hand to Chloe, she said, "If you should need anything, day or night, please don't hesitate to call."

"Thank you."

Tate walked the detectives out, closing the door behind him. With the door between them and Chloe, he asked, "What the Hell was that all about?"

Rita stood to her full five-foot-three-inch height and looked Tate dead in the eye. "I'm not sure what you mean, Mr. Becker."

Detective Fulmer stepped protectively up next to his partner and folded his hands in front of his waist.

"Are you kidding me right now? Chloe found a dead body this morning, and tonight her house was broken into, and you're not at liberty to say anything?"

"We," Rita indicated herself and Detective Fulmer, "take our jobs very seriously. When we have more pertinent information, we'll contact you. Goodnight, Mr. Becker."

Tate stood for a brief moment and watched them get into their vehicle and pull out of the yard. Taking a deep breath, he mentally prepared to go back to Chloe.

As he walked back into the family room, she was already on her feet, her hands placed defiantly on her hips, just as he expected.

He held his hands up as if to ward off any verbal blows. "Listen, before you get all hot and bothered because I said you were staying here, let me clarify. I will be on the couch, and you can have my room."

Her arms dropped. The fight drained out of her, literally right before his eyes. And she simply said, "Thank you."

"No problem. Let's get you upstairs."

Tate gave a sharp whistle, and Bo bolted up the stairs leading the way. Tate noticed Chloe took the time to trail her hand along the smooth banister as they ascended.

"I don't know if I have ever told you, but you do nice work."

"Thanks." Bo stopped in front of the first door, thumping his tail. "Here we are."

"Isn't this your old room?" Chloe asked.

Pleased she remembered, he nodded. "Sure is."

She stepped into the room, and he saw the surprise on her face.

"I blew out the wall between my room and Kurts. I liked being in the front of the house, and with these two rooms combined . . ."

"It makes for a much larger and inviting space," she finished for him.

"Exactly." It seemed as if she wanted to pretend everything was normal, so he went with it.

"I love the large windows, the wide moldings, and the trim. Oh," the word came out almost like a purr. "I love the matching barn doors and the rustic hardware."

He led the way through and rolled open one door. "This is the bathroom." He flipped a switch. "Use whatever you need." He indicated the open shelves and the plush, dark brown towels stacked neatly on them.

Then he rolled its twin in the opposite direction, entered his closet, and dug out a T-shirt. "Here's a shirt if you want to sleep in something more comfortable. But just so you know, house rules state that you are allowed to walk around in your underwear," he said casually.

"I think I'll stick to the T-shirt."

"Suit yourself." He grabbed a pillow and blanket out of his closet. "If you need anything, holler. I'll be right downstairs. If you like, Bo can stay in here with you."

She nodded, leaned over, and patted Bo. "I'd like that very much."

Tate crouched down and rubbed Bo's head; scratching under his chin, he whispered, "You stay here and protect our girl."

Bo gave a soft ruff in acknowledgment as if he understood exactly what Tate had murmured. Tate released him, and the golden retriever padded over to his cozy bed and curled up.

Chloe reached for Tate. He encircled her in his arms and kissed her forehead tenderly. He felt her tremble.

"Thank you, Tate," she whispered. Letting go, she walked to the bed. "I couldn't have stayed there tonight. I appreciate . . . everything."

"No problem, anything for you. Oh, and Chloe?"

"Yeah," she said distractedly, picking up the faded Hershey Bears T-shirt he'd laid out for her.

He pointed at his big, king-sized bed and flashed a quick smile. "You owe me twenty bucks."

TWENTY-SEVEN

Sunday

Chloe picked her way through her room, stepping over clothes, her jeans, shorts, and an old swimsuit, her eyes on the floor, avoiding the mirror. She didn't need to look at it to know what it said. Her name, written in blood red, was seared into her mind.

She snagged a pair of panties off the bed, wadded them into her hand, and sank down on the corner of the bed, overwhelmed. Her eyes filled. The tears threatened to fall, but she willed them not to.

She could hear the guys downstairs working, installing the new deadbolts and changing the locks. The sound of them working was comforting, to have them in the house and know she wasn't alone.

She jumped when a head popped through her bedroom door. "Oh, my word!" Chloe clutched at her heart. "Lucy Jane! You scared the life out of me!" At the sight of her friend, a tear trickled down her cheek. She swiped it quickly away.

"Sorry! I thought you heard me coming up the stairs." She looked around the room. "Looks like you had a wild night without me."

"You could say that."

Lucy picked up a hot pink lace bra and twirled it on her index finger. "Look at you! Hot pink and skimpy! Who knew you were such a wild woman underneath?"

"That's me, as wild as they come," Chloe answered dryly, snagging a tissue out of the box. She quickly dried the tears and balled up the tissue.

Lucy plopped down on the bed beside her and wrapped an arm around Chloe's shoulders. "How are you holding up?"

"I'm fine."

Lucy gave her a look.

"Really. I am."

"Holy mackerel!" she exclaimed doing a double take.

"What?"

Pointing at the mirror, Lucy shivered. "That is some creepy shit!"

"You're telling me."

Lucy got up and went to the dresser. "What is that?" She wiped her finger across it. "Lipstick?"

"Yes."

"It's just the right shade to look like . . ." her voice trailed off.

"Don't say it."

"I won't. I'm assuming the cops already saw this?"

"Yes."

"So, let's get rid of it." Lucy turned and placed a hand on her hip. "Where's the glass cleaner and the paper towels?"

"Under the bathroom sink."

Lucy popped in and out. Squirting the blue-tinted liquid onto the mirror, she started to scrub.

Chloe retrieved the laundry basket from her closet and gathered her clothes. She asked, "So, who called you?"

"Tate."

"He shouldn't have."

Lucy stopped scrubbing for a minute. "No, he shouldn't have." She pointed an accusatory finger at Chloe. "You should have. Why didn't you?"

"I didn't want you to worry. And after Tara . . ."

"Aren't we friends?"

"Is that a trick question?"

"Would you even go so far as to say we are best friends?"

Chloe nodded. Her eyes filled again.

"As best friends, we confide in one another, laugh and cry together, binge on movies and chocolate, and worry about each other. That's what we do; that's what we signed up for when we became friends." She walked over to Chloe and locked her in a hug.

Chloe leaned into her. "I'm sorry. Don't be mad. You already had so much with Tara."

"I'm not mad. I'm terrified and pissed. There's some crazy lunatic out there doing God knows what to God knows who. Spying on women, stalking, and killing them. And for some unknown reason, you're one of them."

"We don't know that this was related."

"Then it's some weird coincidence that your home was broken into the same day you found Tara." Lucy held Chloe at arm's length. "Nothing can happen to you. I wouldn't survive it."

"Nothing's going to happen to me, I promise."

"Make sure you keep that promise."

"I will."

"Make me another promise while you're at it."

Chloe bent over to pick up a T-shirt and throw it in the basket. "What's that?"

"Promise me the next time something happens, good or bad, that I don't find out from some dumb boy what's going on in your life?"

"Who are you calling a dumb boy?"

They both turned to find Tate leaning on the door frame, arms crossed and a look of curiosity on his face. He had that look of an innocent boy locked up in that ruggedly handsome face, which made him seem so sweet and innocent. But Chloe knew better.

"It certainly couldn't be me." He smirked.

Lucy gave him a quick smile. "If the shoe fits."

"Well, this dumb boy just finished installing deadbolts, the locks are changed, and a security bar is on the sliding glass door." He glanced over his shoulder and hooked a thumb. "All with the help of his dumb older brother."

"Hey! Watch who you're callin' dumb, you moron." Kurt stood beside Tate. "Well, well. Isn't this a sight?"

"It doesn't get any better than two hot chicks standing in the middle of some sexy lingerie. Now, does it?" Tate commented.

"Very funny." Chloe made eye contact with Lucy. "I'm going to run this basket full of clothes down."

"You do that. I'll finish getting this off the mirror," Lucy said, patting Chloe on the arm.

"Here, let me help you," Kurt said to Lucy.

Chloe brushed past Tate with her heaping full basket and headed down the stairs to the laundry room, all too aware that he followed her.

"Whatcha doin'?" he asked, tagging along.

"Laundry."

"I see that, but why? Didn't it come out of your drawers?"

"If you must know it's because I can't stand the fact that some stranger touched it, tainted it with his hands."

Tate remained silent and followed her into the laundry room. Bending over, he picked up a silk thong that had fallen from her basket. Dangling it from his fingers, he tried to lighten the mood. He let out a long, low whistle. "Very sexy. Can you model this for me?"

She dropped the basket efficiently on the floor and lunged at him. "Give that here!"

He held it above her head, just out of reach.

"Tate Becker! Stop being so immature."

"I don't think I can." He effectively pulled her in close as she struggled to get the item.

Her face was a breath from his, she stopped struggling, aware of how she was pressing her body into his. The warmth from his muscular body seeping through her thin T-shirt making her brain foggy. She looked into his clouded eyes and became subdued. "Why is that?" she managed to ask.

"Because when I'm around you the blood rushes out of my head and my IQ drops at least ten points." He pressed his lips gently to her forehead and she relaxed into him. Letting herself melt.

A throat cleared.

Both Tate and Chloe turned their heads.

Kurt stood there grinning. "Thought you two were doing laundry?"

"We are," they answered simultaneously.

Glancing down at the basket on the floor, Kurt said, "Well unless those clothes are going to put themselves into the washing machine it doesn't look like you'll accomplish much with your arms wrapped around each other."

"Go away, would ya? I was working on something else," Tate responded, looking down at Chloe.

"Chloe doesn't look overly interested in what you're working on."

"She would be if you weren't standing there in the door gawking at us."

"Is that true, Chloe? You want me to leave you alone with this yahoo?"

Her smile was wicked fast. "No, don't leave me. Nothing good can come out of being left alone with your brother."

"That's what I thought. How 'bout the four of us finish up here, and then grab some lunch at the Taphouse," Kurt suggested.

Tate peered down at Chloe. "Are you hungry?"

"I am."

"Good let's get a load in and get out of here for a while." He dangled the thong he still possessed in his hand. "Here, let me help."

Snagging it, she said, "Not on your life. I got this. Go. I'll be right there."

TWENTY-EIGHT

Chloe tried to concentrate as she sat in front of her laptop. She stared at the vertical black line that flashed off and on against the stark white of her screen. It blinked relentlessly, begging for her to write a paragraph, a sentence, even one word, anything so the screen wasn't completely void of life. Because for her that's what words were - life. Her characters' and hers.

Words. They'd been there for her as a child, little and enthralled with the colorful pages of a children's storybook. She remembered the excitement of snuggling down with her grandmother to hear a story. She remembered sitting on her mother's lap and sounding out her first word or the feel of printing her name across that big line at the top of the page. The wonder of words as they created whole universes in her mind, make-believe and real, enchanted or ordinary.

Not only did words create people and places for her but they were also a type of therapy when she needed it.

She remembered vividly getting her first diary from Lucy for her eighth birthday, the one that had a pale pink cover and a heart that sparkled like diamonds. It even had a small lock, and a shiny gold key to keep it private.

Her words had always been more than just black and white. They had depth, feeling, and color. They were a way to release pent-up feelings whether happy, sad, or angry. She wrote about everything. From her typical day to fun-filled adventures with her friends or vacations with her family.

One diary turned into two, then five. Then she ditched the diary and the pretense that the shabby little locks with the shiny keys could keep anyone out who wanted to read it.

Notebooks, that had been the way to go. They were more affordable and had a lot more space. She had every color under the rainbow and loved to go shopping for them. She was like a kid in a candy store, giddy with her bag full of notebooks and assorted colored ink pens. She generally filled one a month, except for her senior year.

It started the summer before senior year. The summer she fell hard for Tate, head over heels with no heed of warning from her head to her heart. She just tumbled.

Chloe filled four or five notebooks a month on average that year with every single detail. The way he looked. How he smelled. What they talked about. She wrote about everything. Right up until the moment he kissed her in the library . . . and broke her heart.

That's when she stopped. No more journaling. No more notebooks. No more words.

It had been like losing two of her best friends. Tate and her writing. She mourned both, crying her heart out endlessly for hours. It had taken months for her to be able to write again, but once the words started to flow, they poured out easily. Until now.

Tate was back in her life.

Not that he was ever really gone. Just safely tucked out of sight and out of mind. Or mostly.

Now, though, she had seen him every day this week and even spent the night in his house and his bed, finding safety and security there.

Security was an illusion she knew, and it was only represented in her physical safety, but it had been mentally and emotionally draining. Physically, she had been safe from whoever broke into her home, but emotionally, she had been vulnerable, knowing that Tate had been right downstairs. One floor separated them, all she had to do was call his name, and he would have come.

Even now, after replacing the locks, installing deadbolts, and eating lunch at the Taphouse, he was just outside her home working on the porch -- on a Sunday. He was here when he would probably much rather be doing something else, and she was glad. She was still trying to shake the image of her name written across her mirror in blood-red lipstick, and her room ransacked.

With a sigh, she took one last look at the empty, blank screen, acknowledging she couldn't write one word until she properly thanked him.

Closing her laptop, she got up and went downstairs in search of him.

She found him squatting on her front porch, running a hand over the top rail with his dog sitting beside him. Both heads turned simultaneously as she rounded the corner.

"Hey," he said and straightened.

Bo snagged the baseball lying on the porch beside him in his mouth. Padding toward her, he dropped it at her feet. Reaching down, Chloe picked it up.

"Hey, yourself." Holding the ball out to Bo, she asked, "Wanna fetch?"

The front of his body crouched low, Bo's hindquarters popped up, and his tail wagged fiercely in anticipation.

Chloe laughed a little and launched the baseball. Bo took off like a bolt of lightning. She watched him go for a second and then turned her attention back to Tate. Hands on her hips, she looked past him to the porch. "Wow." Gone were the old, faded railings and the splintered wood of the steps from the storm, replaced by stamped concrete and composite vinyl railing that were more durable and modern-looking.

He stepped off the porch, walked over toward her, and stopped. Crossing his arms, he turned around and examined it from her point of view. "You like it?"

"I do. You did a great job. You always do. Thank you."

Bo scampered back and dropped the ball at their feet. This time, Tate picked it up and sent the ball sailing. Golden fur and pebbles scattered as Bo chased after it.

Cocking his head, Tate asked, "Would you go so far as to say it's amazing?"

"I would."

Tate flashed a grin. "The porch or me?"

Chloe couldn't help but laugh. "Both." Shifting, she faced him, taking on a serious tone. "I want to apologize."

Bo came back panting, dropping the ball and watching them hopeful as his tail wagged.

Tate scooped up the baseball and gave it another toss. Looking intently at her with those soul-searching blue eyes, she nearly melted. She hugged her arms to herself, guarding her heart.

Rubbing a hand across his chin, he seemed to be contemplating her and the porch. "I think something is missing. Don't you think?" he asked, turning back toward the house.

She dropped her arms and placed her hands once again on her hips. "I'm trying to apologize."

"I know." He watched her and waited. Now facing her, he furrowed his brow. "I'm not sure what to say."

"You don't need to say anything." Except that you understand. "I just need you to know that I'm sorry."

"You're forgiven. But I guess that means I should apologize, too."

Chloe held her breath, daring herself to ask, "For what?"

"For breaking your heart in high school. I hope you can believe me when I say I had no idea because it's the truth."

Bo padded over and dropped the ball at their feet again. This time, though, he went unnoticed despite all his tail wagging.

"Had I known . . . if I'd known," he corrected. "Things would have been different. I apologize for hurting you and for my dumb teenage self, letting the distance grow between us. I knew there was something wrong, yet I did nothing." He raked a hand through his hair. "I convinced myself it was nothing, and whatever the problem, you'd get over it, and we would return to being friends. Only after that kiss, I couldn't fathom just being your friend."

Her heart pounded. She took a small step closer to him, unable to resist the vulnerability she registered on his face.

"Can you forgive me?" he asked.

Could she? She wanted to. She'd missed him more than words could say. Having him back in her life had been hard this past week, but it had been good, too. "Yes," she whispered, barely able to get the word out.

"We've both made mistakes. It's where we go from here that matters." He reached for her hand. "And I so want to go from here."

Every fiber in her being hummed, tempted as she looked into those eyes. Should she trust him? Could she? Before she could overthink it, her heart pushed her forward. "So do I. But where do we go from here?"

His smile was quick and instant. "I have just the place."

TWENTY-NINE

Tate and Chloe bounced along in the truck on the narrow, deeply rutted dirt lane wedged between a wall of corn and a hayfield. It was barely wide enough for one vehicle as the stalks brushed against the passenger's side mirror. The lane widened, and the fields gave way to a clearing that worked as a parking lot. Tate parked the truck next to several other vehicles.

The late September sun was warm, but the air was growing crisp as the last days of September rolled toward October. The sun was hanging low, and the afternoon rays stretched toward the horizon, casting the landscape in an earthly glow.

She breathed in deep. The air was a mixture of sweet hay, apples, and dried leaves. The scent itself whispered, Fall. Afternoons like this were precious and few.

"A pumpkin patch?" Chloe questioned as globes of cheerful orange peeked out from underneath bright green leaves not far from where she stood.

"Yep."

"What are we doing here?"

"I thought you could use some color on your brand-new porch." He did a slow turn with his arms outstretched. "What better place to get it than here?"

"I love this idea." She didn't even try to hide that he had surprised her and charmed her, all without trying.

"Then let's go pick out a couple of pumpkins." He grabbed a wagon from the nearby corral and tugged it along behind them.

A hundred yards in, they left the wagon on the worn path and picked their way through the open field, stepping over long curling vines.

Tate waited patiently as Chloe took the time to examine each pumpkin, checking the size, color, and shape. There was no comment as she turned them to inspect the bottom for holes or soft spots.

"This is the one." Chloe lifted the bright orange pumpkin triumphantly.

"That's it?" Tate asked, stepping between vines to get closer. He eyed the pumpkin in question. "It's misshapen. A little more oblong than round."

"I know. The pumpkin has character. I like it," she said brightly.

"Alright," he rubbed his chin. "Are you only getting one?"

With her hand on her hip, she scouted the area. "No, I want three. An odd number is better, aesthetically speaking."

He bobbed his head. "I agree with that."

"I have my tall one, and now I need a short, squat one." She held out the first pumpkin for him to hold. Bending down, she plucked another off the vine. "This is it," she declared. "Now for the last one." She scouted the immediate area. "Over there." Chloe pointed. "Medium-sized and round. Oh, and look . . . the stem, it's long and curls around."

Tate stowed them in the wagon. "Anything else?"

"Aren't you going to get a pumpkin?"

"Hadn't really thought about it."

"You need at least one."

They both scanned the pumpkin patch.

If he was only going to get the one, it had to be perfect. She knew instantly when she spotted it. Like a missile locked on its target, she started across the patch with purpose. Stopping, she pointed. "This is it. This is the one you need." She pointed to a giant, bright orange pumpkin still on the stem. She moved to the side so he could see.

He dipped his head. "Yep. That's the one I would have chosen too," he agreed. Side-stepping pumpkins, he rescued it from the entanglement of vines.

Loading the last pumpkin, they headed back toward the barn that worked as a little shop.

Inside, other patrons milled about checking out or examining the fresh produce, baskets of apples, cherries, and tomatoes, crates full of potatoes, onions, and cucumbers.

"Oh, look at those gorgeous lavender Astria," Chloe exclaimed. The small purple blooms and the intoxicating floral smell wafted toward her.

Without saying anything, Tate scooped up two and stuck them in the wagon. Moving through the barn, he rolled the wagon over the dirt floor toward the large refrigerators that spanned the side wall.

"I want to get some apple cider. Do you want any?" he asked as he opened the refrigerator door and bent to examine the different sizes of cider.

"No, thanks, but I will take a peek at the mum's outside."

"Okay, get what you want and meet me back here. Then we can check out."

"I'll be right back." Chloe followed the little gravel path outside the barn and saw hundreds of mums in assorted colors stacked and sorted in neat rows and situated on top of hay bales. Red, yellow, orange, and white flowers stretched out by the hundreds. Tucked up against the building were also shades of pink and purple. The heady smell of mums was like a perfume blanketing the area.

Bending down to examine a pink mum, a shadow fell across her. An involuntary shudder rolled over her. Chloe tensed and waited for him to speak.

"Well, well. If it isn't, Legs," he said in a deep raspy voice.

She straightened quickly, not wanting to be caught in a compromised position, and turned to face Dalton Turk. His eyes were a little glassy, and he seemed a touch unstable. Was he drunk? Placing her hands on her hips, she tried to sound confident. "What are you doing here?"

"I work here on the weekends, so I can help all the hot little numbers carry their fresh produce to the car." His gaze drifted down her entire body. He licked his lips. "Need any help?"

She quivered. "Not from you."

"Think you're too good for me, Legs?" he asked, moving toward her.

Bristling, she couldn't keep the disgust out of her voice. Be firm, she told herself. Don't let him know you're scared. "I'm going to ask you one last time to please call me Chloe. My name is not Legs."

"And if I don't stop?" Dalton asked, a toothy grin spreading across his face. He took a step closer. "What are you going to do about it?"

"I'm going to wipe that smug smile right off your face."

"Really? This I'd like to see." He shifted closer and added with a sneer, "Legs."

Chloe's hand lashed out and connected with his face. The impact was so intense Dalton rocked back on his heels. Her hand throbbed like she'd slammed it into a brick wall. For a brief second, he didn't move, and her heart stopped cold. A prick of fear surged through her. The blood rushed from her head and pooled in her feet, making them heavy as lead. She was frozen in place, unable to move.

"You bitch," he hissed.

Lunging at her, he grabbed both her wrists, pushing her backward. Her feet tangled with the mums as she was shoved back, knocking them over. Pots scattered and rolled. Her back hit the wall with such force the wind was knocked out of her. In one swift movement, one hand went to her neck, and the other pinned both her wrists above her head.

He held her against the wall and leaned in next to her face, speaking into her ear. The stench of beer poured out of his mouth when he spoke. "I'll call you anything I want. You're mine now."

"Get off of me." Chloe's heart drummed against her rib cage, and her breath came out in shallow gulps as his hand squeezed. With all her might, she raised her knee and slammed it into his groin. With a loud groan, he buckled, releasing her.

"Chloe?" Tate called as he rounded the building.

Shoving Dalton over, he crumpled to the ground. She scrambled over the mums toward Tate. "I'm here."

"What the hell just happened?" he scowled, his eyes roaming over Dalton, who was curled up on the ground, groaning.

"Nothing. Let's go." Chloe pushed past him.

Tate gently took hold of her arm and stopped her midstride. "Chloe, tell me what just happened. Did he come on to you?" he asked as he glanced down at the writhing man.

"Yes."

Scrunching up his eyebrows, he asked. "And you laid him out?"

"Something like that."

"Are you hurt? There are red marks on your neck. Did he do that?"

"It's nothing, I'm fine." She pushed his hand away. Pleading to him with her eyes, she said, "Can we just go?"

Tate strode over to Dalton, who was still rolled up in a ball. Tate grabbed the other man by the front of his shirt and lifted him off the ground.

Chloe scrambled over and tugged on Tate's arm. "Please," she begged. "It's not worth it."

Heads turned, and a small crowd started to gather around them.

"Let's go," Chloe pleaded.

Looking directly into her eyes, Tate relented. Chloe could tell that it took every ounce of self-control Tate could muster not to punch Dalton. He released him, and Dalton landed on the ground with a thud.

Tate looked down at him in disgust. "I should kick your ass right now, but that would only be stooping to your level. But if you ever come near her again, I will beat you to a pulp."

Dalton glared back at Tate and spat at his boots as Chloe tugged him away.

"You and that little bitch better watch your back. I'm coming for you," Dalton bellowed as they walked away.

THIRTY

Kimmy spread the blanket out across the uneven ground underneath the old oak tree. The tree had already started to fade from olive green to a golden yellow as the afternoon sun filtered through it.

The dog kept circling her, making her nervous. She'd never been a big fan of dogs, and this one didn't seem to like her either.

The golden retriever steadily barked at her when she first got out of the car and made her way to the door. As she stood there knocking on the big wooden door, he climbed the short set of stairs, sat down, and simply stared at her.

When Tate didn't answer, she grew impatient and tried the door. That was a big mistake. The dog growled. She stepped back, resigned to wait.

And that's what she was doing.

The dog didn't seem to mind that she had set up camp, her picnic, in the front yard. He walked away after circling her and decided she wasn't much of a threat after all. Strategically placing himself on the front porch, he lay at the top of the stairs, keeping an eye on her, effectively cutting off access or any hope she might have of going into the house to use the bathroom. He was a good watchdog, a good protector, she'd give him that. She didn't need to like him to give him the credit he deserved.

With the recent murders and all, maybe she should get herself a dog. Kimmy glanced at the dog again, and those soulful eyes stared back.

She couldn't keep calling him "the dog," especially when Tate came home. What was his name? Barkly. Bert. Joe. Damn. For the life of her, she couldn't remember. That was bad because Tate talked about him all the time. It was evident that he loved him dearly.

She heaved a sigh and flopped back on the blanket, letting the sun warm her skin. Just another thing she'd have to learn to accept if they were going to be a couple, she thought.

Kimmy must have dozed off because she woke with a start to the sound of tires crunching gravel and long shadows stretching across the yard as the sun sunk quickly behind the ridge. She shivered and got to her feet, brushing her hair from her eyes. Tate parked the truck, and the dog immediately came down off the porch to greet him. The minute she saw him, her nerves started to jangle, and perspiration speckled her skin.

"Kimmy?" he called as he unloaded the large pumpkin from the bed of his truck. "Is that you?"

She wiped her sweaty palms on her jeans and gave him her million-dollar smile. "It's me, silly."

"What in the heck are you doing out here on a blanket in my yard, dressed in jeans and a flannel shirt?"

Laughing, she batted her eyelashes at him, glad he noticed the change in her wardrobe. Watching him place the pumpkin on the porch and then stroll toward her, she almost lost her nerve. Instead, she did the only thing she could. Flirt.

She ran a hand down her silky, straight ponytail and twirled the end of it around her index finger.

"Waiting for you, handsome."

"Really? Why?"

She could see his curiosity peaked as he strolled toward her with the dog tagging along.

"What for?"

Her hand swept the immediate area. "I brought you dinner. A nice Sunday afternoon picnic, with all the trimmings."

"That was very thoughtful of you." He stopped at the edge of the blanket and looked down. Then, let out a whistle. "Looks like there's enough food here for an army."

"I wanted to make sure I had all your favorites." Kimmy

glanced down at the food and nervously back at him. What was wrong with her? She was always aflutter when he was around, but this was so much more. This time, she wasn't just flirting. This time, she was really putting herself out there. Here goes nothing. "Come," she reached for his arm and playfully tugged him forward. "Let's sit down and enjoy."

"Kimmy," he said patiently but not moving. "What's up?"

"Nothing, silly." Letting go of his arm she sat down on the blanket and tucked her legs under her. Patting the spot beside her, she asked, "Can't two friends just have a nice, relaxing meal together on a beautiful fall day?"

"They can," he said evenly, holding her gaze. "But this is a little out of character, even for you. Jeans, flannel, the outdoors, it's not really your thing."

"I'm not sure what you mean." This wasn't going according to plan. Kimmy had envisioned him coming over and sweeping her off her feet. Okay, maybe that had been a little too grand of a dream. But this could still be salvaged. Reaching for a take-out container full of wings that had since grown cold waiting on him. She unsnapped the lid. "I brought all your favorites."

"I see that. Kimmy," he squatted down to her level, took the container out of her hand, and placed it back on the blanket dismissing it without even looking at it. "What's really going on?"

Oh, goodness, gracious. What could she say? What should she say? She cleared her throat, but nothing came out.

"Kimmy," he coaxed. "Talk to me."

"I can't."

"Why not?"

"Because your dog is staring at me like he's going to eat me for lunch."

Tate laughed. "Git, Bo," he said, shooing him away.

Bo, of course. Why couldn't she remember that?

The dog gave her one last look, snuffed in her direction, and then trotted off.

"Better?"

"Much."

"Alright, let's hear it," Tate said patiently.

"Well," she started but her heart dropped. If she had to spell it out for him it clearly wasn't going to happen. Or was it? He was only a foot away from her. Without thinking, she moved in and kissed him full on the mouth. Instantly his hands went to her arms, his lips softened, parted . . . for a split second she thought he would pull her in and devour her . . . but he didn't. His mouth turned firm. She increased the pressure against his lips and so did he, pushing her back, gently but firmly away from him.

"Kimmy, stop."

Her hand flew to her mouth. "Oh, gosh. I'm such a fool!"

"You are not."

"I'm so stupid," she hiccupped, pushing down a sob before it could escape. "The new clothes, the food. It's all for nothing."

"You're not stupid. Don't say that. It wasn't for nothing. It's very sweet. I'm flattered."

Scrambling to her feet, she stood. "I'm going to go. I shouldn't have come."

He reached for her arm before she could escape. "Why did you come?"

"Because I thought there was something between us."

"There is."

"There is?" she asked, hopeful.

"Yes, friendship."

She couldn't help it. She physically deflated in front of him. "That's what I was afraid of."

"Listen, it's not --"

"I don't want to hear the whole -- It's not you, it's me, speech." He gave a half laugh. "I wasn't."

Pointing a finger, glaring at him, she said, "You were."

"Okay, I was, but not exactly like you think." He turned serious. "It's Chloe."

"You're into Chloe. That's no surprise; you always have been. Anyone could see that, even me."

"Then why?" He gestured to the picnic.

"I don't know." She shrugged, and sank onto the blanket. She opened a baggie full of grapes, and popped one in her mouth. Thinking for a moment, she said, "Because I was holding out hope that since it hadn't happened for the two of you yet . . ."

"Sometimes it's all about timing."

"Yeah," she agreed. What was he saying? If it didn't work out with him and Chloe there still might be a chance. If Chloe wasn't in the picture, then what? Switching gears, she tried a slightly different tactic. "Listen, I have all this food. How about two good friends just sit down together and enjoy it." She smiled up at him, formulating a new plan.

He glanced up the road, then back down at her. "I really can't."

"Can't or won't?" She applied a little guilt, squeezing out a tear that she let trickle down the side of her face, deliberately waiting to get the full effect before she reached for a napkin and dabbed it away. "I guess we're not that good of friends then." Reaching for the picnic basket, she turned her back to him and began to put away the food.

He sighed. "I guess I could spare five minutes."

Her back still to him, a smile crept across her face.

THIRTY-ONE

Chloe turned down the burner and kept her creamy potato soup warm. Lifting the lid, she gave the pot one last good stir and then topped it with crumbled bacon, shredded cheddar cheese, and finely chopped scallions. Replacing the lid, she glanced at her phone for the third time in the past hour. Nothing yet. No missed calls or texts from Tate. It's fine, she told herself.

Checking the rolls, she noticed they had risen and needed to go in the oven soon. She turned the oven on so it could preheat.

"He said he'd be right back. That was an hour ago. What could he possibly be doing? It doesn't matter," she said out loud. But it did.

With the table set and the food ready except for the rolls, she had nothing left to do but wait. Going into the living room, she started to tidy up. There was no sense in keeping the furniture covered; they were done with the windows and the front porch.

She uncovered the furniture, started a load of laundry, dusted, and vacuumed the floor. With nothing left to do but fluff the pillows on the sofa, she sat down to wait. Ten minutes ticked by.

Chloe pulled out her cell phone and called him. It went straight to voicemail. "He's probably just busy and lost track of time. Or maybe something's happened. What if Dalton Turk tracked him down?" The thought made her shudder. Everything about that man made her skin crawl. "I should get in the car and drive over there," she said to the empty house. To her own ears, her voice sounded hollow and scared.

As she was grabbing her keys off the counter, she heard the

muffled sound of a car door slam outside. "Thank heaven."

Tate knocked and let himself in. "Hey," he said, stepping into the house.

"Hey, yourself," she copied him, relieved. Without thinking, she went to him and wrapped her arms around him. There was no hesitation on his part as he quickly returned the embrace. "I was just about to come over. I was worried something had happened to you."

He bent his head, resting his forehead on hers. She felt him smile.

"You were worried about me?"

"I was."

"There's no need to worry. Nothing's going to happen to me."

She could stay in his arms forever but quickly thought better of it. It was too soon for that. Too soon to depend on him. He had let her down before.

She let go. "Come into the kitchen. I just need to put the rolls in the oven. Everything else is ready." He followed her in and waited as she popped the rolls into the preheated oven. "It'll just be ten minutes for the rolls."

"I forgot you said you were going to make dinner. I'm sorry, I already ate."

"You did?" She looked at the table set for two and immediately was embarrassed. Trying to brush it off, she said, "That's okay. I guess we didn't discuss it. I just assumed since I mentioned it . . . It doesn't matter. It's nothing fancy anyway, just soup."

"It matters." He lifted the lid and inhaled. "Wow. It smells great."

Trying to keep it light, she asked, "So, what were you doing, and more importantly, what did you eat? I've seen the inside of your refrigerator. It's completely bare."

"You're right, it is."

She heard the hesitation in his voice at the same time she registered it passing across his face. "What's the matter? What happened?"

"Nothing happened exactly. I had a visitor at my house when I got there."

"I knew it. It was Dalton, wasn't it?"

He shook his head and gave a weak smile. "No. Not Dalton. Kimmy."

"Kimmy?"

"Yeah."

"Is she alright?"

"She's fine." He rubbed a hand across the back of his neck, clearly stalling.

"Just say it, Tate. What did she want?"

"I just want to preface this by saying I had no idea she was coming."

"Okay." Chloe placed a hand on her hip, raising an eyebrow.

"When I got home, I found her in the front yard with a picnic spread out on a blanket."

"A picnic?" A pit formed in her stomach.

He nodded.

"That's why you've eaten?"

"Yep."

"Let me get this straight. Kimmy came over and camped out on your front lawn with a basket full of food."

"Yeah," he raised his hands as if to ward off a blow. "I know how it sounds."

"It sounds very romantic." She tried to keep the hurt out of her voice, but anger bubbled to the surface instead.

"It wasn't, believe me."

"You could have texted me, then I wouldn't have made all this." She picked up his clean bowl and put it hastily in the sink, the dish clanking loudly.

"Chloe, I'm sorry. I would have, but my cell phone was dead."

"Of course it was." She rolled her eyes, scooped up his silverware, and dropped them in the sink. "I just waited for over an hour to eat with you, and you couldn't even send me a quick text. But it's fine."

"There's more."

She folded her arms over her chest, instinctively protecting her heart. "There's more?"

"I want us to be honest with each other. That's why I'm telling you this, not to hurt you. Do you understand?"

She narrowed her eyes, but gave a slight nod.

"She kissed me."

Chloe pointed at him. "Kimmy kissed you?" She couldn't keep the shrillness out of her voice. "Did you kiss her back?"

"No."

"But you wanted to." She said it as a statement daring him to deny it.

"No," he said again, "I didn't. You're making this a bigger deal than it needs to be."

That cut right to her heart. "I'm making a big deal?" Who was he to tell her how to feel? He wasn't the one who had waited. A sickening pit settled in her stomach, making her ask, "Was this before or after the picnic?"

"Before. Why?"

"Let me get this straight: You didn't return the kiss, which stopped the pass she just made at you, but you stayed for the picnic?" she asked, trying to understand the situation.

"Yes, I couldn't just leave her. She'd made all this food and waited all afternoon . . ." his voice trailed off.

Chloe bristled, opening her mouth to say something as the oven timer went off. She pressed her lips together to deal with the rolls. Shutting off the timer, she opened the oven door, removed the hot pan, and placed the rolls on a trivet to cool.

Tate stood with his hands in his front pockets and waited.

The seconds ticked by as Chloe went about the kitchen, turning off the oven, removing the pot from the burner, and getting out a bottle of wine—essentially ignoring him. Pouring herself a small glass, she anchored herself in the corner of the kitchen against the cabinets and took a tentative sip of wine, savoring the sweet flavor and letting her anger simmer.

"Are you going to say anything?"

Shrugging, Chloe swirled the wine in her glass. "What would

you like me to say?"

"Anything."

"Anything is pretty broad."

"Then let me narrow it down for you. Tell me you're mad."

"I am more hurt than mad." She took another sip, cupping the glass with both hands, she added, "More furious than mad. And disappointed."

"I'm sorry, Chloe. I didn't mean to hurt or disappoint you."

"I'm disappointed in myself. You hurt me once. Shame on you. Twice, shame on me."

Walking toward her, he said, "It's not like that. Believe me."

She held out her hand. "Stop right there. Don't come any closer."

He did as he was told. "I'm telling you nothing other than that kiss happened. Kimmy knows there's nothing between us, that I want to be with you."

"Does she?"

"Of course, she does. I told her so."

"Before or after you spent an hour with her?" Chloe narrowed her eyes and waited for his answer.

He opened his mouth to respond, but nothing came out.

"That's what I thought. You don't even know." Setting her glass of wine down on the counter, she looked at him. "Tate, whether you mean to or not, you're leading her on. She made that picnic for you, hoping it would be romantic and to spend some quality time together."

"It wasn't romantic."

"Maybe not for you."

"Her either. I made sure of that."

"That's debatable . . . But she did get the other half of what she wanted -- to spend time with you. She'll try again."

Chloe walked past him, brushing against him slightly, and headed for the stairs.

Tate followed her. "Aren't you going to eat anything?"

"I've lost my appetite. You know where the door is." She stomped up the stairs and slammed her bedroom door.

"Chloe," he called out.

As much as it hurt, she ignored him. She leaned on her bedroom door and braced against the onslaught of emotions that coursed through her. Tears ran down her cheeks as she heard the muffled sound of the front door closing.

THIRTY-TWO

Monday

Chloe let herself in the side door of Lucy's Corner, toting her laptop. The bookstore was closed on Mondays to outside traffic, but Lucy could always be found there doing inventory, putting away shipments, or ordering new supplies.

The bookstore was a great place to come and write when Chloe needed an escape. And today she needed it. She needed time away from Tate, away from the house, and away from the construction noise.

"Good morning, sunshine," Lucy said with a smile. "What drags you in so bright and early?"

"I just wanted to see my best friend."

"Uh-huh." Lucy eyed her suspiciously. "What's the real reason?"

"Do I need any other?" Chloe hoped she wouldn't pry, but since Lucy was her best friend in the whole wide world, she knew it was inevitable.

"Not typically."

"I usually come in on Mondays," Chloe pointed out.

"Yes, but this is earlier than normal. Something must have chased you out of the house." Lucy paused. "Or someone."

Chloe sniffed, caught. "If you must know, it's Tate. We had a little situation yesterday, and I snuck out while they set up for the day."

"Oh," Lucy wiggled her eyebrows.

She half-laughed. "It's nothing like you're thinking." Inevitably, Lucy was picturing her and Tate with their arms wrapped around each other, all starry-eyed, half-naked, and probably with a can of whipped cream involved. "Keep your mind out of the gutter and the whipped cream in the fridge."

Lucy wiggled her eyebrows. "Ooh, la la! Okay, so you do know me. Doesn't matter. I'll be the one to decide if the details are juicy or not. But first," she waved her over. "Follow me to the backroom. I have boxes to unpack."

They weaved their way through the aisles and into the back. Chloe set her backpack on the large worktable and unloaded her laptop.

Lucy picked up her utility knife and sliced open the first box. "Now, tell me what happened. I saw you in the morning after the break-in. We even all had lunch together. Everything was fine then — despite that."

"I know. It felt right, too — better than it had in a long time. I thought maybe we could move on, push past the old history."

"What happened?"

"He took me to a pumpkin patch."

"He did? That's fun. And kind of romantic." Lucy batted her eyelashes, sighed dramatically, and elaborated. "Walking through the fields, the wind in your hair, the sun at your back. Kissing over the perfect pumpkin."

"There was no kissing. Kissing confuses things."

"I'll say, but usually in a good way. I digress." Lucy waved her hand. "Go on."

"It really was wonderful. The weather was perfect. We found the best pumpkins, and they had beautiful mums," Chloe's voice trailed off.

"And then what?"

"Then Dalton Turk happened."

"Dalton Turk?" Lucy stopped with her hand in midair, ready to slice open the next box. "What was he doing there?"

"Working. Doesn't matter. The point is he came on to me and ruined the whole experience." Chloe ran through the ordeal quickly for her friend, trying not to make it seem quite as scary as it had been, even though if she closed her eyes, she could still feel his hands around her throat. She deliberately kept her eyes open and shoved the mere thought of him away.

"That's the second run-in you've had with him in a week."

"I know."

"Ever since you struck him out at the game, he seems to pop up everywhere. You don't think he's the one that trashed your bedroom, do you? That maybe he's following you?"

"The thought did cross my mind."

"Did you tell the police about Dalton?"

"No."

"You should," Lucy chided.

"I don't know. I don't have any real proof that it was him."

"You don't need proof. That's for the police to find."

Chloe flipped open her laptop and powered it on.

Lucy leaned across the table and looked at her friend. "You can call now. It's not too late."

"I can't." Her voice sounded small even to herself. Chloe risked a look at her friend and saw the concern etched in her face. "I'm just not up to it."

Lucy sighed heavily. "Well, before you leave here today, you're going to call."

"We'll see," Chloe mumbled, and the room fell silent. She didn't want to call, and she didn't want to think about Dalton Turk, so she wouldn't. Chloe typed in her password and pulled up her work in progress.

The silence was broken as Lucy went back to opening boxes.

Could opening a package sound mad? Chloe wondered. Because if it could, Lucy was accomplishing it. She pulled packaging material from the first box, fished around, found the pink packing slip, and tossed the paper on the table.

Lucy muttered something inaudible to herself. Louder, she said, "We can let Dalton go for a moment. But back to Tate, what happened with him after the whole Dalton -- pumpkin patch fiasco?"

"If I tell you, are you going to let me write in peace?"

"Depends."

Chloe gave her a grim look and updated her on the dinner

debacle.

"Yikes!" Lucy shook her head in disbelief. "And Tate being the guy that he is, didn't have the guts to tell her to get the hell off his lawn, that you and him were a couple. Is that about, right?"

"Something like that. But," Chloe protested by raising her shoulders, "we aren't a couple."

"You could have fooled me." Lucy leaned forward and laid her hand on top of Chloe's. "Are you alright?"

Two women had been murdered in her hometown, her house had been broken into, and Dalton had made inappropriate advances to her, essentially attacking her in broad daylight. And now? Tate -- she couldn't even think about it. No, she wasn't alright. She may never be. But she couldn't bring herself to say anything, even to Lucy. Instead, she sagged, feeling defeated.

"I'm sorry he shouldn't have done that, but in Tate's defense, you shouldn't be surprised."

Bristling, she asked, "And why shouldn't I?"

"Tate may be a lot of things." Lucy held up her hand and started listing things on her fingers. "Cute, charming, a big fat flirt, but one thing he's not is mean. He probably had every intention to come right back, but if Kimmy turned on the waterworks, which you can bet she did, you know he caved. He was not about to send her packing. She would have known that and used it to her advantage."

Chloe drummed her fingertips on the table, contemplating. "That's entirely possible." Flopping back against her chair, she sighed a long, cleansing sigh.

"You're darn right it is. When have you known me to be wrong?"

"At least a half dozen things immediately come to mind."

"Which isn't bad, considering you've known me most of your life." Lucy wagged the utility knife at her.

"Even knowing that, though, it still hurts. Just when I thought we could move on, move past the hurt -- this happens."

"I think you need to give Tate another chance," Lucy suggested.

"I don't know. I'm not sure my heart can take it."

"Your heart can't take what?" a deep voice asked. Both women jumped.

"Geeze, don't you knock?" Lucy asked Eddie. "The bookstore is closed, you know."

"I know, but I saw Chloe's car, and the back door was unlocked." He shrugged. "I figured I should come in and check on you with the two murders that just happened. You really should keep the door locked if you're here alone."

"You're right, I should. Look what wandered in when I didn't." Lucy laughed as he wrinkled his nose at her. "Now, what can we do for you?"

Eddie directed his attention to Chloe, effectively dismissing Lucy. He looked slightly irked. "Don't you ever answer your phone?"

"I do. Why?"

"I've tried calling you several times."

"I came in here to write. I always turn it off when I plan on writing for a while. Sorry."

"You should be."

Lucy raised an eyebrow and looked at Chloe, jerking a thumb at Eddie. "Now, who's got their panties in a wad."

Not acknowledging the comment, Eddie plowed ahead. "I received the paperwork from Belov Productions this morning."

Chloe perked up. "You did?"

"Yes, it's a good deal. I won't bore you with all the legal jargon, but suffice it to say, I think you should take it."

"Do you have the papers with you?" Chloe asked.

"I do."

She held out her hand. "Then let's have them."

"This is so exciting," Lucy said. "I can't believe I'm here to witness you signing a movie deal."

"I know. It's all so surreal."

"Are you going to have your lawyer review the contract before you sign?" Lucy asked, fishing out another packing slip and setting a stack of new paperbacks on the worktable.

"I already took care of that," Eddie said dismissively. Laying the briefcase on the table, he snapped the clasps open and pulled out the manilla file folder with the contract. Setting it on the table in front of Chloe. "May I?" he indicated the chair next to her.

"Of course."

"Just so you know, we are not finished talking about you-know-who," Lucy added as she gathered up the packing materials and put them in her recycle bin.

"Who?" Eddie questioned.

"Tate and Chloe. And the fact that she is still hung up on him even after all these years."

"You are?" Eddie asked, his voice pitched on the last word.

"I'm not."

"She is," Lucy corrected. "They're in a relationship."

"We're not." Chloe fidgeted in her seat, uncomfortable as Eddie stared at her, seemingly judging her. She wished to high heaven that Lucy would just be quiet.

"It's good that you're not because this movie deal will keep you busy, and I don't want you to lose focus on some on-again, off-again fling with Tate."

"I wouldn't call Tate Becker a fling," Lucy chided.

"Let's not talk about that right now. Bring on the papers," Chloe said, holding out her hand.

He opened the file and glanced at Lucy. "Would you mind giving us some privacy?"

Lucy balked. "Seriously? This is my workroom."

"I am very serious."

"Boy, are you in rare form today." Lucy tsked at him.

"She can stay. I want her to," Chloe said, defending her friend.

Lucy stuck out her tongue at Eddie. "Ha! I get to stay."

"If you insist," he grumbled. "I thought it would be our moment, but whatever."

Chloe patted him on the hand. She felt more and more that she kept having to appease him. "It is our moment, and having Lucy here to witness it makes it even more special."

"I guess." He took a deep ceremonial breath and said, "Here we go."

"Nervous?" she asked, noticing his hand shook slightly.

"Is that obvious?" he chuckled. "It's only the biggest deal of our lifetime so far." Eddie leafed through the pages. "I already have where you need to sign marked with these red arrow tabs."

"Don't you think you should read before you sign your life away, Chloe?" Lucy asked.

Feeling Eddie flinch, Chloe glanced at him.

"We've gone over these papers before," he answered with a tone. "I told you that."

Chloe hesitated. "I know we did, and I know you have my best interest at heart, but you did say some things changed. I can read through it quickly."

His jaw clenched, and Chloe could see him grinding his teeth together in frustration. "I'm a fast reader," she said, trying to placate him.

Eddie nodded as she began to read.

"Do you have any bottled water or a soda?" Eddie asked Lucy.

"I have both." Lucy pointed to the built-in mini fridge under the back counter. "Help yourself."

Eddie got up and retrieved a bottle of soda from the fridge. "Anyone else want one?"

"No, thanks," Lucy said, unpacking another box of books.

When Chloe didn't answer he twisted the top off his soda, tossed the lid onto the table, and took a small sip.

The minutes ticked by as Chloe read, Lucy sorted, and Eddie paced.

"Geeze," Lucy groaned after a couple of minutes. "Can you stand still? You're getting on my nerves."

"Sorry," Eddie grumbled. "It's just that this is a pivotal moment for us."

"I get that." Lucy bobbed her head. "Good thing I have hardwood floors, or you would have worn a hole in the carpet by now. Wanna help me? It would give you something to do."

"Not particularly," he said, dismissing her.

The silence was palpable as Chloe scanned the last document, and Eddie hovered nearby.

"Finished," Chloe said, straightening the papers.

"Great!" he set his bottle down on the table, pulled out the chair, and sat. "Let me get some pens." He unearthed a couple from his briefcase, turned to hand her one, and knocked over the open soda. The brown liquid bubbled out fast, ran across the table, and soaked into the papers.

Eddie scrambled to retrieve the spilled bottle as it rolled. "Damn it! I'm such a klutz."

"Quick! Grab the paper towels!" Lucy pointed behind Chloe.

Chloe grabbed the roll and started to mop up the liquid. "The contract is ruined," Chloe said, holding up a piece of paper that dripped dark liquid. "Are you able to print another one?"

Lucy brought over a trash can. "Throw it in here."

They deposited the mess in the trash can, and Lucy wiped the table down.

"Luckily, I have another copy. But first --" Eddie made a show of putting the cap on the bottle and discarding it. Then he pulled another copy of the contract from the briefcase. "I'm glad I always bring a spare. Let's get this signed before anything else happens."

Chloe was silent as Eddie flipped through the pages, pointing to the arrow at the spots where she should sign. She couldn't believe this was happening. The movie deal seemed surreal. Signing the last line, she sat back and watched Eddie add his signature beside hers.

"That seemed like more papers than I read before."

Eddie shuffled the papers together quickly, tapping them back into a neat stack. "The next thing is to get a schedule figured out."

"A schedule for what?" Chloe asked.

"I have a couple of podcasts lined up to interview you, and there's that blog you agreed to do. We need to nail down what days of the month that will come out. I have a couple of sponsors who agreed to advertise with you during the podcasts, on the blog, and on your website." Pulling up his calendar on his phone, he scanned the month of October.

"Sounds like you have the next month all planned out for her," Lucy commented.

"Month?" Eddie questioned. "I think you mean year. We're going to be doing a lot. But don't worry." He reached out and squeezed Chloe's hand. "I'll be there to facilitate everything."

THIRTY-THREE

The sun sank fast as Tate packed up the last of his tools. Bo trotted over with his ball in his mouth and dropped it by their feet.

"Looks like your dog wants to play," Kurt said, storing his own tools.

Bo barked and nudged the ball with his nose.

Kurt picked it up and gave it a fling. Bo raced after it.

"Have you seen my favorite bat?" Tate asked, leaning in the cab, searching under the seat.

"You already asked me that."

"I haven't seen it since Tuesday night. I can't imagine where it's gotten to." Tate closed the cab, frustrated. "You didn't pick it up by accident, did you?"

"I don't think so. But I can check my gear again when I get home."

"I'm missing that bat and the new aluminum one I bought this spring."

Bo dropped the ball at their feet again. All three heads turned when they heard the SUV pull in.

"Well, look who's home," Kurt said to his brother. "Looks like now's as good as any time to apologize and get out of the dog house."

"I'm not sure if I should have to apologize again."

Slapping his brother on the shoulder, Kurt said, "Then you're probably not going to get out. Hello," he called to Chloe as she approached.

"Hello to you too," she said, smiling at him. "Are you done for the day?"

"Yep, I'm heading out. Have to stop by the other job site before they call it quits for the day." Behind her back, Kurt gave Tate the thumbs up and a sheepish grin. "See ya later." He jumped in the cab and pulled the door shut.

They both turned to watch him go. Only when he drove onto the road did Chloe turn to face Tate.

"Are you leaving too?"

"I was hoping to stick around and talk to you." He swallowed hard forcing down his pride, thinking of what his brother had just said. "I wanted to apologize for yesterday."

She waved him off like it was nothing. "It's fine," she said, bent down to pet Bo as he stared up at her adoringly. "You don't need to apologize. We didn't have any set plans. If you want to see Kimmy, I won't stop you."

He could hear the sting of hurt laced in those words. Squatting down to her level, Tate reached out and gently touched her hand as it stroked Bo. She stopped and looked directly at him, nearly ripping him in half as he searched those fierce green eyes. Her words, the indifference in them, were like rubbing salt in an open wound. They burned. He fought the urge to shake her to her core until she realized all he wanted was her. "But I don't want to see Kimmy. I told her that. I only want you."

They both stood simultaneously, facing each other. The silence was like a sharp knife.

She was the first to speak. "Tate, I . . ."

He couldn't let her finish. "Don't say it. Don't say you won't give us a chance. Not until you've heard me out." He was too afraid of what she might say. "We have so much to talk about. There are so many questions that each of us needs answered, and I promise we will work through each and every one. But first, I want to show you something." He held out his hand, silently begging her to take it. "Please?"

Chloe nodded as she looked at him almost empathetically. Taking her hand, he linked his fingers with hers. He marveled at how perfectly their hands fit together, making it feel like the most natural thing in the world. Leading her around the house, he wondered why he didn't always have her hand in his.

She gasped. "What a beautiful outdoor dining set. But why is it on my patio?"

"Because you need somewhere to sit." She slipped from his grasp and he watched her walk around the rectangular table made of cedar that he had stained in a rich walnut brown. "A place to work and relax. Despite what you may think – I listen and notice things."

She ran a hand over the smooth finish. Chloe all but sighed. "I can't accept this. It must have cost you a fortune."

"It wasn't that much. I used wood I had left from another project."

"You made this?"

He nodded, pleased she liked it.

"For me?"

"Just for you."

"It's gorgeous. I love the deep green cushions and the squared-off style." She pulled out a chair and sat. "This is so sweet, but aren't you almost done with the house?"

"We are. Just a few minor things to finish up. Trim work mostly. But that doesn't matter. It's for you to use if we are here or not. I wanted you to have it sooner." He shrugged. "Time isn't always on our side."

"I don't know what to say."

"You don't have to say anything. Except ..." Tate stuffed his hands in his front pockets and rocked back on his heels.

"Except what?" Chloe asked quietly.

"Except that you forgive me." He said it despite what he'd said to Kurt. In his heart, he knew he had hurt her, even if he hadn't meant to. He couldn't stand the thought of her being angry with him or, more importantly, disappointed.

She gave him a leveled gaze, one that had him nearly undone. There was a long, drawn-out moment of silence. She seemed to be full of them. He couldn't decide if she was just torturing him or truly making a decision at the moment. He hoped it was the latter.

Just when he thought he could no longer bear it, she said, "You're forgiven." The words came out soft and wispy, like the first notes of a bird's song. "Thank you, Tate. I'll cherish it -- always."

A silent understanding passed between them. A look. She stood then, walking toward him, but stopped. She was but a few mere inches away from him, representing everything he desperately wanted. A ghost of a smile played across her delicate features, and his heart, which had been squeezed tight a moment ago, loosened slightly.

That moment was like an invisible hand with a key turning a lock in a door that had been closed years earlier. The lock released, the door unlatched, and eased open a crack. He knew it wasn't much, just a sliver, a slice, but it was the start of something more.

THIRTY-FOUR

Rita plopped down in the wobbly kitchen chair in the precinct's small lounge. She leaned over, snagged the pink and white cardboard box, pulled it toward her, and lifted the lid.

"Slim pickin's," Fulmer said, noticing her jab a glazed donut with her index finger.

"That's for sure." Rita retracted her finger and rubbed the sticky, sweet icing on a napkin. "Think I'll pass. We should get some real food. I'm half starved."

"Probably a good idea. But how about we settle for coffee right now?" he asked, raising the half-empty pot off the burner.

"Is it still hot?"

"Yes, and fairly fresh."

Fulmer tossed two files onto the table. "Look at those while I pour."

Rita pulled the manilla folders toward her and flipped open the one labeled Tara Zimm. "This the autopsy report?"

"Yep."

"Well, it's about damn time."

"Grabbed Jane Doe's as well. Thought we could compare." Putting the pot back, he carried both cups to the table.

Rita lifted an eyebrow, curious as to what the similarities could possibly be. Rita skimmed over Tara's report. "Blunt force trauma to the back of the victim's head. Same as Jane Doe."

"Yep," Fulmer said, taking a big gulp of coffee. "That's the only real similarity that I see. If you remember, Jane Doe had an extremely high blood alcohol content and high content of antihistamines. Tara Zimm didn't." Pointing, he added, "If you continue reading the toxicity report, you'll find no traces of any substances in her system at all, but her windpipe was crushed. The coroner indicates asphyxiation was the cause of death. Hence, the leash around her neck was what killed her."

Opening the other file, Rita held both autopsy reports side by side, comparing. "The dimensions of both women's blunt force traumas are very similar. Most likely the same weapon."

"Looks like the coroner agrees." Fulmer pointed to the note in the file.

"But actual death in Jane Doe was alcohol poisoning, and in Tara Zimm, it's strangulation." Rita rolled the thought around in her overly taxed-brain. "Let's speculate for a moment -- the perp was plying Jane Doe with drinks. It could have been an accident, not knowing how much alcohol was in her system. Alcohol poisoning depends on a person's size, sex, and weight."

"Also, how fast they're drinking," Fulmer added. "Add in the antihistamines . . ."

"Good point." Rita held her mug like it was an anchor holding her in place while her mind raced down different avenues, checking off details and creating hypotheses. "What if when they went to leave, she was heavily intoxicated and couldn't easily be moved or manipulated? Dead weight, so to speak. So, the perp got her to the alley, hit her over the head, and left her to die. Letting the blunt force trauma and alcohol pumping through her system finish her off." Rita shifted in her chair, thinking out loud. "But where did he get something to hit her with?"

"We didn't find her right outside the bar or wherever they were drinking. He must have moved her with a vehicle."

She sipped her coffee. "He used whatever he had on hand to hit her with, like some sort of tool in his trunk."

"Here's another angle – she could have easily fallen, being that intoxicated, and simply hit her head. The perp panics and flees the scene."

"That's plausible," Rita agreed

"Yeah, I think so too, if we didn't have this other victim with the same blunt trauma."

"Miss Zimm, on the other hand, wasn't inebriated. My guess is he somehow managed to get the leash around her neck, probably grabbing her from behind and strangling her while she bucked and fought. There were abrasions around her neck and claw marks at her throat as if she tried to free herself. I'm guessing he strangled her first and simply hit her in the head after she was already dead."

"But why?" Fulmer asked, holding his cup in mid-air. "Doesn't sound like he needed to. She was already dead. Blood had already started to pool around her neck, bleeding out at the point of contact was minimal. If there weren't the blows to both victim's heads in the same general area, we might never have connected the two deaths together."

"Let's not get ahead of ourselves yet. That's really the only thing tying them together – that and the fact that they both have a small cut above their right eye. Coincidence?"

Fulmer shrugged. "But you're right, two good-looking women murdered, within a few days of each other, approximately the same age, hair color . . ." Fulmer's voice trailed off. "Do you really think they're not related?"

Rita was silent for a long moment. Laughter could be heard down the hall as others went about their day, but here in the tiny kitchenette, murder was being contemplated, two homicides in her town, and it was no laughing matter.

She got up and crossed the room. She was getting jittery, which always happened when she was trying too hard to crack a case, and the coffee didn't help. She dumped the contents of her cup down the sink. Thinking, she began to pace back and forth.

Rita leveled her gaze at her partner. Something clicked. "That's why he hit them over the head. He wants us to know." She gave Fulmer a grim look. "And I have a sneaky suspicion he's not finished."

THIRTY-FIVE

Perched on the hood of his vehicle he tipped back the bottle and drained it. Smacking his lips together, he thought of the surprise he'd left on the other side of town, the destruction, and the mess. That had been a prelude to what was about to happen. And it wouldn't hurt to keep the cops off his trail through a little random violence. He sneered as he chucked the bottle into the long grass and wished he had grabbed one more.

Listening carefully, he heard the tick of the engine as it cooled, the rustle of the long grass beside him, and the distant hoot of an owl as he settled into the dark surroundings to wait and watch, wanting to make sure he was in the clear.

Twisting the hardwood of his weapon of choice in his hands, he watched the little house. It was picture perfect, nestled at the foothills, tucked neatly in the little valley. He waited for any signs of life, plotting his next move.

Excitement skittered across the flesh of his body, and he realized it was time to set his plan in motion.

In the pitch black of the night, the images of the other women came to him. Over and over again, he relived their deaths in his mind, thinking about how he controlled each situation -- the place, the time, how he had chosen each woman, and how he relished the feeling of power he held in those brief encounters.

The first was a stranger -- a woman who was easily flattered and thrilled even at the prospect of a sophisticated man showering her with compliments and free drinks. She was putty in his hands. At first, the encounter had been what he needed, what he craved. It had been easy to kill her -- too easy. She meant nothing to him, and it left him wanting more.

The second woman was different. She was a casual acquaintance and not as seasoned as the first. Every emotion could be read on her face. When he approached her, she was startled, causing the adrenaline to pump through his veins. She had recognized him, which made the game of cat and mouse even more thrilling.

She tensed as terror swept her entire body when his intentions became clear. In the end, the life had escaped from her in one last shallow gargle of air, he had a brief moment of pure ecstasy.

The room had grown quiet as he stood behind her, relishing the speed at which he could take a life, how destiny could be altered -- his and hers.

He had released the leash. The braided cord made a muted thud on the back of the couch as she slumped awkwardly. He wielded the weapon he'd used on the first woman, holding it above her head, knowing that if he struck her, they'd probably be able to link the two deaths, but he didn't care. He swung anyway. Bringing it down in one fell swoop.

The crack of wood against bone sent a delicious chill through him all the way down to his toes. Even now, he couldn't keep the smirk off his face, remembering how he stood over the crumpled woman in pure and unadulterated dominance.

Just imagine what it would be like when he stood over Chloe Harris, his ultimate prize, the person he coveted, the person he wanted most to control. He wanted everything -- her attention, her body, her money, her fame, but most of all . . . her mind. What would he do with her once he had her, he licked his lips . . . the possibilities were endless.

The grin on his face spread.

First, though, he had a little surprise for her. He slipped off the cool metal of the vehicle and walked boldly toward the house, already swinging.

THIRTY- SIX

Tuesday

Chloe's eyes fluttered open, trying to focus still in the dredges of sleep. Struggling to wake, she was caught precariously between her dreams and reality. The sound of agitated horses whining carried through the night. Shattered glass bounced off the edges of her mind. The cluck of chickens, the beating of wings, and a squawk cut off in mid-crow turned that dream into a ghoulish nightmare.

Straining to sit up, she rubbed her eyes, flung back the covers, and tumbled out of bed, the thrashing of wings echoing in her ears. She was barely able to function as she fought off the last dredges of sleep. She stumbled across the room. A spike of fear shot through her heart as she saw movement, but she was quickly relieved as she recognized her own dark reflection in the mirror. The image of her name written in lipstick popped back into her mind. She snagged her cell phone off the nightstand and took a deep breath.

A lone squawk rang out into the night.

Torn between fantasy and reality, unsure what was tangible, she looked around for a weapon.

The only thing she could find was a hairbrush. She clutched it, knowing it was most likely useless, but the metal handle felt good in her hand.

She eased open the bedroom door, and one lone, white feather drifted across her vision as she crept out to the loft. Snagging it out of thin air, she examined it.

"What in the world?"

In the spongy darkness of the silent house, her voice sounded unnerving even to her own ears. Peering over the railing, she gasped.

Something light speckled the hardwood floor and floated lazily through the air as the ceiling fan spun, catching the small objects in the updraft. Feathers? Padding down the stairs, she stopped halfway, desperate to fathom what had happened. Then she saw it.

The sparkle of glass.

The curtain fluttered in the breeze and stirred a pile of . . . feathers? Feathers trailed and scattered across the floor. And a large grotesque lump in the corner shifted. Slowly, she started to piece the eerie sounds from her dream together. Chloe descended the rest of the stairs in the eerie darkness and flipped on the light. She recoiled at the sight. Her stomach pitched and rolled as her eyes took in the scene. The chicken lay broken and bloody on the hardwood floor, still twitching.

She tip-toed to the front door and forced herself to open it. Her hand flew to her mouth as she slowly peered out, cutting off her own scream. Feathers and chickens, battered and bleeding, lay scattered all over her yard. Blood dripped off the newly installed siding and across the railing. She sank to her knees as she recognized the rooster with his neck broken, which lay across the top step. Crimson blood peppered the stamped concrete, the chickens were slaughtered. The sun slowly crept out from behind low hills, turning the horizon from black to gray, casting the disturbing scene in a ghastly light.

The air was unseasonably warm for this early in the morning, hot and muggy for the first day of October. The sun was barely over the ridge, and the sky had gone from an unnatural gray to a clear blue, so bright that it hurt to look at it. Tate stood stock still and knew that somewhere over the horizon, a storm was brewing, even if he couldn't see it yet. He could feel it in his bones. He had sensed it in the wee hours of the morning before he'd even gotten out of bed. He tucked the soda he'd purchased from the convenience store under his arm and dug the keys out of his pocket as he walked back to his truck.

The big brown delivery van barreled into the parking lot and screeched to a halt directly behind his pickup. Tate cringed when Dalton Turk rolled the door back and stepped out.

"You blocked me in, Turk," Tate stated.

Dalton paraded past him, boxes in hand. "You can wait."

"Inconsiderate, son of a . . ." Tate cursed under his breath. He twisted the top off of his Coke and took a long swallow of the dark liquid. Leaning back on the truck, he put the top back on. He didn't know why he was in such a foul mood. Like the storm looming somewhere over the horizon, Tate felt an unease. One he couldn't quite put a finger on, except maybe now, waiting for Dalton to emerge from the store.

"Can't get much work done standing there."

Tate glanced over his shoulder to find Eddie walking toward him, clicking the keyless remote locks on his Jag.

"Hey, Eddie. You're out and about awful early."

"I could say the same to you," Eddie said, stopping a couple of feet from him.

"I'm always up early, starting at the crack of dawn. Already been to a jobsite to meet a delivery. How 'bout you?" Tate took Eddie slowly in and forced down the irritation he felt. Eddie always looked professional and exuded the image of having money, from his dress shirt to his precisely pleated black pants and shiny black shoes. But Tate much preferred his own worn jeans and boots. "Where are you headed? The bank?"

"Funny, but no. I have a meeting later. Just stopped to get some coffee. Are you waiting on someone?"

Jerking a thumb in the direction of the delivery van, he said, "Blocked in."

Eddie shook his head. "Hope you aren't in a hurry."

"Dalton did it to piss me off."

"Oh?" Eddie raised an eyebrow. "Why is that? For retribution from the baseball game?"

"More likely because Chloe and I had a run-in with him on Sunday."

"Is Chloe alright? She didn't mention it."

"A little shaken up. Otherwise, fine." Tate glanced at the door, not wanting to elaborate or think about how Dalton had his hands all over her. "Here he comes now." Pushing off the truck, Tate's irritation bubbled easily to the surface. "'Bout damn time, Turk."

Ramming a shoulder into Tate's as he passed, Dalton sneered. "Lucky for you, I'm on the clock, or I'd have left your ass blocked in all damn day."

Seeing red, Tate counted to ten, trying to control his temper. "Save it for the ball field. Looks like we'll be playing you tonight. If you can handle it, or would you rather me put you back on the ground like you were on Sunday?"

Dalton sneered, stepped up close, his breath hot and stale mere inches from Tate's face. "I can handle it, just like I handled your woman on Sunday, with my hands wrapped around her pretty little neck and between her . . ."

Tate's hands were out of his pockets and seizing the rough polyester of Dalton's uniform before either one of them was prepared for it, slamming him up against the truck. "You stay away from Chloe, you hear? Or the next time you so much as glance at her, your head will be so far up your ass you won't be able to see the light of day."

A slow and dangerous smirk crept across the other man's face. "You can't be with her twenty-four hours a day, Becker."

Tate gave Dalton a shove and released him. "Like hell, I can't."

"Aren't with her now, are you? Weren't last night either," Dalton spat, as his eyes drifted off Tate's, locking on something behind him.

Tate's blood ran cold. "How in the hell do you know that?"

"Is there a problem, gentleman?" Detective Rita Sorenson asked as she emerged from Turkey Hill with her morning coffee.

Dalton spat on the ground again. "No, Detective. No problem at all." Walking backward to the van, he licked his lips and smirked at Tate. "Tell Legs I can't wait to see her tonight."

Tate took a step toward Dalton, and Eddie grabbed his arm, holding him in place. "Don't. It's not worth it."

Seething with anger, Tate reigned it in. He knew Dalton was right. He couldn't be with her all the time. But how the hell did he know he wasn't with her last night? Unless . . . his blood ran cold. Had he been by her house?

"Who was that," Detective Sorenson asked.

"Dalton Turk," Tate answered with a scowl.

Rita stood next to Tate and gave him a slow measuring look. "Want to tell me what just happened?"

"That jack . . ." remembering who he was talking to, he stopped himself. "He's been harassing Chloe," Tate answered, swallowing down the fear that had lodged in his throat. Watching Dalton pull away from the convenience store, he pulled out his cell phone to call her. She was fine, he told himself, but he would call anyway just to be safe. That's when he noticed the battery was dead. He'd forgotten to charge it again last night.

Rita's phone vibrated. "Hold that thought. We're not finished." She looked at the caller ID and immediately answered. "What's up, Fulmer?"

Both men turned to face her, watching her intently. Detective Sorenson locked eyes with Tate but her face remained neutral, unreadable. Even still, Tate tensed. He could feel a storm bubbling inside himself and her.

"I'll meet you there in ten," she said, then clicked off.

"What's happened? Is it Chloe?"

Rita nodded slightly. "Don't panic. She's alright but . . ."

"But what?" the question coming out a little harsher than Tate had intended.

"Something's happened. I'm headed out there now to check it out."

"Not without me," Tate stated.

"Us," Eddie corrected.

Tate could feel the storm pressing in as one lone, dark cloud floated across the horizon.

THIRTY-SEVEN

From the moment Detective Rita Sorenson stepped out of her car, the crime scene was hers. Even though Detective Sorenson wasn't a big woman, every officer and lab technician obeyed her command. Chloe would have called her petite. Her five-foot-three height, slender build, and fine features reminded Chloe of a pixie. Her short, stylish hair and her flash of kind green eyes only added to the image. Chloe half expected there to be wings on Detective Sorenson's back as she turned slowly around taking in every detail.

None of this had registered the first couple of times Chloe had spoken to her but then again, the circumstances had been different.

This time, Chloe stood between Tate and Eddie and watched the investigation unfold.

"Chloe, why don't I take you back to my place, away from this . . . this madness," Eddie offered.

"No," she stated flatly. "I'm staying put." Her voice softened slightly as she registered the hurt on Eddie's face. "I didn't mean . . . I'm sorry, Eddie. It's just my chickens were slaughtered outside my house while I slept. I'm not leaving. I want answers." Twin electric jolts of fear and anger coursed through her.

"I just wanted to take you away from this mess. The gore of it all."

"Thank you." She placed a hand on his arm to appease him. "I do appreciate the offer, but I'm staying. I hope you can understand."

"I do. But it makes me sick to think you were just inside when this all went down," Eddie said, shaking his head.

Detective Sorenson walked over. "Why don't you go inside? We're wrapping up. I'll be in to talk to you shortly."

"Of course. Thank you, detective," Tate said, answering for all of them. He turned to Chloe. "Let's go in." Tate linked his fingers with Chloe's and tugged her forward, leading her into the house, through the back door, and into the kitchen. "Why don't you sit down and try to relax," he coaxed.

"I can't." Chloe couldn't sit. She felt confined, cornered. "I should make some coffee for the detective," she said to no one but herself, needing something to do.

"Chloe, I don't think that's necessary," Eddie started to say but stopped when she simply looked at him. He raised his hands in defense. "Go ahead if it makes you feel better."

"Would you like help?" Tate offered.

"No, thank you," Chloe said, getting out the makings for coffee. She went about the mundane task of setting the container on the counter, putting the paper liner in the basket, and filling it with coffee grounds. Then, she turned on the tap, filled the pot, and poured the water into the cavity, pushed the button and waited for the liquid to leak through.

"I know," Eddie said, pulling out his cell phone and filling the silence. "I'll call an acquaintance of mine over at the rendering company and have them come out and clean up this mess."

Chloe bristled. "I can do it myself."

"Why would you want to do that?" Eddie asked.

Clenching her fists, she balled them at her side. "I can . . ." her voice trailed off as Tate put his hands on her shoulders, and she felt the tension there. A tightness she didn't know she was holding in.

"Relax," he murmured softly in her ear. "No one is saying you can't."

As his hands lay reassuringly on her, she felt a little of the tension seep out.

"Eddie's only trying to help," Tate added. "It's a good idea. They can discard the bodies."

There was a knock on the back door.

Detective Sorensen opened it. "May I come in?"

"Of course," Chloe answered. She pointed to the kitchen table and pulled out a chair. "Please have a seat," Chloe offered. "The coffee is almost done. Would you like a cup?"

"I would."

Chloe got out four mugs and filled them. She handed one to each person and then set out the cream and sugar. "Can I get anyone anything else?"

"This will be fine. Please, Miss Harris. Have a seat. Why don't you tell me from the beginning what happened."

"Okay," Chloe nodded, picking up her coffee cup to warm her icy hands. Despite the unusually warm day, she felt a chill down to her toes. She ran through it quickly for the detective, starting at the beginning.

Detective Sorenson was quiet while Chloe spoke and remained that way until Chloe ran out of steam.

"What time did you wake up this morning?" Rita asked.

She shook her head, trying to clear her mind. "I'm not sure. I didn't look at the clock. My guess would be around five."

Nodding, Rita clicked her pen and jotted down a quick note. Looking up at Chloe, Rita sat a little straighter in her chair. "This is the second major incident at your house. Can you think of anyone that might have a vendetta against you?"

Chloe shifted in her chair, unable to make eye contact with the detective. Should she say anything about Dalton Turk? He was creepy and aggressive, but surely, he wouldn't stoop to breaking into her home, and now this?

"Chloe, you should tell her about Dalton Turk," Eddie insisted.

"What about him?" Detective Sorenson asked.

"Eddie," Chloe scolded. The decision had been taken from her. "It's not your place to mention that."

As if sensing Chloe's frustration and hesitation, Detective Sorenson asked, "Gentleman, could you please give Miss Harris and me a minute alone?"

"Of course," Tate said, standing and taking his empty cup to the sink.

Eddie followed suit. "If you need me, I'll be right outside." Chloe flinched involuntarily as Eddie laid a hand on her arm as he passed. She needed to relax and remember that he was only trying to help.

Chloe simply nodded, and the men filed out of the kitchen.

When the door was firmly shut, Rita leaned forward in her chair. "Miss Harris, I notice your hesitation. What is it you're not telling me?"

"As Eddie said, there is Dalton Turk."

Rita folded her hands into her lap, waiting.

Chloe saw a flicker of recognition in the detective's eye.

"The delivery man at the bookstore?" she questioned.

Chloe nodded.

"I'm listening."

"It all started a week ago today." Again, Chloe ran through it quickly for the detective, starting with the baseball game to the interaction with Dalton at the bookstore and then at the pumpkin patch.

"And prior to the game, what was your relationship like?"

"There wasn't one. I knew of him and ran across him in town a few times, but no conversation was exchanged. He's a few years older than me, and we simply don't run in the same social circles."

"What about Tate Becker or Eddie Lambert? What's your relationship with either of them?"

"Both men are friends. Eddie is in the same industry as I am, and Tate is my . . ." Chloe didn't know what to say or how to classify Tate. They were friends surely, but were they more? Even though it felt like they had crossed that line into something more, now wasn't the time to analyze it. "Neighbor -- friend," Chloe finished lamely.

The detective nodded at that statement as if it made sense, so Chloe didn't elaborate.

Detective Sorenson held her gaze for a moment. Chloe

thought the detective was about to ask her to elaborate, but the bell literally saved her as the detective's phone rang.

Detective Sorenson looked at the caller ID and said, "I need to take this."

"Of course."

Chloe got up and went to the sink to give the detective a little privacy. She started the tap and listened to the one-sided conversation as she washed the coffee cups.

With very few words spoken on Detective Sorenson's part, she clicked off then stood. She crossed to the sink and deposited her cup in it like the others. "I'm needed across town. Seems like there's been more than one break-in last night."

Before Chloe could ask, Detective Sorenson moved swiftly across the kitchen.

"Thanks for the coffee. I'll be in touch." Without another word, she disappeared out the door.

THIRTY-EIGHT

"I don't need a babysitter," Chloe said.

Tate flashed her a grin as bright as a 100-watt bulb. "I know you don't. But I don't want you left alone after all that's happened. Plus," he reached over, squeezing her hand, keeping the other one on the wheel." I like having you with me."

"Slick, aren't you?" She couldn't help but smile. "Think you're charming, don't you?"

"I like to think so. Besides, what else did you have to do today?" he asked teasingly as they drove across town.

"It's Tuesday, Tate," she said, slightly annoyed. "I should be writing. Not to mention the mess I have at the house." If she was being honest, she didn't want to be alone, but going to the Taphouse was the last place she wanted to be.

"Right. And that's why I had you bring your laptop and sent Kurt over to fix the window. The rendering crew Eddie hired will dispose of the poultry, and the cleaning crew will do the rest."

"I still think it was overkill on Eddie's part. We're talking about a dozen birds. I could have –"

"For once, I agree with Eddie. He wanted to help. So, we let him. Hopefully, most of it will be put back in order by the time we get done at the Taphouse." He gave her a sideways glance. "I know it might be awkward, but I'm sure Kimmy won't mind if you sit in a booth and write while Neil and I work."

"Awkward?" Chloe said the word out loud. "That's an understatement." Chloe knew Kimmy wouldn't be happy to see her despite what Tate said. Not when Kimmy, obviously, had a thing for him even though he insisted he set her straight. "I should have gone to the bookstore and stayed with Lucy."

"You could have, but then you wouldn't have been with me."

"I need a shower and a change of clothes," she protested. "I never got the chance this morning. I just threw something on before the police arrived."

"I like your outfit." He peered over at her and wiggled his eyebrows at her. "Jeans and a T-shirt. Classic."

Chloe rolled her eyes at him as he turned the corner and pulled in alongside Neil's truck, parking. Digging in her backpack, she located a hair tie. Running her fingers through her hair, she hastily pulled it back into a messy bun.

"You look beautiful."

Furrowing her brow, she protested. "I feel gross. I need a shower."

He leaned over, tugged her forward a couple of inches, and gently placed his mouth on hers. She sighed into the kiss, and the tension between her eyes eased. It was hard to stay mad at him when he did stuff like this. It seemed so natural, so easy.

His mouth was still on hers when his lips turned up into a devious smile. "We can talk about that shower later, and maybe I can even help you with the hard-to-reach places."

"Keep dreaming."

"Believe me, I am."

There was a rap on the window. "Are you two going to make out in there, or are we going to get to work?" Neil asked as he pressed his face to the glass, grinning from ear to ear.

"You've always had the worst timing," Tate said loudly. "Let's make him wait a little longer." He kissed her once more.

"Okay, okay," Chloe laughed, pushing him back. "It's time to work. For both of us."

"Okay, boss. Whatever you say."

"Hey, Tate?" she said softly before he got out.

"Yeah?"

"Thanks."

"For what?"

"For taking me out of there. For distracting me."

"That's what I'm here for." He opened his door. "I'm just sorry it has to be here with Kimmy."

"It's okay," Chloe said, resigning herself to the fact that she would have to see Kimmy sooner or later.

"Come on," he jerked his head toward the window. "Neil's getting antsy."

Despite the circumstances, she grabbed her backpack and got out, feeling better than she should have. She had to admit Tate had a way of doing that.

Kimmy popped her head out of the back door of the building. Her smile was wide but seemed forced. "There you are! I thought I heard someone pull in." That brilliant smile dimmed considerably when she spotted Chloe. "Hello, Chloe. Are you working for Tate now, too?"

"Not quite." She spared a leveling glance at Tate to say, I told you so. "Mind if I find a booth in the corner somewhere out of the way to work?"

"You came here to write?"

"Is that a problem?" Tate asked Kimmy.

"No. I . . ." Kimmy shook her head as if dismissing the comment on the tip of her tongue. "Of course. Make yourself at home," Kimmy said in a clipped tone. She held the door wide. "But I must warn you, the place is a disaster."

"Sounds like you had a little excitement last night," Tate said. "Let's take a look, and then we can come back out for our tools."

They all navigated through the small storage area in a single file line.

"Have the police already been here?" Tate asked, bringing up the rear.

"Yes, they've come and gone," Kimmy answered.

"What about your insurance agent?"

"He's been here too." Kimmy stopped just inside the restaurant.

Neil let out a low whistle as they came into the bar. Broken bottles and shards of glass covered the counter and the floor, sparkling in the dim light. The smell of alcohol and fermented beer hung heavily as it slowly dripped off every surface. The shelving on the back wall hung precariously, and the mirror behind it was shattered in the center. A spiderweb of tiny cracks snaked out in every direction.

Chloe gasped, and her hand went to her mouth. "Oh, Kimmy."

Tears bubbled to the surface; Kimmy choked back a sob. "I know, right? It's terrible. Just awful." She looked over at Tate, all teary-eyed. "I didn't know who else to call."

Tate draped an arm over Kimmy's shoulder. "You called the right people. Don't worry. It looks worse than it is. We'll get this cleaned up, replace the mirror, and rehang the shelving."

"He's right," Neil agreed. "It's all fixable."

"When did this happen?" Chloe asked.

"I was here until midnight, so sometime after that." Kimmy sniffled. "Do you think I'll be able to open today?"

"It's already almost lunchtime, so that's not likely, but we should be able to get you open for dinner."

"Where is your staff?"

"I called them and told them not to come until the police had gone. I was just about to call them and have them come in." Tears trickled down her face. "They should be here shortly to help."

"We will grab our tools and get started," Tate assured her.

Chloe set her backpack in a corner booth, writing, and her animosity toward Kimmy had already been forgotten. She took Kimmy by the hand and said, "Show me where you keep your cleaning supplies."

Blinking, Kimmy used the back of her hand to wipe away the tears. She nodded and clasped Chloe's hand tightly. "Thank you."

They worked steadily for a few hours when they heard someone call from the back room.

"Hello! Anyone here?" Eddie poked his head into the dining room.

Kimmy answered, "We're in here."

"What's going on? The front door is locked. Didn't you open for lunch? It's already after three."

"Not today," Kimmy replied as she wiped down the counter. "Didn't you see the closed sign?"

"I did." Eddie glanced around and saw Tate and Neil up on ladders, reinstalling the shelving.

"What happened?"

"Someone broke in last night," Kimmy replied as she dragged over a trash can full of glass.

"You too?" Eddie asked, surprised.

"What do you mean you too?" she questioned as she tied the trash bag shut.

"Someone was at Chloe's house last night and slaughtered her chickens," Eddie answered. "Didn't she tell you?"

"Oh, Chloe!" Kimmy exclaimed. "I had no idea. And here you are cleaning up my mess when you should be home."

"You didn't know," Chloe said. "How could you?"

Eddie wasn't about to be deterred from the reason he was here. "Are you going to open? I'm starving, and it looks like everything is almost cleaned up."

"I'm not going to open until at least four, maybe five. We are behind on food prep."

"Let me get this last bag of trash for you, and then you can go help them with prep." He tried to take the bag from her hand as Kimmy lifted it from the trash can.

"I got it, Eddie. Don't touch it. There's glass sticking out."

He ignored her, grabbing the bag with both hands. When he picked it up the contents split the already compromised plastic.

"Eddie!" Kimmy scolded. "I told you to be careful."

"I'm sorry." He bent down to pick up a large piece of glass. "Damn it!" Eddie cursed as blood squirted out of a deep cut in the center of his palm.

"Now you've done it. Quick, come to the sink before you get blood everywhere."

They ran his hand under the water.

"I told you not to pick up the bag. It wasn't tied shut properly and was already ripping in places," Kimmy reprimanded him.

"I'm sorry. I just wanted to help so you could open sooner."

"Kimmy already told you she can't open for at least another hour," Chloe said, coming over with a wad of paper towels. "Here." She pressed the paper towel into his palm. "Apply pressure until we can get a bandage."

"I'll get the first aid kit." Kimmy disappeared into the back room.

"Sit down." Chloe pointed to a barstool. "And pay attention to what you're doing."

Hauling out ladders, Tate and Neil stopped by the counter to see what was going on.

"What happened?" Neil asked.

"He cut his hand," Chloe supplied.

"How bad is it? Does he need stitches?" Tate asked.

"Probably, it's pretty deep."

Furrowing his brow, Tate asked, "Can he pitch tonight?"

Chloe shook her head. "I doubt it."

"I have the first aid kit," Kimmy said, brandishing it in the air as she returned.

Tate's brow furrowed even more. "Now, what are we going to do? I sure as hell don't want to forfeit to the likes of Dalton Turk."

Eddie winced in pain when Kimmy applied the antiseptic.

"Don't be such a baby," Kimmy clucked.

"Chloe can pitch," Eddie said between clenched teeth.

"No way," Tate was quick to reply.

Chloe lifted an eyebrow in question. "Why not?"

"Because I don't want you anywhere near Dalton. That's why. You need to stay as far away from him as possible."

"Do you think he's the one that's been breaking into Chloe's house?" Eddie asked.

"I wouldn't put it past him," Tate answered.

"But why?" Eddie questioned. "Because she struck him out at the last game?"

"It's possible."

Chloe wasn't about to let her fate be decided right in front of her. "I was planning on going to the game anyway, so you might as well let me pitch. You know you need me."

Kimmy finished wrapping Eddie's hand and stood up. "You should let her play, Tate."

"No, I said it before. I don't want you anywhere near Dalton."

"What if it's not him?" Chloe asked. "And you make me stay home. Then I'm home alone while you're all at the game. Think about that for a second." She let her words sink in. "I'm safer either way at the game with everyone there together."

"She's right. She's safer at the game than at home," Neil agreed.

"And we are assuming he's the one that broke into my house and killed my chickens, but we don't know that for sure."

"I think we do," Tate said grimly.

"How?" Chloe poked a finger at his chest. "What do you know?"

Sighing, Tate relented. "I saw Dalton at the gas station this morning, and he said he knew you were home alone last night." He waited a beat, letting the comment sink in. "How would he know that, Chloe, if he hadn't been at your house?"

Chloe stayed silent for a long moment.

Tate gave it one last chance. "Kimmy, could you stay with her?"

"I – uhm," Kimmy stammered.

"Don't put her on the spot like that, Tate. It's not fair," Chloe protested.

"Thank you, Chloe." The women exchanged a look. "It's not that I don't want to help, it's just I thought I would like to come out and watch the game since it seems like it's all you talk about when you are here. Besides, after this . . ." Kimmy moved her arms to encompass the entirety of the restaurant and its damage. "I need to get out."

"You, see?" Neil pointed. "Yet another person that will be at the game. The more people, the better."

"Fine," Tate relented, then pointed a finger at Chloe. "Don't leave my sight."

"Believe me, I won't."

THIRTY-NINE

The sun bled behind the ridge while foreboding clouds rolled in overhead, creating a wall of slow-moving darkness with a ribbon of red between it and the mountain range. Cars pulled into the quarry with headlights on. The beams bounced off the carved rock walls, slicing the darkness and creating an odd effect of light and shadow.

Tate went to the equipment shed, unlocked the door, and flipped on the park lights. Immediately, the diamond was washed in a swath of white light.

A sense of urgency could be felt among all the players as the humid air that had hung thick all day pressed in. The gravel crunched under cleats, and worn gloves snapped as ball met leather.

Chloe deposited her bag on the bench, tucked her glove under her arm, and reached for her water bottle. Twisting off the top, she took a long, slow drink, trying to quench her thirst as well as her nerves. She told herself she was all right, but the minute she saw Dalton step out of his truck, her nerves skittered out of control. Dalton's face was pinched with concentration as he scanned the diamond, the bleachers, and then the dugout. The minute his eyes landed on her the scowl vanished. A slow, devious grin crept across his face. His eyes locked with hers.

Maybe this wasn't such a good idea after all.

Lucy dropped her bag beside Chloe. "I'm so late." Lucy bent and rummaged through her bag. "The bookstore was really busy this afternoon."

"Don't worry. You still have time to warm up."

Straightening, Lucy tucked her glove between her legs and pulled a hair tie off her wrist. She smoothed back her hair and pulled it into a hasty ponytail. "Are you okay?" Lucy asked. "You look a little rattled."

Chloe turned her back on Dalton. "Yeah. Just a little nervous."

"You're bound to be with all that's been happening." Lucy leaned in and gave her a quick hug. "Everything's going to be fine."

"I know."

"I need to warm up. You coming?" Lucy asked as she walked backward to the field.

"I'll be right there."

Nodding, Lucy turned and jogged out to first base.

Chloe felt him before she saw him.

The intake of breath was meant to be loud, followed by a low whistle. "Looks like we meet again, Legs. I thought you might be too scared to come tonight, to face me in the box."

Chloe straightened her spine and turned to look at Dalton Turk. "I'm not scared of you," she said.

He stepped in closer. "Really? The look on your face says different."

Tate came up beside Chloe and put his hand on the small of her back reassuring her he was there. Kurt quickly came around and flanked the other side.

"Aren't you on the wrong side of the field, Dalton?" Tate asked, his voice dropping low. "You shouldn't be over here unless you came to forfeit."

Dalton rocked back on his heels. "Forfeit?" He rolled with laughter. "To the likes of you? Hardly."

"Then you better get back to your side so we can get the game started." Kurt glanced up. "It doesn't look like the weather's going to hold for much longer. Clouds are moving in fast."

"It's on." Dalton started to back away, not taking his eyes off Chloe.

"If we have to call it, the rules state whoever's ahead at the bottom of the fifth wins," Tate reminded him.

"I know the rules, Becker. Besides, this game will be over long before then." Dalton gave one last parting comment, "Try to get the ball over the plate, Legs. I'll be looking forward to that first pitch."

※

Rita had both files laid out on her desk. She picked up the photograph of the first victim and studied her face, taking in every detail.

Reaching for the second woman's photo, she held them side by side. It was like looking at a brain teaser, where identical photos are shown but a few random things have been changed, and you need to spot the differences. Both faces were very similar, but something about that bothered her. She just couldn't quite put a finger on it.

Rita stared at each face, slowly memorizing every detail. Their frown lines, a random freckle, and the upturn of a nose. Then she saw it.

Once she did, she couldn't unsee it. Where had she noticed that before?

Then it hit her.

She needed a photo of Chloe Harris. She went to her laptop and typed in Chloe's name in the search engine. Images of books popped up on the left, and a Wikipedia entry with Chloe's professional headshot on the right of her screen, followed by multiple sites where her books could be purchased. Clicking on the photo, Rita enlarged it, until the photo of Chloe's face filled her screen. And there it was.

The smallest scar at the edge of her brow. The two victims had a scratch in exactly the same spot. Was this a clue that they had been looking for to tie all the crimes together? How could something so simple, so small, be potentially so significant?

Rita was so deep in thought that when her partner stuck his head in her door she jumped. "Holy crap, Fulmer. Can you be any sneakier?"

Fulmer chuckled. "Sorry. Next time I'll stomp down the hallway so you know I'm coming."

"What's up?" she asked as she turned her attention back to the photos.

"Have a bit of news for you." Fulmer leaned his lanky frame against the wall just inside the door.

"Oh, yeah?" Rita said distractedly. "What would that be?"

"You know the break-in at the Taphouse?"

She put the photos down. "Yeah?"

"What made you widen the sweep of the perimeter?"

Rita shook her head. "A gut feeling. Why? Did they find something?"

He shrugged, "Maybe."

"Let's have it," Rita said, lifting a folder off her desk. "It wasn't just a smash-and-grab, was it?"

"Essentially." He shifted, rubbing his back against the wall to scratch an itch he couldn't reach, stalling.

"Spill your guts. I don't have time for your games."

"They found a baseball bat tucked behind the dumpster. Figure that's what the perp used to smash and destroy the bar."

"Is that it? Or is there more to it?"

"Yeah, a couple of things. I followed up with the rendering company that removed the poultry from the Harris property. The manager said the chickens were busted up so badly that it was like they had been beaten with a baseball bat."

Rita straightened and laid the folder down on her desk.

Holding up his hands, Fulmer said, "Those were his exact words. I kid you not."

"What else?"

"It was a wooden bat with a couple of drops of dried fluid on it. There were dark reddish spots, which they believed to be blood. The wood was also slightly splintered, and there was a hair attached."

Inhaling deeply, Rita asked, "Where is it now?"

"The bat? It's in the evidence room. DNA samples have been taken and sent to the lab."

"Good. That's good." Rita ran her hands through her pixie-cut hair, fluffing it slightly, giving herself time to think. "What about our other sample? The scraping from underneath Jane Doe's fingernails."

"No match yet."

She picked up Jane Doe's folder, flipped through to the autopsy, and read out loud. "The contusion in Jane Doe's skull is concave and approximately two and a half inches wide." She pointed at the other folder. "Read me Tara's."

Fulmer reached for the folder containing the case. He scanned it. "Tara Zimm's skull contusion measures two point six inches. It's also concave, dish-shaped." He glanced up at his partner.

"How big is the end of an average baseball bat?" Rita asked.

Pulling out his phone, Fulmer searched it quickly. "The average length is thirty-four inches with a maximum diameter of two point six one inches."

Rita sat back in her office chair, the weight of evidence heavy on her chest. But one by one, like pins and tumblers of a lock, the clues slowly slid into place. "I think we just found our murder weapon."

FORTY

Kimmy pulled into the lot, parked her car next to an old truck, and exited. Emerging from her air-conditioned vehicle, she noticed the humidity had cranked up another notch and the wind with it. A storm was definitely brewing.

Smoothing her hair as best she could with one hand, her keys, and her phone in the other, she strolled over to the baseball diamond and found Eddie sitting alone on the bleachers.

"Hey, you," she said cheerfully.

"Hello," he grumbled.

"No other spectators but you?"

"Guess not. Everyone's afraid of the storm that's rolling in."

"How is your hand?" she asked as she sat beside him, laying her stuff down on the bench beside her.

"Hurts," he said gruffly. "It took seven stitches to close it."

"I'm sorry. I'm sure you wish you were out there playing." Kimmy glanced up at the scoreboard. "It looks like they're in the lead, though."

"Yeah, they are, thanks to Chloe," Eddie said, not taking his eyes off the pitcher's mound.

Kimmy followed his gaze and saw Chloe prepare for the next pitch. She released. The ball sped through the air rapidly. The batter swung, connecting. A line drive was hit directly at Tate.

He was a man in motion, fielding the ball easily, scooping it up, and throwing it to first base. Kimmy sighed a little, watching. The ball reached Lucy's glove at top speed, her glove snapped closed. The third out of the inning, and the batter wasn't even close to the base.

"Seriously?" Eddie asked, sounding annoyed.

Kimmy flinched at his tone. "What?"

"Are you really sitting here next to me drooling over Tate?"

"I am most certainly not drooling over Tate," she denied. Even though it was the truth, she couldn't help herself. She sat a little straighter as the team ran towards the dugout and prepared to bat. Tate glanced up at the stands, noticing her, and gave her a head nod. She returned his greeting with a flirty little wave.

"Good grief." Eddie shook his head. "You know he's into Chloe, right?"

"I know," Kimmy answered. And she did. But she just couldn't help herself, wondering what would happen if Chloe wasn't in the picture. She berated herself mentally for the thought, especially after Chloe had spent part of the morning and half the afternoon helping her clean up the Taphouse when she had a disaster of her own at home. But still, she couldn't help but wonder if Chloe weren't here, maybe she'd be the one he took home after the game. "What about you?" Kimmy asked quietly. "Seems like you're interested in Chloe for more than just her writing skills."

"Hardly. Our relationship is purely professional."

"Keep telling yourself that." Kimmy saw Eddie's jaw clench, clamping closed.

"Does he come when you call?" Eddie asked, not taking his eyes off the dugout.

"Who Tate?"

"Who else?"

"Well, that's kind of a random question, but . . ." Kimmy thought for a moment, unsure what Eddie's angle was or why he cared. "Not that it's any of your business, but yes, he does."

Lightning flashed and split the sky. A burst of cool air swept across the field, bringing with it the smell of rain. The metal bleachers rattled and lifted slightly off the ground.

"Oh, heavens! I think we'd better run!" Grabbing her keys, they both scrambled down.

Lightning cracked. The ground shook, and pebbles bounced as thunder rolled. Suddenly, everyone was scrambling. Scattering. Equipment was hastily thrown in truck beds or stowed in trunks. Lights popped on cars as the world around them grew dangerously dark. The ball field lights flickered and then went out, plunging them into an eerie darkness. Vehicles pulled out and formed a line, one by one creeping toward the exit.

Kimmy ran to her car and saw Tate and Chloe get in his truck. "So much for that."

The sky burst open like a whole sack of seed split along the seam, pouring out in a flood of water. The rain was so heavy her windshield wipers could barely keep up. She inched her car along until it was in the procession to vacate the lot. Try as she might, she wasn't able to keep track of Tate's truck through the heavy rain. She could barely see five feet in front of her.

Kimmy couldn't make out the road even with her windshield wipers on full blast. She did the only thing she could -- she inched forward, following the stream of red taillights. Once outside the quarry, though, all bets were off as those red taillights turned off in different directions leaving her wondering if she should have stayed in the lot until the storm passed.

Taking her time, she rolled forward, straining her eyes to see the painted lines on the road. She knew the way home. All she had to do was stay straight on this road for a couple of miles, just past Tate's house, make a right, and follow that road into town.

She cursed her precarious situation as the wipers beat out a steady rhythm way too fast for her liking. She should have stayed at the restaurant. Her little car had never been any match for the weather, and this torrential downpour had her nerves on edge.

A spot of red to the right caught her eye. Coming up on a stop sign, Kimmy was just able to make out the street sign above it between swipes of her wipers. It was exactly four miles from here to the road that would lead her into town. All she had to do was watch the mileage and keep it between the lines. Watching the odometer, she pressed gently down on the gas and prayed she could do just that.

FORTY-ONE

"It's raining cats and dogs," Tate stated, his knuckles white as he clenched the wheel.

"You're right. These raindrops are as fat as baseballs," Chloe agreed. "And hitting the windshield just as hard."

"In case you're wondering, I'm taking you to my house tonight." He afforded her a glance, barely taking his eyes off the road.

When she remained silent, he filled the hole in the conversation. "I was right there, and Dalton still came over to badger you. He can't help himself, not where you're concerned. I'm certainly not leaving you unattended all night in your house, at least not until we have this thing all sorted out."

Chloe watched the wipers battle the onslaught of rain that beat against the windshield. "If you want me to argue, you're going to be disappointed. Because I'm not going to." She looked directly at him. "I can't believe I'm actually going to say this to you, but -- Dalton Turk scares the living daylights out of me."

He pulled into his lane, drove up the driveway, and hit the garage door button with his index finger. He waited patiently as it rolled up and then pulled the truck inside, parking it beside his old pickup. With the engine off and the garage door down, he finally spoke. "You should be scared."

Pushing open her door, she hopped out and skirted the truck. The water that rolled off of it pooled on the cement. "Thanks for the vote of confidence. I feel so much better for confiding in you."

Tate caught her arm at the door. As she reached for the knob, he gently laid his hand on top of hers.

"Chloe," his voice was deep and kind. "That's not what I meant, and you know it."

"Do I?" she questioned, stiffening her spine. "If I didn't know any better, I'd almost think you want me to be frightened. After all, you get what you want if I am."

She looked up at him and shot daggers at him with her eyes.

"Whoa, relax." He chuckled, clearly unfazed by her expression. "That came out wrong. All I meant was you're right to feel scared. It's only natural. Hell, I'm terrified for you." He wrapped an arm around her waist and pulled her against him.

His body was warm and inviting despite the fact that she held herself stiff against him.

His smile was swift and keen, and his tone was teasing. "If it makes you feel better, I'll admit that I want you here with me because I'm scared. I need protection. Will you, Chloe Harris, stay and protect me?"

He bent and nipped at her bottom lip. She couldn't help herself, and a tiny sigh escaped her. Leaning in closer, he pressed his lips to hers.

The overhead light in the garage went out as the timer on the door lift clicked off, plummeting them into the pitch black.

"Let's go in," Tate whispered. "I sc - scared of the d - dark."

She smiled at his antics, glad he couldn't actually see her face. "Alright, you big baby. Let's go in."

The second the door opened, Bo greeted them with his tail swishing.

"Hey, Bo," Chloe said, bending down to pet him. "How are you?"

Tate flicked on the light in the mud room and slipped off his shoes. Following suit, Chloe did the same and placed her purse on a hook, still talking to Bo. "I bet you were wondering if we were ever coming in."

Bo barked and pranced around, excited to have company. Lightning flashed, and thunder rocked the house. The golden retriever whimpered and bumped into Chloe.

"Oh, hey. You're okay," she soothed.

"Why don't you take him to the couch? I'll light a fire."

The three of them padded across the floor and into the living room as a unit. Tate reached for the matches he kept above the mantle and struck one. Bending down, he held it to the kindling already placed in the hearth. The tiny flame flickered as it toyed with the paper, catching.

Tate flicked the match into the hearth and stood just as his cell phone chimed.

The lights flickered when another round of thunder rattled the house. Tate looked at the message, and a crease formed between his brows.

"Who is it?" Chloe asked as she sat down on the sofa. She patted the cushion for Bo to climb up beside her.

"Kimmy."

"What does she want? Is she okay?"

"She's stuck. Needs help getting her car out." Tate looked at Chloe and shrugged.

"Where is she?" Chloe questioned. Of course, Kimmy had texted him for help.

"She never made it out of the quarry."

Chloe remained quiet for thirty seconds, trying to put herself in Kimmy's place. She was caught in a torrential downpour and stuck. "You should go. She needs help."

"She can call a tow truck just as well as me."

"Ask her if she's done that."

His thumbs quickly tapped the text.

The response was quick.

"She says she has. It will be at least two hours before they can come."

"I'm sure that's true in this weather." Chloe let out a breath and shivered slightly. "You should go. No one should be out in this storm."

"I need to stop being the one to come to her rescue." He turned around, perched his arm on the mantel, laying down his phone. Watching the logs snap and pop, he said, "Now I see what you have been saying all along."

"And what's that?"

"How needy she is. How she depends on me." Tate turned to Chloe, wearing his heart on his sleeve. "I don't want to be needed by Kimmy. I want to be here for you."

He looked so sweet and vulnerable that Chloe couldn't stand it. She slipped out from under Bo and went to Tate. "You're a good guy, Tate Becker. A good friend. I know that. Just because you help Kimmy doesn't diminish what we have or what we might have. I see that now."

She lifted herself slightly on her toes and placed her lips tentatively on his. He pulled her in against his body, pressing her chest into his, warm and tempting. A delicious spike of heat raced through her core as she slid into the kiss. His hands rested on her hips, rocking her against him while his mouth begged for more. She went down fast, a woman drowning on dry land. He smelled like rain, his clothes slightly damp, and his face just a little bit rough from his five o'clock shadow.

The phone on the mantel vibrated again. He ignored it, trailing kisses down her neck.

"Tate," she whispered. She heard the hitch in her own voice. "You should --"

"I should, what?" he murmured against her skin. "Sweep you off your feet and whisk you away upstairs. Because," she felt him smile. "That I can do."

Breaking the spell as the phone vibrated again, Chloe reluctantly pulled back. "You should go."

Her lips still humming with the feel of his, she fought the urge to throw the phone across the room and have him do just what he suggested. Clearing her head with a small shake, she said quietly, "You can't leave her out in this. She needs you."

"I need you," he responded, his voice low and full of longing.

She studied him intently. His eyes were dark with desire, asking for nothing but offering everything. Her heart fell at his feet. Barely audible, she whispered, "I need you too."

The breath escaped him in a long sigh. "God, I have waited

so long to hear you say that." He dropped his forehead to hers, touching it lightly.

"The sooner you go, the sooner you'll get back."

His head moved against hers slightly, and he agreed. "Lock the door behind me, and don't open it for anyone." He straightened and dropped his hand to link with hers. His voice was raw with emotion. "Do you understand? I need you to be safe."

"I'll be fine. Don't worry about me. I've got Bo."

At the mention of his name, he fired off a solid bark.

"See?" she smiled. "We will be fine. Go."

FORTY-TWO

The rain came down in waves, like sheets of wet fabric hurling toward him. The minute Tate pulled out of his driveway, he had to put Chloe out of his mind, or he'd never be able to concentrate enough to keep the truck on the road. The wind had grown even more violent, like a woman scorned, as it beat its angry fist against his truck.

He didn't want to be out here at all. He wanted to be home with Chloe, out of the elements and snuggled up on the couch with that crackling fire.

"Stop it," Tate scolded himself as the wipers beat a small path of visibility on the windshield. "Concentrate." He kept the truck at a steady pace, feeling like a snail as he inched along the pavement at a precarious speed, afraid to be swept off the road at any second.

Fifteen minutes ticked by, and so did the numbers on his odometer. He knew he was getting close now. Making the turn, he breathed a sigh of relief as the walls of rock emerged from the darkness. Turning into the park, his headlights made a feeble attempt to cut through the storm. Barely able to make out anything, he saw a flash of silver between swipes of the wipers and headed in that direction. Stopping the truck behind a vehicle, he determined that at least two vehicles were parked.

Leaving the truck running, Tate reached for the handle. The truck jolted as a man ran full force into his door.

Tate jumped and cursed. "What the hell?"

The man's face was plastered against his side window. Steamy breaths came out in hot puffs of air as he pressed his half-crazed face against the glass. It took a second for Tate to recognize him. But when he did, his blood ran cold.

＊

Chloe watched the vicious storm swallow the truck whole. His red taillights disappeared in a matter of seconds. She jumped as the wind swept a pile of soggy leaves across the porch and plastered them to the window where she stood.

Bo whimpered beside her. Chloe looked down at him, his big brown eyes wide in the dim light.

"Nothing to do now but wait." She bent and wrapped her arms around his neck reassuringly. "He'll be back soon," then she added, "Don't worry." But she felt that was more for herself than the dog.

Bo swished his tail.

"Let's find your ball, and then we can curl up on the couch." She stood, and they moved through the house together. "Where could it be?"

Bo trotted off, headed straight for his cozy cushion in the corner, and retrieved his ball.

"Of course." She smiled at the golden retriever. "Why didn't I think to look there? You're such a smart dog."

Chloe heard the muffled ring of her cell phone. She turned a slow circle. "Now, where did I leave my purse?" The phone continued to ring. "The mud room. Maybe it's Tate. I'll be right back."

A flash of light, followed by a sonic boom, shook the house's very foundation. The lights flickered and then went out, pitching Chloe into the dark. She tripped over a shoe and stumbled into the dark mud room, groping for her purse. The ringing had stopped when she fished out her cell phone. "Oh, for heaven's sake," Chloe grumbled. She checked the recent list on her phone and saw the missed call from Detective Sorenson.

A pounding started on the front door. Bo barked, and Chloe jumped. "Tate!" she yelled, thinking the worst, running to the front door. Checking herself before she turned the lock, she squinted out into the darkness behind the safety of the glass. Bo kept barking.

"Chloe?" She heard the woman's voice. "Is that you? Please let me in!"

Staring back at the drenched woman, Chloe realized it was Kimmy. "Stop, Bo." Without hesitation, she twisted the lock, opening the door. A gust of wind and rain swept in, pushing the door open further. "Thank God you're alright. Come in," Chloe said, ushering the dripping woman in and closing the door behind her. "You're back faster than I thought you would be. Why are you limping?"

"I twisted my ankle," Kimmy said, shivering.

"Let's see." Chloe bent down, lifted the soaked material of her pant leg, and examined Kimmy's ankle. "It's starting to swell. Can you take off your shoes?"

"I think so."

"Let me get a towel, and then we will get you off your feet." Accustomed to the dark now, Chloe made her way to the mudroom to retrieve a couple of towels and a kitchen chair. She was back in a matter of minutes.

Placing the chair by the fireplace, Chloe took the towels to Kimmy.

"Here," Chloe said, handing Kimmy a towel. "You must be frozen."

"I think I only ran a half mile, but it felt like a hundred. I never thought I'd get here." Kimmy wrapped the towel around her shoulders and shuddered. "Thank you."

"Let's get you to the fire."

Bo danced around them, sniffing at Kimmy's wet legs as the two women hobbled to the fireplace.

"Why were you running, and where is Tate?" she asked, placing Kimmy in the chair. "Hold that thought. I'll get you another chair to prop your leg on."

Chloe disappeared and emerged from the dark house with another chair. "You need to keep that leg elevated to keep the swelling down."

Kimmy's teeth chattered as she spoke, "My car went off the road about a half mile past here. This was the closest house, and I have no idea where Tate is. Why would I? He left with you." Kimmy raised her leg gingerly, wincing, she placed it on the chair. "I assumed he was here."

"But you texted him," Chloe said confused. "Your car is stuck at the quarry."

Shivers racked Kimmy's body as she inched the chair closer to the fire, a puddle of water forming around her as the wet dripped off. She shook her head. "No, I didn't. I couldn't. I don't have my phone."

"What do you mean you don't have your phone? You have to," Chloe said, confused. "You texted him about thirty minutes ago."

"It wasn't me." She wrapped the towel tighter. "If I had my phone I would have stayed in the car until a tow truck came, not run a half mile in this torrential down pour. The last time I remember having my cell was at the game. I must have dropped it when we ran to our cars right before the storm hit."

"But if you didn't text him, who did?"

"I don't know but it wasn't me. Why would he lie?"

Chloe pictured his face when he'd read the text. The concern mixed with the frustration. "He wouldn't. Someone must have used your phone." Chloe tried to think, piecing it together. "Someone could have picked it up,"

"I guess. But how would they know it was mine?"

"Your phone is easily recognizable; you have the Taphouse logo printed on the case. Who else has that?"

Smiling sheepishly, Kimmy said, "No one, I guess."

"Anyone at the quarry would recognize it as yours. We're all locals."

"You're probably right," Kimmy agreed.

"But they would have to know your password."

Kimmy frowned. "I don't have a password on it."

"Really?"

"I have a hard time remembering passwords, okay? I have

enough to remember with the business. I need my phone to be simple, easy to use."

"I'm not berating you. I'm just frustrated." Chloe started to pace back and forth. "So, if it wasn't you, then who was it? Who would want him to come out in this weather?"

"Someone crazy, that's who. Or mad at him."

Chloe stopped in her tracks. "What did you just say?"

"Someone who's mad at him."

Chloe's heart dropped. Sick to her stomach, she could barely speak his name, "Dalton Turk."

"You really think so?" Kimmy asked, her eyes huge in the dim light.

"Who else would do such a thing?"

"I don't know," Kimmy answered truthfully.

"I have to go. I have to help him."

Chloe ran through the house and into the mud room, searching for the spare set of keys for the other truck.

"What about me?" Kimmy called from the other room. "You can't leave me here alone in the dark!"

Finding the keys on a hook, she slipped her shoes on. Chloe yelled back, "You'll be fine. Bo will protect you if it comes to that. Just stay put. I'll be back soon." With that, Chloe rushed out the door.

FORTY-THREE

Rita swore under her breath as she hit redial on her cell. "Come on, come on, pick up." She couldn't shake the feeling that getting a hold of Chloe Harris was imperative.

"Any luck?" Fulmer asked, sticking his head in her office.

"Straight to voicemail."

"Could be the weather."

"Could be. But I have this awful feeling in my gut."

"Never argue with your gut." He came through the door. Pointing at her desk, he said, "Try using the landline. See if that helps."

"Then I'd actually have to punch in the numbers," she said grumpily.

He chuckled. "Then read off the numbers, and I'll do it."

Rita read off the numbers to him. He held the phone to his ear and waited. When it started to ring, he handed it to her.

"Beginners luck," she grumbled.

He smirked.

Rita's voice caught when she heard someone pick up. "Chloe?"

"Yes."

"You sound like you're in a tunnel. Where are you at?"

"I'm driving."

"You shouldn't be out in this weather." Rita placed her fingers between her brow, trying to ward off the headache forming there. "I've been trying to reach you. Is Tate Becker with you?"

"No, he's not."

"I have some new information about your case."

"You're breaking up. It's hard to hear. What did you say?"

"We found the weapon used to kill your chickens."

"What was it?"

A flash of lightning directly over the building flooded the room in an eerie light. "A baseball bat."

"What was it?"

"A baseball bat," Rita paused, debating, choosing her words carefully. "With the initials TB engraved in it."

There was no response except for an ear-shattering crackle of static.

"I think Tate's in trouble. I'm going --"

There was more static. Chloe's voice cut out and came back. Rita could only make out a few words.

"-- now."

"Chloe? Did you hear me before?"

There was no response, and Rita's heart dropped. Was this woman driving right toward danger?

"Chloe! Where are you headed? What's your location?"

"-- Quarry Field."

The line went dead.

FORTY-FOUR

Before Tate could react, the door was yanked open, and he was pulled from the cab, landing face-down in the mud. With the taste of dirt in his mouth and mud in his eyes, Tate struggled to get leverage.

Stepping on his back, Dalton pressed him down as he maneuvered, trying to get into the truck.

Tate flipped, spewing mud. Reaching out, he caught Dalton's leg and wrenched him backward.

Dalton staggered to get his footing. Adrenaline pumped through his veins, Tate rushed him, and tackled Dalton to the ground.

"You son of a bitch! Get off me, damn it!" Dalton cursed, swinging at Tate. "Get the hell off before the bastard comes too."

Dalton's fist caught Tate's mouth. There was the instant taste of blood. Tangy and metallic. The rip of skin as hard knuckles connected with his face. Dalton bucked, trying to throw him off, but Tate braced, held his ground, and landed a blow to the head.

He saw his attacker's eyes dim and wide in the flash of lightning, fighting to stay conscious. In the next flash, he saw them focus, sharp and clear, on something over Tate's shoulder. Then he saw the fear.

The blow connected with his ribs. His body unprepared for a direct hit from the right. The crack of metal as it made an eerie aluminum clang. A shot of pain coursed through him. Bat - registered in his mind. But from where?

The second blow, was like an electric shock. He felt his bones crack. He cried out and rolled off Dalton. To the left. Away.

Bracing for the next hit.

❉

Chloe shrieked, dropped the phone, and yanked the wheel, swerving to avoid the large branch that landed on the road. Her heart hammered against her chest at the near miss. Taking the curve at the bend in the road, her cell phone skated across the floor of the truck, out of reach, landing next to a bag of balls.

Needing to pay attention if she wanted to make it there in one piece, she tried to put the conversation with Detective Sorenson out of her mind. But it wouldn't stay there. She must have heard her wrong. It sounded like the Detective was implicating Tate in some way. But that couldn't be. She must have misunderstood. Tate couldn't be involved, could he?

The rain seemed to be lessening just a little. Chloe was able to make out the sign through the steady rain for the ballpark. She turned in, her headlights sweeping over the rough walls. Seeing Tate's truck with the lights on, Chloe breathed a sigh of relief.

She pulled up behind the truck, her lights illuminating a couple of men. It was like a scene right off the big screen as she sat frozen in horror, watching. Fist flew. Arms swung. Bodies weaved and staggered. Even through the roar of the rain and wind, Chloe could hear the grunts and groans of the men. One staggered back into the beam of her headlights, and for a split second, she saw his face. Dalton Turk.

She cut the lights, threw the truck in reverse, and backed up.

FORTY-FIVE

Tate must have blacked out for a minute, but when he came to, the pain ricocheted through his entire body, causing him to spasm, jolting him back into consciousness. He tried to focus as the pelting rain beat on his face. The crack of metal and the shatter of glass behind him caught his attention. Holding his ribs, Tate struggled to turn and face the sound.

Eddie stood less than ten feet away from him, swinging an aluminum bat. He brought it down hard, just missing Dalton and striking the hood of his pickup instead.

Dalton scrambled for purchase. Eddie swung, and the bat connected with Dalton's knee.

Crying out in pain, Dalton slithered back.

"That one was for Chloe, you bastard!" Eddie cursed.

"Eddie!" Tate shouted, raising his voice to be heard over the rain. "What the hell are you doing?"

Turning toward him, Eddie smirked. "What you've always wanted to do but never had the guts to. Kicking Dalton's ass." He cocked back the bat like he was getting ready for batting practice, but hesitated as Dalton dragged his body backward. Eddie ran at him, and Dalton flattened himself and rolled under the truck, getting out of reach in the nick of time.

Eddie didn't falter, he let it rip, smashing in the door right where Dalton had been only seconds before. He walked to the front and smashed in the headlight of Dalton's truck. Glass flew. "Ah, that felt great." He flipped the bat in his hand and held it out to Tate. "Wanna give it a try?"

Tate was on his feet now despite the excruciating pain across his abdomen. "Are you crazy? Have you lost your mind?"

With a roar of laughter, Eddie took a step toward Tate. "Maybe. I think I lost it a long time ago. Between you and Chloe, I don't know which one pushed me over the edge first."

"What the hell is that supposed to mean?"

"You always thought you were just a little bit better than me at everything, especially baseball and girls. I wanted to play shortstop, and every year, you beat me out without even putting forth any effort. Me? I had to work my ass off, and still, you got the position." He took another step closer. "And don't even get me started on Chloe."

"What about her?"

"I wanted her, and you took her. She was supposed to be mine."

"I didn't take her. She's not someone or something you can just take or possess."

"That's easy for you to say -- You've always owned her heart." He swung the bat, slicing through the rain, missing Tate by mere inches. "The minute you kissed her in the library in front of everyone, you sealed my fate. She was never the same after that. You broke her, ruined her for me and everyone else."

He turned around suddenly, swung, and smashed the truck's side mirror.

"Dalton's going to kill you when this is over."

"No, he won't," Eddie said confidently, walking around to the front of the pickup. "Will you Turk?" Eddie screamed, beating the truck with the bat.

Lightning flashed, and Tate saw Dalton's face beneath the truck in the eerie light. He looked dazed and confused. Tate glanced around, trying to locate something he could use as a weapon.

"Not that you really care, and why would you? He's a coward, always has been. But don't worry, before I'm done, he will be face down in the mud, unconscious and half dead. When I'm through, he won't remember what happened."

"And what exactly is going to happen?" Tate asked, a shudder racking his body as the rain continued to hammer them from above.

"Don't you know?" Eddie sneered.

"Why don't you enlighten me," he said, trying to match his tone to Eddie's.

"You're the one who will take the blame." Eddie flipped the bat back over and swung, hitting the windshield and cracking the glass. "Everyone in town knows you don't like Dalton Turk. There's this unspoken rivalry between you, all the way back to high school, starting with baseball. How you unseated him from his starting varsity position when he was a senior."

"That was a long time ago."

Eddie shrugged. "Maybe so, but some things can't be forgotten. And then there's Chloe."

At the mention of her name, fear snaked its way into Tate's body.

Eddie took a step toward Tate, seemingly oblivious to the persistent rain. "It's a shame, really, how Dalton's been harassing her. First at the bookstore, then at the pumpkin patch. Who's to say he wasn't the one that destroyed her bedroom and killed her chickens." Eddie slung the bat over his shoulder.

Tate could feel Eddie's pride emanating from him, rolling off him like water off a duck. "That was you," Tate stated, the truth registering. "But why?"

Eddie ignored the question. "It sounds to me like something Dalton would do. Doesn't it? People would understand that you would want revenge, that you couldn't wait for the police to investigate, and that you needed to take matters into your own hands. Settle this thing that's been brewing between you once and for all."

The fear turned to anger and settled like a fist in his gut. "People that really know me know I would never stoop to that level."

"Maybe," Eddie smirked. "Maybe not, but if there's a witness who can corroborate . . ." Eddie's voice trailed off as he took a step closer to Tate.

"And how exactly would the story go?"

"I'm no professional writer, not like your girlfriend anyway. Oh, wait. Is Chloe your girlfriend yet?"

"Leave Chloe out of this."

"Oh, I'd like to. But I'm afraid she's going to be a big part of your demise."

Tate was having trouble concentrating. Even the slightest movement shot unbridled pain through his entire body. Black orbs circled his vision as he leaned back against the vehicle behind him, trying to stay conscious.

"Isn't she the one that gave you your lucky bat for your fifteenth birthday? The one with your initials engraved in it. The one that's been missing for a good portion of the week, along with this one I stole out of your equipment bag."

Tate bit back bile as a wave of nausea swept over him. "Yeah, why?"

"No reason, except it's in the police precinct right now in the evidence room. If they have any brains, it'll have been linked to several crimes. Even murder."

The shock of Eddie's last comment had Tate focusing. Determined not to slip into the darkness. He welcomed the pain to keep himself awake and alert. "How do you know that?"

"You'd be surprised by the things I know."

A shiver racked Tate's body. He was soaked from head to toe, like Eddie, but Eddie seemed unaware of the wet or the cold.

"You murdered those two women?" Tate questioned.

"I did."

"But why? What did they ever do to you?"

"Nothing," he said simply. "But remind me of Chloe."

"That's just sick. You are sick, Eddie."

"I'm not sick. I have needs, wants, and desires. And what I want is Chloe. I want to teach her. Mold her into the woman I know she can be. Her mind is brilliant and worth a fortune if cultivated correctly, promoted, and marketed so that the world can know her as I do."

"And you think that's what she wants?"

"She does. She just doesn't know it yet."

"And you're the one that can do this? Mold her and teach her?"

"Yes," Eddie said it so simply as he paced back and forth, a deranged look in his eyes.

"You know nothing of the real Chloe Harris if you think she's going to fall for this."

"I know more than you." He spat. "You know nothing of her world as an author."

"You're right. I don't know much about her writing or being an author, but I know it's hard work. I know she pours her heart and soul into everything she writes." Tate straightened despite the pain. "I know where she comes from. I know who she was and is."

Eddie gave a half laugh. "That's not nearly enough."

"It's a good start."

"Hardly. When I'm through with her, she will be famous. And I'll be rich."

"You'll be rich? Is that what that movie deal was about that you took her to in Philly? Is that why you pushed her into signing the contract with them? So, you'd be rich? So, you'd make money off of her?"

"I guess there's no harm in telling you." Eddie sneered. He couldn't help himself. "You'll be in prison. And it's my word against yours."

Tate saw Eddie's chest swell, the pride showing through as he tapped the end of the bat into his free hand. "She didn't sign with them. She signed with me. The whole thing was an act. Those men that she met with – they're nobodies. Those guys owed me a favor. I own Chloe Harris. Now and forever. From here on out, every single word she writes is mine. As brilliant as she is, she's also a fool."

"She trusted you."

"She's naïve. But I'll fix that because I'll be there to guide her. Shape her. Mold her."

Tate's gut wrenched. Was that true? Was it possible that Chloe had unknowingly signed her life away to this backstabbing crook who pretended to be her friend? Anger burned deep inside him. Rage bubbled up and over. Unable to accept it. "She said she read the contract."

Eddie sneered then. "She did. Every damn word. I knew she would, so I created two documents. The one I let her read and the one I had her sign." He guffawed. "It was brilliant, really."

Tate slid his hand ever so slightly around to his back pocket.

"It's not there."

"What?"

"The phone you're reaching for. I made sure of that while you were blacked out." He took a step closer to Tate and tossed it on the ground. The phone sank down into the mud. "Besides, you forgot to charge it again. It's dead." Eddie placed his shoe on it and pressed it down deeper. "Your time is running out. By the time I finish with Dalton, he will be as good as dead. And you'll be to blame. Your life as you know it is over, even if you manage to walk out of here alive." Eddie walked forward, swinging.

"You won't get away with this."

"If I were a betting man, I'd say the odds are in my favor. Every clue the detectives found, which wasn't much because I was very careful. They all lead straight to you."

"I'll take that bet," she said, her voice, strong and unwavering, carried above the wind and rain.

Eddie turned, trying to locate her.

The ball came out of nowhere, striking Eddie in the head. He shrieked in pain. Grabbing at the side of his face with one hand, he swung the bat wildly with the other. He lunged at Tate.

Tate weaved, slipped, and sprawled out in the mud. Another ball connected with Eddie's back. The smack was loud and wet. Before Eddie could recover, another baseball hit between his shoulder blades.

That's when Tate spotted her, like David facing Goliath, she emerged from the darkness, armed with only a bag of baseballs. Her beauty and determination couldn't be hidden behind the onslaught of rain. Every fiber of her being vibrated as she stepped closer, the ball clutched in her hand.

Chloe moved out further into the open. Steam rose in white puffs around her head like a halo as the temperature plummeted. But she stood her ground, tall and definite. Anger flashed in her eyes like the lightning that ripped the sky wide open behind her. "You son of a . . ." she flung a ball at Eddie, hitting him square in the chest. "How could you?"

Eddie gasped for breath. "Chloe?"

Walking toward him at a steady clip now, unafraid, she hurled another baseball, and another, and another, peppering him in the upper arm, the shoulder, his right leg, and his gut. Try as he might, Eddie couldn't deflect or anticipate the next ball.

His cry was cut short as the next baseball hit him directly in the neck. He drug in a haggard breath. Clutching his throat, Eddie dropped the bat and gasped for air like a fish out of water. Tate scrambled up from the muddy ground, pushing down the pain, and ran at Eddie, taking him out at the legs as another ball hit him between the eyes.

Eddie flopped to the saturated ground unconscious.

Chloe dug through the bag, searching for another baseball. Tate scrambled off Eddie, slipping and sliding in the mud, and ran toward Chloe, pulling her away.

"Chloe, stop." He said gently, pinning her arms at her sides. "He's down. He's unconscious."

"No! He lied. I have more baseballs! I'll . . ."

He held on tight as she struggled to control her emotions. She dropped the bag at her feet, and then the last ball. He felt the fight drain out of her.

Leaning into Chloe, he shifted and wrapped his arms tighter around her despite the excruciating pain that racked his body.

Sirens cut through the night as the rain continued to fall.

"I thought he was going to kill you. I couldn't let that happen."

"And you didn't. You stopped him. You, Chloe Harris," his eyes searched hers, caught and held. "You stopped him."

His lips brushed her wet cheek. Blinking back tears, she looked at him, her eyes as big as saucers. The rain poured down around them. He cupped her face, brushed wet hair from her eyes, and murmured into her ear, "Chloe Harris, you saved me. Even after all these years, you're still my hero."

EPILOGUE

"Keep your eyes closed," Tate said as he made a right turn and bounced along on the bumpy road.

"I am." She could feel his eyes on her even without looking at him. "Keep yours on the road. Are you trying to hit every pothole?"

"Seems that way, doesn't it? This gravel road is rough."

"Are you sure you should be driving? It's only been six weeks since –"

"The doctor said six weeks. I did what I was told. Took it easy and healed fast." He reached for her hand and brought it to his lips. "I healed quickly, thanks to you and the extra TLC I received." He kissed her hand and kept it in his.

She rolled her eyes at him behind closed eyelids even though he couldn't see it. "I know, but it is exactly six weeks today. You could have waited at least one more day."

"I waited six weeks. I'm driving, and that's that." He slowed the truck and made another turn. "Besides, this is important, and it couldn't wait.

"How much further?" she questioned in a playful tone.

"You're worse than a little kid. Almost there."

Not that she really minded. She was enjoying the warm fall day. They were getting fewer and further between as they were deep into November now. She leaned back in the cab, with her hand still in his, and welcomed the sunshine that poured in through the open windows. The sun's rays danced over her face as Tate drove down the tree-lined road. She knew without looking that a scattering of leaves still clung to branches but had lost their fall luster. The color had drained off them and the countryside, leaving the muted brown before the encroaching winter.

It was hard to believe it had only been six weeks since that terrible storm and that awful night with its devastating turn of events. So much had happened in the wake of it all.

When the police arrived, they found her and Tate clinging to each other with an unconscious Eddie at their feet, Tate barely able to stand.

Dalton was still under the truck, unable to crawl out with his shattered kneecap and going in and out of consciousness with the excruciating pain he was in. Eddie had worked him over good before Tate had arrived.

Eddie had regained consciousness when they loaded him into the ambulance, yelling, swearing, and insisting that Tate had attacked him.

Despite Dalton and Tate's differences, Dalton had been essential in having Eddie arrested, as he had witnessed and heard most of what Eddie had said and done.

Chloe shook her head, thinking about Dalton. He had a long road to haul with surgery and rehabilitation for his knee, but he had seemed genuine at the hospital when they had spoken, wanting to put the past behind them and move forward. Only time would tell.

Chloe remembered how hard that night had been. Her emotions had run the spectrum from thinking she'd lost her career -- her rights to her books and the movie deal. But when they had wheeled Tate away from her, not knowing the extent of his injuries – that had her completely undone.

From the moment they'd brought him back to her in the hospital, she never left his side.

Even though Tate had been on strict orders to rest, he had helped her sort through the whole mess of the signed contract. Much to Chloe's relief, they were able to determine that since the contract was signed under false pretenses, it was null and void.

Detective Sorenson was able to tie both murders back to

Eddie with the bat and the DNA sample they had collected from under the first victim's fingernails. It turned out Eddie had been wearing collared shirts more than usual to cover up the scratches on his neck.

Tate's hand slipped from hers as she felt the truck slow, and he put it in park. "We're here. You can open your eyes."

Chloe blinked against the sun as she opened her eyes and took in a cute little farmhouse. She could see a pretty little barn and hear some dogs barking in the distance. "What are we doing here?" she asked.

"You'll see." His smile was instant. "Come on. Let's get out."

No sooner were they out of the truck than an elderly man came out onto the front porch. "Howdy," he called, lifting his hand in the air. "Are you Tate Becker? Are you the guy?"

Tate linked hands with Chloe and tugged her gently forward. "I'm the guy."

"Thought so." He came down off the porch and shook Tate's hand. "Ma'am." He said, shaking Chloe's hand as well. Then looked from Chloe to Tate and smiled an all-knowing grin.

Tate gave Chloe a nervous smile and said, "This is Fred."

"You wanna just get to it?" Fred asked.

Tate took a shaky breath. "I guess so."

"Let me call my grandson." Fred gave a loud whistle, and a teenage boy rounded the corner with a trio of dogs.

"What's going on?" Chloe asked, suddenly suspicious. "Where are we?"

"Fred fosters dogs and puppies until they are adopted. This is where Bruno has been for the past month and a half."

Chloe recognized the little black lab before Tate finished the sentence. "Oh my," Chloe whispered. "Hasn't he grown?"

"I'll say," the man said. "Growing like a weed. Friendly, too. And he's a fast learner. My grandson has him trained pretty well." To demonstrate, Fred said, "Bruno, sit."

The little puppy plopped his butt down.

"He shakes, too," the boy added. "Squat down to his level and ask him," the boy encouraged Chloe.

Chloe bent down and held out her hand. "Hey, Bruno," Chloe said softly. "Do you remember me?"

He sniffed her hand and cocked his head.

"Shake Bruno," the boy said from over her shoulder. Instantly, Bruno lifted a paw.

Chloe laughed and took it. "Smart dog. Aren't you." She patted his head, and he moved toward her, lavishing her hands with puppy kisses. "You're so sweet. I haven't stopped thinking about you." He flopped onto his belly, and she rubbed it. "I wondered where you had gone and hoped someone was taking good care of you."

"He can stay and roll over, too," the boy said proudly, anxious to show off what Bruno knew.

Tate cleared his throat, getting her attention. "He's yours if you want him."

"Really?" Chloe asked as her heart swelled. She was touched that Tate would have thought of something so sweet and special.

"The papers are already signed. All you have to do is say yes," Tate said.

Chloe nodded, her heart full. "Of course, I'll take him. I would love to."

A look exchanged from the old man to Tate. "Perfect. My grandson has one more trick to show you."

"Oh?" Chloe asked, interested. "What's that?"

"He can fetch, too. Watch this." The boy pulled a small black ball from his pocket. "Bruno fetch," he said, tossing it.

Bruno scampered after it and leaped, snatching it neatly out of the air. The little lab trotted back and dropped it at Chloe's feet.

"He wants you to have it," the boy said, backing up.

"Here, let me," Tate said, kneeling down beside the puppy. On one knee, he retrieved the black ball.

"What is that thing? Chloe asked, wrinkling her nose at the soggy black lump. "It doesn't look like much of a ball."

"It's not." Tate pulled a layer of black wrapping off of it and produced a little black box.

"Tate?" Chloe's voice caught as he held it up and flipped it open. A diamond sparkled in the sunlight, nestled in black velvet. All the while, Bruno sat patiently next to Tate, his tail wagging excitedly.

"Chloe Harris," Tate's voice cracked. "Will you say yes to Bruno and me?"

Her heart tripped and fell, landing at his feet. She was head over heels for both the man and the puppy. She knew without a doubt her heart was Tate's. She simply could fall no further.

The End

ACKNOWLEDGEMENTS

Writing a book is a solo effort -- until it isn't. Until you're stuck and need an encouraging word or even some hard-core constructive criticism. That's what this is about. Without these individuals, this book wouldn't have been written.

I owe a great big thank you to my friend and fellow author Jess, whom I met by chance but quickly connected with. Her encouraging words and constructive criticism guided me through the murky waters of this novel. Without her, I may have never finished. I'm excited to see where we both go from here and glad we will get to travel this "writing world" knowing each other and cheering each other on.

To my first reader, Kristy: You never disappoint with your enthusiasm for my work. Thank you for bearing with me through the unpolished draft.

To my daughters, Delaney and Makayla, thank you for reading and rereading, and finding those little flaws and typos. Your attention to detail, dedication, and support helps more than you will ever know. Near or far, you both have my heart.

I also need to thank Liz, another writer I met recently, who didn't hesitate to lend a fresh set of eyes to my story, ensuring everything flowed.

To my Arc readers: Erin, Melisa, Jill, Pam, and Amy. Thank you for giving me your time and your willingness to read. You have my sincere appreciation.

To my readers, your choice to invest your time with me is truly humbling. Being a part of your world, even in a small way, brings me immense joy. Your feedback, whether in words by email, text or in person, fuels my passion and drives me to create more. Thank you for allowing me to be a part of your entertainment and for the opportunity to connect with you.

I also want to give a shout-out to Claudia and Diane. These women dedicate their time and energy to their local library — creating events and fun environments where anyone can go and read, encouraging authors like me, and helping us get exposure to more readers. You rock!

Last, but certainly not least – to my family, thank you for your unwavering patience as I wrap up one more paragraph, one more sentence. Your steadfast belief in my abilities fills me with confidence and empowers me to reach for the stars. Your support is the cornerstone of my success, and I am endlessly grateful for your love and encouragement.

BOOKS BY THIS AUTHOR

You Can Hide

Jayde Walker is left for dead. Surviving, she is the only witness to the murder of her best friend.

Fighting amnesia, she tries to get on with her life with the killer still on the loose. Then, one night, she remembers, and the truth terrifies her.

Leaving behind everything and everyone she knows, she runs.

Halfway across the country, lost in the Midwest, Jayde makes a wrong turn, desperate to disappear.

The tall, green cornstalks in the vast fields of Iowa call to her. Without hesitation, Jayde steps in and disappears.

Who can save her? Her fiancé, whom she left behind? The detective she trusted? The farmer who rescued her? Who can she trust with her life? And her heart?

In The Shadow Of The Black Moon

Bree Thompson has suffered a life-altering, devastating loss. One from which most people wouldn't recover. She needs a drastic change in her life, or she's afraid she won't survive it. Bree drives across the country to the East Coast, determined to find what she thinks she needs in the sand and the surf, leaving it all behind.

She wants a place to call home, somewhere completely different from where she came from, so every time she turns around, it doesn't remind her of what she once had. But someone lurks in the shadows watching, waiting.

Slowly, she starts to find her way and believes it is possible. She finds the perfect house on the water and a construction crew that can rebuild her fixer-upper, and maybe one of them can even mend her broken heart.

But that's when the trouble starts. Someone doesn't want her to have it all. Instead, they want to take it all away.   Someone wants her life to end in the shadow of the black moon.

Cherry Hollow

For Cami Parker, Cherry Hollow represents . . .
Twins.
Tragedy.
An old stone manor.
Her best friends and a high school crush.
But after being away for ten years, she also wants it to be her future.
She returns with big dreams, determined to make them a reality. Wanting to start a new business, rekindle old friendships, and find out the truth about the tragedy that haunts her.
But not everyone is happy to see her. Not everyone wants her to uncover the truth. Some things are better left buried in the past.

JOHN 3:16